DEADLY GREETINGS

A Card-Making Mystery

Elizabeth Bright

A SIGNET BOOK

SIGNET
Published by New American Library, a division of
Penguin Group (USA) Inc., 375 Hudson Street,
New York, New York 10014, USA
Penguin Group (Canada), 90 Eglinton Avenue East, Suite 700, Toronto,
Ontario M4P 2Y3, Canada (a division of Pearson Penguin Canada Inc.)
Penguin Books Ltd., 80 Strand, London WC2R 0RL, England
Penguin Ireland, 25 St. Stephen's Green, Dublin 2,
Ireland (a division of Penguin Books Ltd.)
Penguin Group (Australia), 250 Camberwell Road, Camberwell, Victoria 3124,
Australia (a division of Pearson Australia Group Pty. Ltd.)
Penguin Books India Pvt. Ltd., 11 Community Centre, Panchsheel Park,
New Delhi - 110 017, India
Penguin Group (NZ), cnr Airborne and Rosedale Roads, Albany,
Auckland 1310, New Zealand (a division of Pearson New Zealand Ltd.)
Penguin Books (South Africa) (Pty.) Ltd., 24 Sturdee Avenue,
Rosebank, Johannesburg 2196, South Africa

Penguin Books Ltd., Registered Offices:
80 Strand, London WC2R 0RL, England

First published by Signet, an imprint of New American Library,
a division of Penguin Group (USA) Inc.

First Printing, June 2006
10 9 8 7 6 5 4 3 2 1

PUBLISHER'S NOTE
This is a work of fiction. Names, characters, places, and incidents either are
the product of the author's imagination or are used fictitiously, and any resemblance to actual persons, living or dead, business establishments, events, or
locales is entirely coincidental.
  The publisher does not have any control over and does not assume any
responsibility for author or third-party Web sites or their content.

Alphabetically
To Laura C., Nancy C., Elizabeth D.S., Earlene F.,
Nancy M., Rosemary M.(S.), Tamar M., Sarah S.,
and
to Carolyn H., Charlotte M. and Agatha C.
for leading the way.

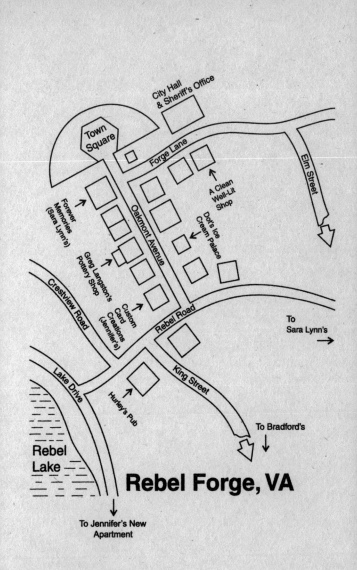

Rebel Forge, VA

City Hall & Sheriff's Office

Town Square

Forge Lane

Elm Street

Forever Memories (Sara Lynn's)

Oakmont Avenue

A Clean Well-Lit Shop

Dot's Ice Cream Palace

Greg Langston's Pottery Shop

Crestview Road

Custom Card Creations (Jennifer's)

Rebel Road

To Sara Lynn's

Lake Drive

King Street

Hurley's Pub

To Bradford's

Rebel Lake

To Jennifer's New Apartment

Chapter 1

I never really believed in ghosts until Frances Coolridge tried to kill me two months *after* she died. I've made a ton of handcrafted greeting cards for hundreds of occasions, but never anything remotely like the one I wished I could create for her. I might head it "WISH YOU WERE (STILL) DEAD," or maybe even "YOU'RE INVITED TO YOUR VERY OWN EXORCISM," but I doubted either one would do much good. It was pretty apparent that Frances didn't want me living in her apartment, and just as obvious I wasn't about to move out. We were at a stalemate, and while it was true that I was going to have to get used to Frances's presence, it also meant that she was going to have to get used to mine. I loved my new quarters at Whispering Oak, and it was going to take more than a scatterbrained poltergeist to make me pack up my stuff and leave.

My name's Jennifer Shane, and I own Custom Card Creations, a small handcrafted-card shop in Rebel Forge, Virginia. My business is on one end of Oakmont Avenue—a road that runs through the heart of downtown—and my sister Sara Lynn's scrapbooking store is on the other. I'd worked for her at Forever Memories before opening my card shop, but I loved being on my own, even if I *was* constantly just a sale or two away from putting up my very own GOING OUT

OF BUSINESS sign. Though our parents died in a car accident years before, I'd never felt totally orphaned. After all, my brother, Bradford, is the sheriff for all of Rebel Forge, and my aunt Lillian helps me out at the card shop. Sometimes the pluses and minuses of living in a small town are one and the same. My family is close, both in proximity and in our hearts, but it can be stifling at times. As the youngest of our clan, I often find myself chafing against their desire to protect me, even though I know they are motivated out of love.

"What do you call that ghastly hue?" my aunt Lillian asked as she came into the card shop one morning the week before. I was displaying a new shade of paper I'd made in my small workshop in back, and I was proud of it.

Without glancing in her direction, I said, "Don't you like it? It's called 'Lillian's Dream.' "

"It's more like one of my nightmares," my aunt muttered under her breath as she waved a hand in the air to dismiss the topic. "But never mind that. You've got to close the shop and come with me at once."

"Lillian, I'm barely making enough to feed Oggie and Nash, let alone myself. I can't afford to shut the place down." My cats, though not fancy eaters, were finicky in their preference of national brands over generic fare. Hoping to squeeze another nickel out of my budget, I'd tried them on Stylin' Stew and Jumpy Cats, but they'd refused to touch either one.

Lillian flicked a strand of dyed henna hair out of her face as she said, "Jennifer, you still hate your apartment, don't you?"

"You know I do," I said, remembering what had happened there the month before that had completely robbed me of my sense of security. Someone had made a rather concerted effort to scare me, and they'd done a pretty good job of it. The memory of the threat at my door lingered every night as I tried to sleep.

Lillian nodded. "Well then I've got just the place

for you. We have to go now, though, before someone else grabs it." My aunt was a woman of action, proved by a string of seven ex-husbands; she was only half teasing when she said that she was always on the lookout for number eight.

"Do they allow cats?" I asked as I slid the rest of the paper onto the display.

"My dear, they embrace them. Now let's go."

After grabbing my coat, I flipped the sign on the door to BACK IN FIFTEEN MINUTES and locked up. Honestly, I had no idea how long we'd be gone, but I was hoping whoever saw it would hang around, since I couldn't afford to alienate the few customers I had.

"So where are we headed?" I asked as we hustled toward her car, a classic candy-apple-red Mustang in mint condition.

"Have you ever heard of Whispering Oak?"

I thought about it a second before answering her. "Wasn't he an Indian guide around here two hundred years ago?"

Lillian shot me one of those looks that spoke volumes about her thoughts on my sanity, but I was being serious.

She explained, "Whispering Oak is a fine old house on the outskirts of town. There's even a path from your doorstep to the lake. It's wonderful."

"If it's so wonderful, why is it vacant?"

Lillian took a curve sharp enough to fling the paint off her car, and by the time I caught my breath she had shot down a side road at the edge of town that I'd never noticed before. I've lived in Rebel Forge nearly all my life, and I'd always assumed the graveled path was a driveway to the house facing the road. Instead of pulling into the Jackson place though, we followed it on through the woods until we came to an ancient Victorian home, replete with fancy shingle siding, gingerbread trim adorning the porch and a pastel palette that belonged on a greeting card.

"This place is for rent?" I asked, knowing full well I couldn't afford to live there on my modest income.

"Not the entire house, Jennifer," she said. "However, there is a free room upstairs that would be perfect for you."

"If it's free, then I guess I'm willing to look at it," I said. "That's about all I can afford."

"You know perfectly well I meant it was available, not without cost." She bit her lower lip, then said, "It is reasonable, though, less than you're paying now, I'll wager."

"I'll take that bet," I said. One of the few advantages of my current apartment was that the rent was within my means, though just barely.

Lillian parked, then I followed her as she walked to the front door with a purposeful stride. I was expecting her to knock, but she strolled right in like she owned the papers to the place. There wasn't much for me to do but follow. The foyer had been divided into a vestibule with two doors that were obviously later additions. "Which one are we going to look at?"

"Neither one of these," Lillian said as she pointed to a narrow staircase in back that I'd missed at first. "We're going up."

I eyed the tight passage suspiciously. "I'm not sure I'll fit, let alone the cat carriers."

"Jennifer, can you really choose to be that particular, given your budget?"

"Okay, fine, I'll look at it," I said, doubtful it would suit even my meager needs.

The stairs went on and on, but we finally made it to the top. There was a narrow door there, perched on a landing barely big enough for the two of us.

I was getting claustrophobic without even going inside. "What is it, the attic?"

"Certainly it was at one time, but it's a perfectly delightful space now." Lillian reached under the rug and pulled out a key. As she slid it in the lock, I said,

"I just love these modern security features, don't you?"

Lillian ignored my comment as she unlocked the door and flung it open. I moved past her as we stepped inside, finally having enough room to stand without her imprinting her elbow into my side.

I thought I'd hate it. In fact, I was already planning a few choice words that involved chasing wild geese and hunting snipes.

Then I looked around. It was nothing short of charming. While it had been an ordinary attic in another incarnation, it was now the perfect studio apartment. The bead board walls enchanted me, painted a pastel green that reminded me of springtime. Light bounced around the room, filtering in from large windows on either end while two dormers also served to illuminate the place, making it bright and airy, nothing like what I'd expected when I'd realized it was a converted attic space. It was fully furnished with antiques built in the Shaker style, and while some folks would find the clean design rather plain, I adored it. A handcrafted quilt covered the queen-sized bed, and a faded Oriental rug adorned much of the open floor, leaving just enough of the honey-toned heartwood pine beneath it to make me want to roll back the rug.

"I don't have to share a bathroom with anyone, do I?" I asked, searching for any flaw I could find.

"No, the middle dormer has been outfitted as one. Granted, it's not all that large, but you live alone. There should be plenty of room for you and your cats here."

I shrugged, not willing to commit to it yet. "So what's the catch?"

Instead of answering my question, Lillian said, "Jennifer, look through that window."

I did as I was asked and peered out. To my surprise, I found a small deck just outside, replete with an iron chair and a charming little table. For a finale, Lillian pointed through the canopy of leaves beyond. "The lake is just a few steps away. Autumn is nearly here, and you'll soon have a glorious view of the lake. Isn't it delightful?"

I couldn't have agreed with her more, but I realized Lillian must have misunderstood the price. "I can't imagine how I can come anywhere near to affording this place."

When she told me the rent, I didn't need to know anything else. "Where do we go to sign the lease?"

Lillian smiled in approval. "I took the liberty of acquiring one from Hester Taylor." Hester was one of Lillian's best friends, operating a combination copy store/apartment rental agency/ice cream shop in town ever since her husband had disappeared one day ten years ago. The rumor was that he'd taken their cash, their car, and their dog with him when he vanished. Hester claimed that besides the cash, the only thing she really missed was the dog.

"So where do I sign?" I asked.

Lillian gestured to the places Hester had marked, then took the document from me. "Don't worry about the deposit or the first and last months' rents. I've got those covered."

When I started to protest, Lillian said, "Think of them as housewarming gifts."

"I'd rather think of them as paid by me," I said. "I'm not letting you do this."

"It's too late," Lillian said, laughing. "You already signed the lease."

"Then I'll default," I said. "Or you will. I mean it." I'd learned early on that if I didn't stand my ground with her, I'd be stampeded.

She huffed out, "Blast it all, child, do you always have to get your way?"

"Think of it as a character defect I inherited from my favorite aunt," I said.

Lillian thought about it a few moments, then said,

"Let's compromise. You can pay me back, but only after your store makes a profit two months in a row."

"Are you sure you can wait that long?"

She scolded, "Have faith in your card shop, Jennifer. I do."

I knew better than to push her any more than I had. There was only one thing left I could do, and that was to accept as graciously as I could. "Okay, thanks, I can live with that."

"You're most welcome," she said as she hugged me. We were downstairs, ready to go back to the card shop, when one of the tenants on the main floor came out into the foyer. "Who are you?" an elderly man with a black cane asked us fiercely.

"I just rented the apartment upstairs," I said. "I'm Jennifer Shane," I added as I offered my hand.

He refused it, then took a step back from us. "You can't be serious."

"Why? What's wrong with it?" I was beginning to think that there might be something I'd failed to ask.

The man shook his head. "You really don't know?" He lifted his cane and shook it in Lillian's direction. "You should be ashamed of yourself, Madam."

Lillian laughed. "I often have reason to, but I rarely am. Now go away."

With a grunt, the man retreated back into his apartment, slamming the door in our faces.

"Gee thanks, Lillian, it is so sweet of you to make such an effort to get me accepted by my neighbors."

"Pooh, he'll come around. Give him time."

An odd-looking tiny woman with blue hair and a nose like an ice pick was standing on the porch when we walked outside. I'd seen her around town from time to time, but we'd never really spoken to each other.

Lillian said, "Hester, what are you doing here? I told you I'd take care of this."

The woman fluttered her fingers in the air like a

hummingbird's wings. "I just thought . . . I was nearby. . . . Did she sign it?"

"I'm standing right here. Ask me yourself," I said.

Hester continued to ignore me. "Do you have the lease agreement?" she asked Lillian.

"It's right here, Hester. Now calm down before you have a heart attack or, worse yet, give me one."

Hester grabbed the lease Lillian held out and without another word she bolted for her parked car, a Cadillac that was tinted the most unpleasant shade of green I'd ever seen in my life.

I turned to Lillian and asked, "What in the world was that all about?"

"Hester always was a tad high-strung."

I touched my aunt's arm. "Lillian, stop dodging. There's something you're not telling me, isn't there?"

"Jennifer, I knew if I said anything, you'd miss out on a wonderful opportunity. It's all nonsense anyway."

"I wish I'd had a choice, but I'm already committed. So what is it you haven't been telling me?"

She frowned a moment, then admitted, "There's just one thing I neglected to mention. Honestly, it shouldn't matter one bit."

"Come on, Lillian, out with it."

My aunt scowled, then finally said, "Very well, if you must know, some folks think the place is haunted."

"The entire house?" I squealed. Great, that was just what I needed, moving into Amityville. Suddenly my apartment didn't seem all that bad.

Lillian shook her head. "No, the rest of the house is fine. It's just your apartment that's said to have a ghost."

And that was the first time I'd ever heard of Frances Coolridge's demise.

"So now I'm living in a haunted house?" I tried to keep my voice from shrieking, but it was tough to do.

She frowned, then said, "It's all nonsense, Jennifer. Honestly, I expected you to be more levelheaded about the whole thing."

"Well, I expected my aunt to look out after my best interests. The world's just full of disappointment today, isn't it?"

Lillian took a deep breath. "Let's discuss this as we walk by the lake. The air has such a soothing quality to it."

I stood my ground. "I'm not taking another step until you tell me what this is all about."

Lillian frowned, then said, "I know you; you won't quit until I tell you, so you might as well hear it all at once."

I planned to stand right there until she told me, but Lillian had other ideas. If I wanted to hear why my new apartment was haunted, I was going to have to follow her as she walked down the path toward the lake.

"Jennifer, first of all, you must know that I would never put you in harm's way. Will you at least give me that much credit?"

I wasn't ready to give her anything, but I knew until I threw her some kind of bone, I was going to be doing laps around the lake until my shoes wore out. "I know you wouldn't do it knowingly," I said grudgingly.

She paused, glanced at me for a second, then nodded. "Fine." Lillian's step faltered a moment, then she said, "Frances Coolridge was a friend of mine in another lifetime."

"Oh please don't tell me you're going to say you two shared a past life. Who were you, Cleopatra?" Some folks around town thought my aunt was eccentric, but I'd always stood up for her. It was starting to look like I'd been a tad hasty in my support.

"Don't be ridiculous," she said. "Do you want to hear this or not?"

I was beginning to wonder that myself. Maybe I should just trot over to the library and look it up in the archives. Then again, the newspaper would report just the facts, and I knew I could count on Lillian to supply the backstory, and that was often more telling than what found its way into print. "Sorry, I'll try not to interrupt again, but I'm not making any promises."

"As I was saying," Lillian continued. "Frances and I knew each other a lifetime ago. We were locker mates in high school, and the very best of friends."

"Then how come I never heard of her until today?" I asked. "You think I would have, if the two of you were so close." I didn't mean to interrupt, but I couldn't help myself.

Lillian chose to ignore it. "We had a falling-out at our graduation party. I should have apologized to her, but I kept delaying it until the issue became bigger than it really was; all the while a wall built up with every minute our conflict continued."

This was getting good. "What did you do? It must have been something huge."

"Jennifer, the details aren't important. All you need to know is that we became estranged that night."

"Aunt Lillian, there's not a chance in the world I'm letting you off that easy. Tell me what you did."

She stopped and looked at me long and hard. "I told you, it doesn't matter."

"Then I don't want to hear the story," I said as I turned around and started back to her car. She was stubborn, but I'd gotten my mulish streak from her, so I knew I could outlast her if I put my mind to it. Sometimes it was hard to get Lillian to talk about herself, but once she got started, I knew she'd have a tough time stopping until she finished.

I was twenty steps back up the path before she said, "I danced with her boyfriend one night."

"When you say 'dance,' what exactly do you mean?"

"Jennifer, don't be vulgar. It was one dance, no more and no less. Frances was in the powder room, and Herman asked me. I still don't know why I said yes."

I couldn't hide my smile. "You had the hots for a guy named Herman?"

Lillian said frostily, "He was rather dashing, as I remember him. Now do you want to hear the rest of this or not?"

"You've got my undivided attention," I said.

At least Lillian dropped her plan to circle the lake. She stood there and continued. "Frances never spoke to me again, a difficult thing to do in a town this small. She moved away soon after high school, but came back here to live after her parents died. They were quite wealthy. The family fortune started with a gold mine in North Carolina, but they quickly branched out into acquiring properties all over the South. After that, they started buying up businesses here and there as a hobby. The rumors around town were that the family barely left anything to Frances, choosing a charity in Richmond to receive the bulk of their wealth instead. The only things Frances inherited were a pair of doorstops, a swamp in Georgia and some other equally worthless things, or so the story goes."

"So why is she haunting my room? How did she die? And why didn't I ever hear about this?" It was hard to believe that someone could die in Rebel Forge without the entire town knowing about it.

"Frances's dead husband was related to the Dunbars, and the owners of the newspaper weren't about to let one whisper of the scandal out. For once, something happened here that no one else knew about. As for the rest of it, you'll have to get the details from your brother."

Great. Grilling Bradford was the last thing I wanted to do. "Lillian, you started this story; now finish it."

"Bradford really should be the one to tell you. After all, he was the one who cut her down. You see, she hanged herself."

A feeling of dread swept over me. "Please tell me she didn't do it in my beautiful living room."

"Of course not," Lillian said, and I felt instantly better. Then she added, "There probably wasn't a good place to attach the rope in there. That's why she used your bathroom."

So there it was. I was going to be taking a shower in the middle of a place where someone died. How in the world did Lillian think that would be better than my old apartment? "I never should have signed the lease," I said. "At least no one ever died in my old apartment."

"Not that you know of," Lillian said.

"Why, what have you heard?"

She shook her head. "Jennifer, I assure you, there's no such thing as ghosts. You'll be fine living here, I promise."

"If you're so sure, then why don't you move in with me?"

Lillian looked shocked by the suggestion. "I have my own place, my dear girl. Besides, there's no room for both of us up there."

"Okay then, I'll move into your house and you relocate here. The cats will love romping around in your big old house." My aunt had converted one bedroom of her rambling old house into a closet, and I knew her clothes alone wouldn't fit into the attic.

Lillian said, "Jennifer, you're delusional. I'll tell you what I will do, though. Spend one week here. If you absolutely hate it, you have my blessing to move out and I won't hold it against you."

"Do you honestly expect me to stay here for a full week?" I looked up at my room and saw the curtain fluttering in the breeze. There were just two problems with that: there wasn't the slightest whisper of wind in the air, and that window had been closed when I'd left it.

She said, "Oh, pooh, don't be so dramatic. Now let's get back to the card shop. You really shouldn't leave it unattended this long."

I didn't even know how to respond to that. While it was true I was eager to leave my apartment, I hadn't expected to go someplace worse. Still, Lillian had paid for two months there; if I could stand it for a week, maybe I could get used to rooming with a ghost.

Honestly, how bad could it be?

Chapter 2

At least I had a few days before I had to move. I probably should have spent more time fretting over my new domicile, but Custom Card Creations took up most of my conscious thought. Lillian and I were back working half an hour later. Unfortunately, the mob of customers clamoring to get in was more in my dreams than my reality. From the look of things, no one had even noticed that we'd been gone.

I was restocking some of our stickers when Lillian approached me. "Jennifer, this new gizmo came in yesterday. Would you mind showing me how to use it?"

My aunt Lillian had become a card-making fanatic since she'd come to work for me—something I was grateful for most times—but it was a tendency that could drive me crazy when I had work to do at my card shop. Still, I couldn't expect her to help customers if she didn't know how to make cards herself, so I put the stickers down and took the box from her. We'd just received a new embosser, and I needed to run it through its paces, trying papers from my supplier and some samples I'd made myself, before I'd recommend it to my customers.

I pulled out the tray, pegs and stencils, then quickly set it up for her, explaining as I went along. "It's the simplest thing in the world to use." I held one of the stencils up. "See the cutouts? These will end up embossed in your paper." There were swirls, curlicues and leafy vines cut out of both pieces of the hard plastic. "You put the base stencil down, then the top one above it. Pin it with a peg, slip your paper in, pop a few more pegs in to hold it all together, and you're ready to go. Think of it as a plastic sandwich with paper in the middle."

She studied it a moment, then asked, "But how do you get it to emboss? Is it some kind of press?"

I held up a burnishing tool, a gizmo that looked like an ink pen with a little silver ball on either end. "Press this into each opening. No, not like that. Trace the pattern. Don't worry about filling it in, just go around the edges."

She worked at it a few minutes until she'd traced every opening, then frowned. "I must be doing something wrong. This looks terrible."

I fought to hide my smile as I pulled out the pins, took off the top stencil, then handed the card stock to Lillian and waited for her reaction. While I hadn't used that particular brand before, I had embossed quite a bit myself, so I knew the process.

Lillian studied the results closely, then said, "That's absolutely incredible. Now this is what I call elegant," she added as she held it up for me to see.

"The pattern's a little ornate, wouldn't you say?" I said as I took the card stock from her. Lillian had used every shape on the pattern sheet, raising nearly every square inch of the paper. I couldn't see how anyone could add the simplest greeting to it.

"Oh pooh, Jennifer. Not everyone likes your simple stylings. You really must unleash that inner artist and let yourself go."

I took the embosser from her and said, "Okay, no more self-help tapes for you. Have you been listening to them while you walk again?"

"Scoff if you must, but they truly work." She gently

took the embossing stencil from me. "I'd like to try one of the other sheets, if you don't mind."

"Knock yourself out," I said. "I've got to finish restocking these collage stickers." The sticker set images came in everything from wedding gowns to teapots to floral bouquets. They were an easy way to make an elegant card quickly, and regardless of what Lillian thought, I could make an ornate card with the best of them. I was just finishing up when the front door chimed. Not only was it not a customer, as I'd sincerely hoped; it was someone I really didn't want to talk to at the moment.

"Jennifer," my brother, Bradford, said, "have you lost your mind completely?"

"Sometimes I wonder," I said. "What's got you in an uproar now?"

Decked out in his full police uniform, my brother spun his cap in his hand, a sure sign that he was truly angry and not just posturing. I could usually tell how mad he was by the velocity of the cap. Judging by its current blurring motion, I was guessing he was pretty steamed. "You moved into a place where someone died," he said.

"Would you like to field this one, Lillian?" I asked.

"No thank you. Goodness, look at the time. Jennifer, I have to dash, but I'll be back anon."

She was past me before I could grab her arm. So much for family loyalty. There was a real friction between my brother and our aunt, and I was guessing she'd just turned up the heat another notch. Well, if she was going to bail on me, I was going to return the favor and sing like a mockingbird in love. "I rented the place before I knew about its dubious history. Lillian told me about it."

"Just tell me you didn't sign a lease," he said.

"I could, but you know how I hate to lie to you." My brother was used to respect and consideration from nearly everyone in Rebel Forge, but I was one of the lone exceptions. He might be the law in our town, but he was still my brother, first and forever.

"Grab your jacket," he said as he stormed toward the door. Only when he saw that I wasn't following him did Bradford stop and turn back to me. "Why aren't you coming?"

"As flattering as your invitation is, I'd like to know where we're heading before I'm willing to leave."

"I'll tell you exactly where we're going. Hester Taylor is going to tear up that lease if I have to throw her in jail to get her to do it."

"Then I'll just have to sign another one," I said, standing my ground. If Bradford had approached me in a calmer manner, I might have taken him up on his offer of support. In fact, if the oaf had left me alone a few hours, I most likely would have hunted him down and pleaded for his assistance myself. What I wasn't about to stand for was letting him make my decisions for me. Suddenly I knew that I was staying at Whispering Oak, whether my brother or Frances the ghost liked it one bit.

He stared hard at me, something I was sure made criminals quiver down to their socks, but I returned as good as I got. Finally, he said, "I never thought much of our aunt, but she's really crossed the line. I can't believe she'd do this to you."

I didn't feel much like defending her, but I wasn't about to let Bradford take that swipe at her. "She thought she was doing what was best for me."

"I can't imagine how," he said. Then I saw a grim smile on his face.

"What's that all about? What are you up to?"

He shrugged. "Me? Sis, I'm not going to say another word. I'm just going to mind my own business." He glanced at my clock, then said, "Sorry I can't stay and chat, but I've got a date for lunch."

"Are you taking Cindy out? Good, your wife deserves a break from the library."

He shook his head. "No, she's volunteering at the school today. I'm taking Sara Lynn to lunch."

"Bradford, don't bring her into this."

He tried to look innocent and failed miserably. "Jen, she's my sister, too. If your name comes up in the course of our conversation, it's perfectly natural that I tell her your latest news."

I could see it now, the two of them ganging up on me after they had a quick bite to eat. It was time to stop his schemes now. "I'm moving to Whispering Oak. It's settled. You can tell Sara Lynn that, and I'll tell her the same thing when you both casually 'stop by' here after lunch."

I could tell by his flinch that I'd wrecked his plan, which did my heart good. I love my brother, but sometimes I have to step on him a little harder than I want just to get his attention. Touching his cheek lightly, I said, "Bradford, I know you love me and want to protect me, and I appreciate it, I honestly do. But I'm a grown woman. I'll be fine, I promise you."

He grunted, uncomfortable as always with exhibits of emotion. "You'd better be. If anything happens to you, I'm holding Lillian responsible."

After he was gone, my stomach grumbled, and I realized that I was alone. The only way I was going to get anything to eat myself was to shut the card shop down, and I couldn't afford to do that. I rummaged through my purse and found a few peanut butter crackers, then grabbed the last Diet Coke from my minifridge. If my questionable nutritional practices didn't kill me, how much luck could a ghost have?

Lillian came back to the shop soon after Bradford left, and I wondered if she'd been waiting in the shadows for his departure. I didn't care. She had a bulging bag from Granville's Deli, a new sandwich shop that had opened where Carly's House of Style had recently been. We were all accustomed to watching shops come and go on Oakmont, but I'd hated to see Carly's shut down. Contrary to its name, the boutique was run by an older man named Georges, who had better taste in clothing than I ever had. We'd become friends since I'd opened my place, but Georges couldn't afford to stay in business and he'd shut his doors, a prospect that haunted my dreams nearly every night.

Lillian handed me a sandwich, and I took it eagerly from her. "Don't you at least want to know the choices?"

"If it's not still moving, I'll eat it." I took a single bite and discovered that I'd chosen a club sandwich, one of the worst ones I'd ever had in my life. The bacon was still raw, barely warmed, while the bread was at least as old as I was. If tomato and lettuce were present, they were hiding from that bite. The rest of the meat was frozen into a solid block. Lillian glanced at my expression, then wisely examined her sandwich before sampling it. Without a word, she wrapped her sandwich back up in its paper. "Give that to me," she said, gesturing to mine.

"You know, I'd love to be able to say that it's not that bad, but I'm not that good a liar."

I handed it back to her, and as Lillian headed for the door she called out, "I'll be back shortly."

I was glad I didn't own Granville's. It was going to be hard enough for them to keep afloat while the greatest influx of our tourists was absent. While it was true we had hikers during autumn and skiers during winter and on into spring, there were no crowds like our summer people, and I was hoping to hang on for their return myself.

As I waited for a real meal, I was in a pretty foul temper, hungry as a bear after hibernation, and I was in no mood for any foolishness. When I saw Bradford drive up, I rushed out the door to send him away.

One look at the expression on his face told me that he wasn't there to chide me about my new living quarters. Something was wrong.

"What is it? Did something happen to Sara Lynn?"

He shook his head. "No, it's nothing like that. Jen, you mentioned that Maggie Blake was one of your customers, didn't you?"

"Sure, Maggie's in my card-making club. We meet every Thursday. She makes the most hilarious gag cards I've ever seen. Why?" Suddenly I wished I hadn't asked. Maggie was a real jewel, always ready to tell a funny story on herself, relaying something that had happened to her with the most hilarious results. Her sense of humor was barely inside the boundaries of good taste, but the cards Maggie made were so outlandish they were funny. She was at least as old as Lillian, but while my aunt fought every advancing wrinkle with creams and ointments galore, Maggie embraced her age, reveling in it, and I'd always admired her for it.

Bradford's voice caught in his throat before he managed to say, "I'm afraid she had a car accident. After I left you, I got a call on my radio. From the look of things at the scene, she must have taken her eyes off the road for just a second. Cargill Road turned, but her car kept going straight. If she'd had her seat belt on, who knows? But she didn't. I'm sorry, Jennifer, but she didn't make it."

Oh, no. I hated the thought of Maggie not being around anymore.

"Sis, are you okay?"

"I'm not, but I will be. Life's short, isn't it, Bradford?"

He rubbed his neck, then said, "I see it all the time, but it doesn't make it any easier to accept, does it? Anyway, I was on my way out there and I wanted to stop and tell you about it first. I know she was a friend of yours."

I hugged my big brother, hanging on longer than I needed to, but sometimes it was nice forgetting that I was grown-up. Bradford wrapped me up in his arms, and I let it out, mourning for my lost friend. After a few minutes, I felt better than I had any right to expect. I pulled away, wiped the last tears off my face, and kissed Bradford's cheek. "Thank you," I said.

He looked down at me and smiled. "Any time. If you need me, call, okay?"

"I will," I said as I touched his shoulder lightly. At that moment, his radio crackled. "Boss, we need you here on Cargill."

"What happened?" he asked, his face suddenly taut.

"No big deal, but a couple of rubberneckers watching the tow truck rammed into each other."

"Can't you handle them, Wayne?" I'd recognized the voice as belonging to one of my brother's deputies. Bradford had a blind spot when it came to Wayne Davidson, but I knew he was a total creep, and I did everything in my power to avoid him.

"Well, I could, but seeing how one of them's the mayor, I thought you might want to trot on back and take care of this one yourself."

Bradford rolled his eyes, then said, "I'll be right there." Then he turned to me. "Sorry Jen, but I really need to be there."

"I'll be fine," I said. "Go."

By the time Lillian came back five minutes later, I'd repaired my makeup, but my heart was still in bad shape. If I tried, I could almost hear Maggie's laugh, and it was a sound that should have given me comfort, but couldn't anymore.

"Child, what happened?" Lillian asked as she dropped two bags from Hurley's on the counter. Hurley's was an upscale pub that served some of the best food in Rebel Forge.

"Maggie Blake is dead," I said, not meaning to blurt it out like that.

Lillian shook her head sadly and asked softly, "Was it her heart?"

"No, she had a car accident on Cargill Road. Why, did she have heart problems?"

Lillian frowned. "Not that I know of, but it's a likely suspect when folks get to a certain age."

I decided not to say anything about my aunt's years. I didn't want to even think about her mortality. "I'm going to miss her," I said, managing to hold in my tears, though barely.

Lillian accepted it a lot more readily than I did. "She was a bright light, wasn't she?" Then my aunt turned to the food. "I've got hamburgers here just the way you like them. I'm afraid Granville's isn't going to make it till Christmas."

I couldn't believe how cavalier my aunt was being. "I can't possibly eat anything now. A friend of ours is dead, Lillian. Don't you care?"

My aunt's voice was stern as she said, "Jennifer, when you get to be my age, losing people is something you must accept with all the grace and dignity possible. Maggie had a good, full life, and from the sound of it, she didn't suffer much in the end, not like other friends of mine have. I'll miss her too, but there's nothing either one of us can do about it. Starving yourself won't bring her back." Lillian must have realized how callous she sounded. Her tone shifted as she added, "The best memorial we can make to the ones who've gone before is to live our lives to the fullest. Are you certain you don't want this?"

She unwrapped the burger and handed it to me. Lillian was right, but it was tough to act as if nothing had happened. My stomach rumbled again, and I decided to follow my aunt's advice. We ate in silence, every one of Lillian's attempts at conversation dying in the air between us. I'd have to make the best card I was capable of in Maggie's memory, but I didn't know who I could possibly give it to.

After our meal, I told Lillian, "If you don't mind, why don't you work the front. I want to inventory our stockroom."

"Jennifer, are you really in the mood to crawl around those dusty and dirty shelves counting stock today?"

"Grunt work is exactly what I need right now. If you run into any problems, just call me."

As I worked, I tried to put Maggie's death in perspective. While it was true that Lillian had been confronted with the loss of family, friends and loved ones a lot more than I had over the years, I'd lost both my parents, two people I loved with all my heart. Losing them had been a blow, and maybe the fact that they'd been killed in a car accident too made Maggie's death a little tougher for me to take.

I heard the front door chime, but I didn't think anything about it until a head poked into the back room. "Hey, any chance you haven't had lunch yet?"

Gail Lowry, my best friend since the third grade, was standing there. I didn't want to cry again, but seeing her suddenly brought it all out. She was dressed in a suit that was worth more than my car and I was covered with dust, but Gail didn't even hesitate to hug me. "What happened?" she asked finally as I wound down and pulled away.

"One of my favorite customers in the world just died in a car wreck."

"I'm so sorry," she said. "Is there anything I can do?"

I looked at her smudged suit. "Oh no, look what I did. You're a mess."

She brushed a few bits of dust off her jacket. "Don't worry about this. I wanted an excuse to skip out this afternoon anyway. I don't even know why I'm working. I already made my sales quota for the month, and then some. Anything I make from here on out will just go to taxes."

My best friend was extremely successful selling heavy equipment to construction companies. Her startling blue eyes and thick black hair got their attention, but her brains were what persuaded them to buy, and keep on buying. One of the things I liked best about her was that she didn't try to hide her extra twenty pounds, having her suits tailored to show off her curvy figure, enhancing instead of disguising.

Gail said, "Listen, why don't you play hooky with me? We can catch a movie or something."

I was tempted, but there was no way I could afford the time away from the shop. In all honesty, I wasn't even certain I could cover the cost of the ticket. "Thanks, but I've got to work."

"Suit yourself," she said, knowing better than to offer to pay. "While you're slaving away, I'm going to get lost in a movie star's eyes."

"Tell him I said hi," I said.

"I'll do no such thing. When I'm in the theater, they only have eyes for me."

I felt much better after talking to Gail. It was time to stop worrying so much about myself and think about how the other members of our club would deal with our loss. We'd have to do something special in her memory at the next meeting. Then I wondered if anyone knew to call the rest of the group and break the news to them. Our new club consisted of Hilda Bunting, Dot Crane, and Betty and Howard Hudson, seniors all. While I'd hoped to get a few folks under sixty to join, I was still happy with my group. Even Howard, Betty's husband and an ex–war vet, had thrown himself into card making, though from what I'd heard, Betty had blackmailed him into attending with her at first. I decided I needed to call them myself be-fore they read about Maggie's death in the newspaper.

When I picked up the phone to call Hilda, instead of getting a dial tone, the line was open. "Hello?" I said, wondering what was going on.

"That was fast," Hilda said. "I barely finished dialing your number."

"It didn't even ring," I said. "I was just calling you."

Hilda paused before replying. "That's odd, isn't it? I'm guessing we're calling about the same reason. You heard about Maggie too, huh?"

That really caught me off guard. My brother had just told me, and if Hilda had a better pipeline to the police department than I did, I wanted to know what it was. "I just found out. To be honest with you, I'm surprised you know already."

"Don't be. I've got a police scanner. I've been sitting here listening to them in a state of shock. Poor Maggie."

"It's terrible, isn't it? Should we cancel our meeting this week?" I wasn't sure I could face everyone so soon after losing one of our members.

"It's up to you—you're in charge—but what do you think Maggie would say?"

I thought about the card crafter and how much she loved our get-togethers. Maggie had instituted a refreshment policy that required everyone to take turns with a dessert, even Howard. He'd had the rotation during the last session and had brought Rice Krispies Treats. Betty swore he'd made them all by himself, following the recipe on the box.

Suddenly I knew exactly what our friend would say. "We'll have the meeting, just like we always do."

Hilda said, "That's the spirit. Maggie would be proud."

"Have you already called everyone else in the club?" I asked.

"No, you're the first one on my list. Would you like to call the others yourself?"

I thought about it, then said, "Why don't you take Dot and I'll call Betty and Howard?"

"I can do that," she said softly.

"Thanks, Hilda, I appreciate your help."

"Hey, she was quite a gal, wasn't she?"

"She was." I hung up the phone, then dialed Betty and Howard's number. If I was going to get through this without crying, I needed to make that phone call fast. I was hoping Howard would pick up, but Betty answered instead.

"Betty, I'm afraid I've got some bad news."

"You're not canceling the meeting this week, are you? I just read about a new technique I've been dying to try."

I fiddled with a calligraphy pen, not sure how to break it to her. "I'm sorry to be the one to tell you this, but Maggie Blake is dead."

While I wasn't expecting Lillian's calm reaction to the news, I still wasn't prepared for Betty's shriek. As I heard the phone hit the hardwood floor, I felt helpless listening to her wail. In the background I could hear Howard trying to comfort her. A minute later he picked up the phone. "Hello? Who is this?"

"Howard, it's Jennifer Shane from the card shop. I'm so sorry I caused this."

His voice grew tense. "What did you say to her?"

"I told her that Maggie Blake was dead."

There was enough silence on the other end of the phone that I wondered if I'd killed them both. "Howard, are you still there?"

"I'm here," he said, his words barely above a whisper. "Thanks for calling." And then he hung up on me.

I was suddenly very glad I didn't have to make any more telephone calls, and hoped that Hilda had better results with Dot than I had with the Hudsons. I was about to go back to my inventory when the telephone rang. As soon as I answered it, I found myself wishing that I'd just let it ring.

Chapter 3

"Jennifer Shane, it appears that I gave you more credit than I should have. Explain yourself, young lady."

It was my sister, Sara Lynn, and as greetings went, I wished I could say that this one was more abrupt than her usual manner, but if I did, I'd be lying. "Do you really have the time for that particular conversation? Because I know I don't."

"You know perfectly well what I mean. I just heard from Bradford. I cannot believe you had the shortsightedness to rent that apartment."

I took a deep breath, then said, "Sara Lynn, I've got more problems than you can imagine. My housing situation is the least of my worries. If you want to scold me, you're going to have to wait till later. I don't have the time or the heart for it right now. Good-bye." Then I startled myself by hanging up on her.

It felt good cradling the telephone back in its base, even though I fully realized that I'd pay for it later. I knew my sister meant well, but that excuse for her abrupt manner only went so far, and I was in no frame of mind to be on the end of one of her scoldings. I wasn't in the mood to work on the inventory anymore, so I dusted off my jeans and tried to make myself presentable enough to wait on customers, if we had any.

Lillian was waiting on a handsome man in his mid-

thirties, his dark hair already beginning to dust with
touches of silver. Of course she got to help him. No
doubt my next customer would be a third grader
working on a school project or a ninety-year-old man
with wandering eyes. Sometimes life just wasn't fair.
I tried to look busy at the counter, sneaking a peek
every now and then at Lillian's customer. To my surprise, she caught me looking, and I could see a smile
barely crease her lips as she called out to me, "Jennifer, could you come here a moment?"

I started to stick my tongue out at her when her
customer turned in my direction. "I'd be happy to."

I joined them, fighting the urge the entire time to
smooth my hair and brush off my jeans yet again.
"How may I help?"

He said, "I'm looking for a present for someone,
and it has to be perfect."

"What's the occasion, if I might ask?" I didn't see
a ring, so hopefully he wasn't buying an anniversary
present for his wife.

"My mother's turning sixty-five in a few days, and
I'm at a loss what to get her."

"We've got just the thing." I led him to our selection of gift baskets and wondered why Lillian hadn't
taken him there first.

He frowned. "I've seen these already. They just
won't do, not for my mother."

"Okay," I said. "Perhaps we can do a custom basket
designed exclusively for her."

"That's what I need, something unique for the perfect woman," he said as he smiled.

I'll say this for him: the man knew his mother's
every whim and taste. After I talked to him for five
minutes, there was no doubt in my mind that there
was room for only one woman in his heart, and he'd
known her all his life. I pitied any woman he dated,
knowing that they would never measure up to the
standard he'd set in his mind. We worked together

half an hour, and when there was a choice to make, he always opted for the most expensive item I had to offer. I felt a little bad taking advantage of him, but the man was screaming for it, and I didn't have the heart to deny him. As I rang up his considerable purchases, I said, "If you'd like, we offer a special delivery service for our most exclusive clientele." We did nothing of the sort, but I wasn't ready to let him off the hook yet.

"No, thank you. I want to deliver this myself. You've done a remarkable job on it."

I gave him my best smile. "That's why we're here."

Ten seconds after he was gone, Lillian and I burst out laughing. "Can you believe that man?" I asked.

"You're the one I can't believe. Jennifer, that bill was atrocious. You should be ashamed of yourself."

"Lillian, I just gave the man what he wanted. Think how proud he'll be when his mother gets her present."

My aunt shook her head in amazement. "Right now all I can think about is how he'll react when his credit card statement comes."

"Are you kidding me? It's for his dear precious mother; he'll pay it without batting an eyelash. Suddenly I'm feeling better about the world."

Lillian scowled as she looked over my shoulder. "Sorry, but I have a feeling it's not going to last very long. Sara Lynn's almost at the door, and from the sour look on her face, she's about to ruin that smile. Quick, duck out the back way and I'll stall her."

"Thanks, but I can handle Sara Lynn." While that wasn't even remotely the truth, I knew it was better to deal with her than to run away. Well, maybe just a little better.

Before she could say a word, I said, "Sara Lynn, I'm sorry I hung up on you, I'm sorry I didn't consult with you about my new apartment, and I'm sorry you can't seem to lose those last five pounds you've been battling." That final shot was complete farce, since my older sister was barely as big as a hummingbird. I grinned as I said it, and though I could tell she was fighting it, she matched my smile with one of her own.

Finally, she said, "I don't know how you manage to do it, but I can't stay angry with you."

"Hey, when you get into as much trouble as I seem to, it's a skill worth cultivating. I really am sorry."

Sara Lynn spied the credit card receipt still on the counter. I'd meant to put it in the drawer, but I kind of enjoyed seeing it out there. "My, I don't need to ask how business is, do I?"

I nonchalantly opened the register and put it inside. "We're managing. How's business on your end of Oakmont?"

"Fine, adequate, tolerable—take your pick. Jennifer, I'm not here to discuss the status of our enterprises. Are you really moving into Whispering Oak?"

"I am. Would you like to help? I could use an extra hand. Bailey's invited, too. He can bring his pickup." While I wasn't crazy about the running commentary from Sara Lynn that I was sure to get, I could use her husband's strong back and especially his Ford truck.

Sara Lynn bit her lower lip before she spoke. "I'm afraid Bailey's gone."

"Sis, what happened? I didn't know you two were having problems." Of all the married couples in the world, my sister and her husband were the most married I knew. I couldn't imagine the circumstances that would split them up.

"We're not divorcing, you nit. He's out of town on business. As a matter of fact, I've been looking for something to keep me occupied. I'd be delighted to help you move."

The last thing I wanted on earth was to be one of my sister's projects. "You know, I don't have that much stuff after all. I'm sure I can handle it by myself."

"Nonsense. When are you moving?"

I've long known that my sister has been a thorough planner since kindergarten, so if I was going to dodge her assistance, I knew just what I had to do. The best way to throw her off was to accelerate the time frame right on the spot. "I'm going to move right after work tonight. It's probably going to run pretty late, so I understand completely if you want to pass on it."

I thought I had her, but it just proved I didn't know my sister as well as I thought I did. "Tonight would be perfect. We'll make a party out of it." Lillian had been hovering in the background, no doubt afraid I was going to rat her out again. Sara Lynn turned to her and said, "You're helping too, aren't you?"

"Sorry, I'd love to, but I can't. I'm busy."

If my aunt was seeing anyone, she'd failed to mention it to me. I didn't doubt it was a date with Ben & Jerry, but I wasn't about to push it. I said, "That's fine."

She frowned, then said, "Jennifer, I'll be there to help, you know that."

"Don't cancel your plans on my account."

"Please," she said. "You know that my family always comes first."

"If you're sure." Lillian might have had something going on, but then again, she might not have. Either way, I knew I could count on her.

I hadn't packed a thing yet, hadn't even planned to move until the weekend in fact, so I was going to have to hustle to get ready on the new schedule. I hadn't given notice yet at my old apartment, but it was the kind of place where it wasn't really required, since folks had a tendency to move out in the middle of the night there. After my sister left, it suddenly hit me. Whether I was ready for it or not, I was moving into a haunted apartment in Whispering Oak.

Moving a residence is a real wake-up call. I must have thrown out more than I packed, shedding the remnants of an old life along with the apartment. My cats were taking the changes with their normal reactions. Nash was perched on the TV, watching with disdain as Sara Lynn and I worked, while Oggie had to investigate every box as we packed it. I was going through a stack of old bills, letters and cards when something caught my attention. It was a Hallmark greeting card, something as rare in my place as snow in Miami, and I wondered who'd sent it. I opened it and saw that it was from Greg Langston during one of our "on again" periods. "My Dearest Jen," it said in his clear and firm hand. "Being with you is all I ever want. I love you more than I can say, Greg." Evidently he wrote it a little prematurely, but the sentiment had been sincere at the time. What happened to us, Greg? I thought. Any rational person would think that two broken engagements would be enough to close that door forever, but there was something about that man, something magical when we were together. Maybe that was why I was so abrupt with him all the time. I knew that if I gave him the slightest sign of encouragement, he'd wedge himself back into my heart, and I doubted I could take another breakup with him.

Lillian's voice brought me abruptly back to reality. "Child, whyever are you crying?"

"I'm not crying," I said as I wiped the tears off my cheeks.

"Okay," Lillian said in an even tone, "then what's so mesmerizing about that card? You've been staring at it for the last five minutes."

"It's nothing," I said as I resolutely chucked the card into the growing pile of discards from my life now littering my living room floor. That was best, getting rid of all those old reminders, so maybe they'd stop haunting me.

Five minutes later, I scrambled through the pile, retrieved the card and tucked it safely inside one of my books. Maybe that made me a sentimental slob, but it comforted me knowing that at one time in my life, for however long it lasted, somebody had loved me that much. Sara Lynn had packed up my kitchen while I'd been sorting through my personal items. There was no doubt in my mind she was better at that particular salvage operation than I would have been.

"My goodness, you travel light in this world, don't you?" Lillian said as she surveyed the stack of boxes by the door.

"I'm not a big fan of knickknacks," I said. "I've got everything I need." She was right, though. I had a habit of discarding things the moment they lost their usefulness to me. It was more out of necessity than philosophy, as my apartments tended to be on the tiny side. One large box held my favorite books, and it was going to kill me getting it down the stairs into Sara Lynn's car. Studying the pile of boxes, I thought it didn't look like much to have accumulated in a life-time, but it was still going to be a pain to move it all. Bailey had taken his truck out of town with him, and I wasn't sure how we were going to get what we needed to move without making several trips.

"The next question is, how are we going to get this all downstairs?"

At that moment, Bradford walked into my apartment through the unlocked door. Instead of his uniform, he wore blue jeans and a flannel shirt I loved. He grinned at me and said, "You really should keep this dead bolted, you know."

"Why, when there's a cop right around every corner? What are you doing here?"

He smiled, a gentle reminder of Bradford as a boy. He'd had the best disposition of any kid on the block. No doubt he'd needed it, growing up with Sara Lynn and me. "I'm here to help you move. Cindy took the kids to her mother's house for dinner, but I told her I needed to help you."

I laughed. "Now I know you'd do anything to avoid Clara. Bradford, I don't have anything to feed you. Sara Lynn and I ate before we got started."

"Don't worry about me," Bradford said as he patted his stomach. "I grabbed a bite at The Lunch Box on the way over."

"And you didn't bring me anything? I can't believe Savannah let you out of there without at least a piece of pie for me."

Bradford wiped a phantom crumb off his chin. "That's right; I was supposed to give that to you, wasn't I? If it's any consolation, it was delicious."

Sara Lynn came out of the bedroom. "Glad you could finally make it. Did you bring your truck?"

"You'd better believe it. It would take forever to move with those dinky cars you two have. Where should I get started?"

Sara Lynn instantly pointed to the box of books. "Why don't you take that one?"

Bradford started to pick the box up, and I could see the strain on his face.

"I'm sorry," I said. "Should I break that up into two or three boxes?"

"No, I'll manage it, but dinner with Clara is looking better by the second."

Sara Lynn said, "Pooh, you need a little more real exercise, Bradford; sitting at that desk is making you pudgy."

If Bradford had gained three pounds since he'd become sheriff, you couldn't prove it by me. He protested, "I work out at the gym three days a week."

"And you eat all seven," she said.

Bradford raised his eyes to the ceiling. "I've got a question for you. Did I really need two sisters?"

I laughed. "You love us both. Admit it."

He shrugged. "True, but my favorite changes by the minute." He grabbed the box and took it downstairs as Sara Lynn and I started stuffing my castoffs into trash bags. "Are you certain you wouldn't like to go through this again?" Sara Lynn asked.

"I'm sure. I've got everything I need." As I walked through the apartment one last time, I felt the emptiness, though there was still furniture and appliances there. It was suddenly generic, devoid of my touch and ready for its next occupant.

Sara Lynn said, "After we unpack, we should come back here and clean this place from top to bottom." Sara Lynn was a clean freak, whereas I put things off until I was forced to straighten up so I could clear a path to walk.

"We'll see how long it takes to set up my new place," I said.

"Are you having second thoughts?" Sara Lynn asked me.

"I'm probably up to fifth thoughts by now, but I'm moving anyway. Maybe we will come back tonight." Suddenly I wanted to put this address behind me once and for all. If Sara Lynn was still up for it, I was going to take her up on her offer.

Oggie and Nash were sitting quietly on the couch, side by side and as still as statues. "How about you two? Are you ready to see your new place?"

I swear it had to be coincidence, but Oggie shook his head, as if denying it.

I looked over at Sara Lynn, who had the most quizzical expression on her face. I asked her, "Did you just see that?"

She said, "When it comes to your cats, I'll believe just about anything."

I waited until the last possible second to put them into the cat carriers. Bradford's truck was loaded, and the kitchen items were in Sara Lynn's car. All I had to contend with was moving my roommates. I clucked softly to them as I put them in their carriers, and as we walked out, I spoke to them both, trying to ease some of their anxiety about moving. Okay, maybe I was the one with the anxiety, but it seemed to help all three of us.

.

A light glared from the front porch as we drove up. Was that a courtesy for me, or was it on a timer? I grabbed the carriers and told Bradford and Sara Lynn, "Give me a few minutes to get the cats settled, okay?"

Bradford said, "Fine by me. I never say no to a break."

Sara Lynn ignored his comment. "We'll be up in three minutes, Jennifer. After all, we don't have all night, and there's still a great deal of cleaning to do back at your old apartment if you have any hope of getting your security deposit back."

I refrained from reminding her that she'd volunteered for tonight's duty, and grabbed Oggie and Nash. I was at the top landing before I realized that I didn't have a key to the place. Had Lillian put it back under the mat? Yes, there it was. I opened the door and slid the key into my purse. The second I carried the cats inside, Oggie was eager to get out and explore. After I freed him, I opened Nash's carrier, but instead of leaping out like his roommate had, he stared at me as if I'd lost my mind. "Not you, too. I'm getting enough of that from my siblings. Come on, you'll like it here. Trust me."

He sneezed twice, then stared disdainfully at me as I pulled him out. I swear, cats are crazier than people. Nash's expression probably reflected that exact sentiment in reverse, but I chose to ignore it. While Oggie explored, Nash leaped onto the top of an armoire, wedging himself in a place where he could see just about everything going on inside the apartment with barely a twitch of his neck.

"They repainted the place," Bradford said as he carried the first box upstairs. "It looks good."

Sara Lynn followed closely behind him with the

remnants of my refrigerator. "Where do I put these? This apartment does have a kitchen, doesn't it?"

"Of course it does," I said as I pointed to the corner where a scaled-down stove, refrigerator and sink stood.

Sara Lynn snorted. "I can't imagine you actually cooking anything there more complicated than toast."

"Yeah, but I'm really good at that, if I say so myself."

Bradford looked at Sara Lynn and said, "Take it easy, Sis. The deed is done, so let's make the best of it."

No one said a word about the suicide, though I noticed that Sara Lynn detoured away from the bathroom whenever she was within a yard of it. Bradford, who had every reason in the world to avoid it, had no qualms about storing my towels and extra sheets in the closet inside it. It would have taken me hours to make the move myself, but with my brother and sister helping, we had all the boxes upstairs in hardly any time at all. Like I said, sometimes it was nice having family so close.

Bradford started to open one of the boxes. "Let's get this stuff put away. It's my turn to tuck the kids in tonight." My brother was a devoted father, one of the things I admired most about him.

"Leave them. I'll take care of unpacking later. You've already done the hard part."

"I don't mind hanging around. I've got a little time before I need to get home," he said.

"Nonsense, you've done more than enough. Sara Lynn and I aren't staying, either. We're going back to the old apartment in a few minutes." I reached up and kissed him on the cheek. "Thank you, Bradford, and not just for the strong back."

I didn't have to tell him my added thanks were for not mentioning his thoughts on my apartment choice,

given the circumstances. "Hey, you'll be fine." He
leaned in closer and whispered, "I'd get that lock
changed, though. Would you like me to call my guy?
He can come by tonight if I ask him."

"I'm sure he would, but I'll be fine. I'll call him
myself when I get the chance."

Bradford raised one eyebrow. "Jennifer, I'm serious. You don't have any idea how many copies of that
key are floating around."

"Come on, I've got my two trained attack cats with
me. What could happen?"

Sara Lynn said, "What are you two mumbling about?"

Bradford winked at me, then said, "The ears are
the first to go. Next thing you know, we'll have to
shout at her."

Sara Lynn swatted him smartly. "Just because
you're the sheriff doesn't mean you're safe from me,
little brother."

"Hey, if that's the way you're going to be, I'm getting out of here." Bradford hugged me, then tickled
Sara Lynn until she laughed. It felt good being with
them in my new place.

"We'll walk you out," I said. At the door, I saw that
Nash was still at his post, while Oggie had wormed his
way inside one of my boxes. At least it wasn't one
holding food. I silently thanked Sara Lynn for putting
all of that away. "See you soon. Try to stay out of
trouble."

They both ignored me completely, so at least that
was back to the status quo.

It took us until nearly midnight before Sara Lynn
pronounced my old apartment fit for its new tenant. I
would have left at ten and taken the hit on the deposit
just so I could take a long hot bath and go to bed,
but my sister wouldn't hear of it. I knew I'd thank
her when I got the check, but at the moment I was
tired, dirty and in no mood for company. As we car-

ried the last two bags to the Dumpster, she said, "Aren't you going to miss this place?"

"I'm not the sentimental type—you know that—at least not when it comes to apartments. Do you want to know the truth? I enjoy moving around every now and then. It keeps things fresh."

"Jennifer, if I had to move everything I own, I swear I'd be tempted to take a match to it all and start over with the insurance check."

My sister had to be at least as tired as I was to say something like that. "Shh, somebody might hear you."

"So? I wouldn't deny the sentiment."

"Sara Lynn, with your luck, there will be an electrical fire and Bradford will have to lock you up for arson."

She scoffed at the idea. "I'd like to see him try to put handcuffs on me."

"You know what? I'd pay for a front-row seat for that myself."

After we tossed the last bags, I knocked on the super's door. No surprise, he wasn't there, so I scrawled a note explaining my departure; then I stuffed it in an envelope with the keys and slipped it all into the super's mail slot. We walked back to our cars and I hugged my sister fiercely.

"Jennifer, I can't breathe."

"Sorry," I said as I eased off a notch. "Sara Lynn, you were a lifesaver tonight. I mean it; you were golden."

My sister is not one to suffer compliments well. "It wasn't that much trouble. After all, I didn't have anything else to do."

I kept hugging her as I said, "I'm not letting go until you say 'You're welcome.'"

She struggled briefly, but I was a lot stronger than she was, and besides, I had a better grip.

"You're welcome," she finally said, and I released her.

Sara Lynn looked up at me and said, "Are you going to be all right at your new place? I could stay with you a few days if you'd like."

"You're welcome to visit, but why don't you wait until I get everything put away first?" Before she could offer more help, I said, "If you help me get settled, I'll never be able to find anything. Good night, Sis."

It was a miracle, but she didn't fight me on it. Sara Lynn must have been every bit as exhausted as I was. "Good night, Jennifer."

I watched her drive away, then got into my car and headed to my new place. I didn't even look back at the old apartment. It had been just another place to stay, no better or worse than any of my other homes. As long as I had Oggie and Nash with me, I could stay just about anywhere. I wondered what my roommates were up to, and drove a little faster than I should have getting back. My cats, regardless of their brave fronts, needed time to get acclimated, and I knew the transition for them would be easier if I was right there with them. I parked, walked in and started up the stairs when I saw a stranger standing at my door with something in his hands. He had a scowl on his face, and I wondered what kind of trouble I'd gotten myself into this time.

HANDCRAFTED CARD TIP

Handmade cards were created in Victorian times using paper "scrap," tiny pieces of colorful die-cut paper available for just pennies.

In that tradition, I like to take favorite colors and textures of paper I've stumbled across over the years and incorporate them into the cards I make. It's my own way of creating a little history.

Chapter 4

"Can I help you?" I asked, gripping my keys in my fist like a weapon. I'd teased Bradford about his recent lessons in self-defense, but I wasn't joking at the moment. I had pepper spray too, but unfortunately it was on the other side of the door, along with the baseball bat I liked to keep around for protection wherever I lived. Still, with the keys protruding between the fingers of my closed fist, I wasn't entirely defenseless.

"You must be the new tenant," he said. "I'm Barrett Dawes. From downstairs," he added, gesturing to one of the doors below us.

Okay, so he wasn't some crazy stalker. I slid my keys out of my hands and tucked them into the front pocket of my jeans.

I offered my hand. "I'm Jennifer Shane," I said.

He took it, and I felt a spark from static electricity at his touch. At least I hoped that was what it was. He wasn't a pretty-boy kind of handsome, but he didn't miss it by much. A slightly broken nose and a faded scar on his chin kept him from that status, but he was still one of the best-looking men I'd ever met face-to-face. He ran a hand through his jet-black hair and offered me my first look at his dimples. "Jennifer, it's nice to meet you." He pulled his other arm from behind his back and produced a nice bottle of wine. "Here, this is for you, a housewarming present."

"Thanks," I said as I took it from him. "Your greeting is a lot more cordial than our other neighbor's."

Barrett smiled, his pale green eyes flashing. "So you've met Jeffrey. Don't mind him; he hates everyone."

"Even you?" I asked. Jennifer, get a hold of yourself. I swear, it was all I could do not to giggle like a girl in junior high school.

"We had a rough patch at first, but Jeffrey and I get along fine right now." He gestured to my door. "I won't keep you; I know you just moved in. I just wanted to say 'Welcome to the building.'"

"Thanks," I said. "I'd invite you in, but . . ."

"No, please, I understand. We'll have a proper drink once you're settled. Good night."

"Good night," I said as he headed down the stairs. I unlocked the apartment door, stepped inside, then slipped the dead bolt in place and, after a few moments' thought, wedged a heavy chair under the knob.

"Guys, are you hungry?" I didn't expect Oggie and Nash to greet me with enthusiasm—there was no mistaking them for dogs in any way, shape or form—but I didn't think they'd hide from me either. The new apartment wasn't all that big, so where could the rascals be? I walked to the bed, expecting to find them curled up on my pillow like they always were, but neither one of them was there. There was only one more place I could look, and I'd avoided the bathroom so far. Taking a deep breath, I pushed the door open and looked inside, but there wasn't a cat in sight. Now it was time to panic. "Oggie! Nash!"

Then I heard a low, frightened mew. "Guys, where are you?"

I heard the sound of their whimpers again, and I knew where they were. Huddled inside their cat carriers, both of my roommates were staring out at me. "Oggie, Nash, what's wrong, you two?"

I had a tough time coaxing them out of their carriers, which was a first. Why had they ended up back inside, when they had an entire apartment to explore? They'd both already eaten, but tonight was an exception. I dug through two of the boxes until I found my electric can opener and got out some canned salmon, their utmost number one favorite treat. As they dug into the windfall, I stroked their backs and cooed softly to them. By the time they were finished, it appeared my old friends were back in their true form. Nash favored me with a nuzzle, and his whiskers tickled my nose. "Okay, salmon breath, I'm glad everything's fine now. What happened? Did something spook you two?"

I swear, sometimes I wished they could talk. I got out my comforter and spread it out on the bed. Before I could straighten it, both cats had pounced and were curling up on it. I didn't know how I was going to fit on the bed with them, but tonight I wouldn't have evicted them for anything in the world. I needed their proximity every bit as much as they seemed to need mine. I stared at the boxes by the front door, knowing that I should start unpacking, so there was really only one solution. I turned my back so I wouldn't have to look at them. I'd have enough time to unpack when I wasn't so exhausted. I'd worked hard enough that day, it was late, and I had to get up early for work.

I shucked off my clothes and slipped into my pajamas, which I had, quite by accident, rolled up inside the comforter. I didn't even wash my face or brush my teeth, a rare event for me.

Then, in the middle of a deep and sound sleep, I swear I heard something moving around in my apartment.

The first thing I did was check on the cats. They were both sound asleep on my pillow, and for a second I regretted not having a nice pit bull or rottweiler as a pet. I might as well have wished for wings. I tried to find a light, but it was hopeless. My eyes were adjusting a little to the darkness, and as far as I could tell, there wasn't a single whisker twitch from my roommates. Blast it all, I couldn't remember where I'd put my baseball bat! In desperation I took the drawer out of the nightstand, determined to whack the intruder over the head with it if I could. It felt good having something in my hands.

I would have loved to have had a flashlight, the heavy kind I'd seen in Bradford's patrol car, but I didn't even have a lighter. As I scanned the room, I thought I saw someone frozen in place near one of the windows, though I could barely see his outline. What was he doing? Holding the drawer like a weapon, I crept up on him and swung at his head. There'd be plenty of time to ask questions later after he woke up. There was a loud crash as I swung, and I knew he wasn't getting up any time soon. I searched frantically for a light switch so I could find the telephone to call Bradford. Finally, my fingers brushed against the switch and I flipped it up.

Somehow, in the darkness, I'd managed to kill one of my new lamps.

As I gathered up the remnants of the broken shade, I had to laugh about what I must have looked like. Of course no one could get in my place, but that still hadn't deterred my imagination one bit. I laughed as I worked, proud of myself for downing an innocent floor lamp. Hey, I hadn't known it was harmless. I'd seen a threat and had taken action. Still, I doubted I'd tell anyone about that particular confrontation. After I was finished, I turned off the lights and went back to bed. If Oggie or Nash had moved, I couldn't prove it. "You both missed all the excitement," I said.

They didn't respond, and I was tired of talking to myself, so I went to sleep, too.

* * *

It took me a few seconds to realize what was happening the next morning, but I finally figured out that someone was pounding on my front door. I glanced over at my alarm clock and saw that it was nearly eight. I'd slept in for the first time I could remember in the recent past. While I knew I had a robe in one of my boxes, I wasn't about to spend five minutes looking for it. I did find my coat from the night before, so I threw it on instead. "Who is it?" I asked without opening the door.

"It's Ethan York. Your brother sent me."

"With breakfast, by any chance?" I asked.

His laughter filtered through the door. "Sorry, I would have picked up a few doughnuts for you if I'd known. I'm a locksmith. He said you needed me first thing."

I undid the dead bolt and opened the door. "Well, I'll tell him you're a man of your word. It certainly is first thing, isn't it?"

Ethan was a tall, skinny man with a hawk's nose and a mop of unruly gray hair. He took in my disheveled appearance, then said, "I'm sorry, Ms. Shane, but I had to squeeze you in when I could. This is it, but I could come back next week if you'd rather."

"No, that's crazy." I added with a smile, "Besides, you're already here. I'd offer you a cup of coffee, but I don't have the vaguest idea where my coffeepot is."

"Thanks for the offer, but I'm going to have to jump on this pretty quick. Don't you worry, now; I'll be out of here in ten minutes." He retrieved a brand-new lock set and his toolbox from the hallway, then got to work. I needed a bath, or at the very least a shower, but I wasn't about to take it at the moment. There was only one thing I *could* do, so I started unpacking. Ethan was a chatty fellow, so I wasn't without entertainment as I worked.

"You've got a good solid door here," he said as he started dismantling my lock. "Oak like they don't make anymore. Once I'm through here, it would take an ax to get through to you."

That particular sentiment sent chills through me, and he must have seen the expression on my face. "Not that somebody's going to be coming after you with an ax. Or anything else, I mean. Come after you, that is. Hey, I've got an idea: why don't I just shut up and focus on the job at hand?"

"You can keep talking, but I wouldn't mind if we changed the subject."

Ethan laughed, and it was a lot more potent when we were both on the same side of the door. "You've got yourself a deal." He chatted aimlessly as he worked, fortunately avoiding any further discussions about potential attacks, for which I was eternally grateful. Ethan was as good as his word, and finished the job quickly. "What do I owe you?" I asked as I scanned the room for my purse.

"Your brother's covered it already," he said, and before I could protest, Ethan added, "He told me you'd put up a fuss, but if I took a dime from you, he'd have my head. Please don't put me in that position, Ma'am."

Well, there was nothing I could do about it, I realized that. "Thank you," I said.

He looked relieved, and I wondered what Bradford had told him about me. As Ethan handed me the keys, he added a card. "Don't hesitate to call me, day or night if there's an emergency. Have yourself a nice day, Ms. Shane."

"You too," I said as I closed the door. The lock had a solid thunk to it as it slid in place. Bradford was right; I did feel better. But I wasn't about to let him pay for the privilege.

There was a note on the register when I got into the shop. Written in Lillian's fluid script, it said,

Jennifer, I'll be late today, as I'm just wrapping up my evening at a little past four in the morning. I'll see you at noon with bells on and our lunch in tow.

  Fondly,
  Lillian
  PS Sorry about the short notice, but I'm having a wonderful time and most decidedly do not wish you were here! If you must, feel free to dock my wages. Ta-ta!

Well, at least one of us had a good night. Actually, I shouldn't say that. Once I got over attacking one of my lamps, I had fallen into a sound sleep, but I'd still been groggy this morning, and I'd decided today would be Casual Wednesday at Custom Card Creations, as the first articles of clothing I'd found were faded blue jeans and an old polo shirt.

I tacked the note to the corkboard behind the register so I could tease Lillian about it later; then I got ready to open the shop. Lillian wasn't a big fan of music in any form, so I took the liberty of tuning my radio to a classical station and I enjoyed a little Chopin while I worked. After I was set to go, I flipped the CLOSED sign to OPEN and unlocked the front door. Since no one was clamoring to get in and make a greeting card, I figured it might be a good time to catch up with my mail. I probably should have gone back to inventorying the back, but I decided it could wait until the next time I had to think something through. While I would dearly miss Maggie, I knew she'd live in my thoughts for a very long time, and a better memorial I could not imagine.

There were several bills in the stack of mail, a handful of fliers, and one handcrafted card. I recognized the envelope as one we sold, and I wondered who would be sending me, of all the people in the world, a greeting card.

My hands shook as I flipped the card over to open it and saw the name and return address. Printed in bold letters across the back of the envelope were the words "Do Not Open Unless Something Happens to Me."

Maggie Blake had created a card just for me, and she must have sent it right before she died.

Somehow I managed to tear the envelope open, but I was glad no one else was there to see my fumbling. The front of the black card was decorated with three-dimensional tombstones and skeletons, and the silver words HELP ME were stamped on the front of the card. The edges had been cut in a new scallop pattern using decorative scissors she'd special ordered. I recognized the design because it had just arrived the week before, and I'd tried the scissors myself before I delivered them to her.

Inside the card, Maggie had written a message with a silver marker that stood out against the black background.

It said,

Jennifer, I'm afraid someone's trying to kill me, and I can't for the life of me figure out who or why. I've never harmed a soul in my life. It just doesn't make sense. If I should die, make sure your brother investigates it thoroughly. I'm in the best of spirits, so he can rule out suicide, no matter how likely it may appear. As to an accident, believe me when I say I'm most careful, especially lately. Finally, there is no such thing as a random murder in this case, so if I'm carjacked or a tree falls on me, you can rest assured that someone wanted me dead.

Don't let me down, Jennifer. I'm counting on you.
Your friend,
Maggie.

I dialed Bradford's cell number as I finished reading. He picked up on the second ring. "Shane here."

The card shook in my hand as I stared at it. "Bradford, I need you to come to the store. It's urgent."

"What's wrong, Jennifer? Did someone break in?"

I tried to keep my emotions out of my voice. I knew my brother meant well, but most of the time I'd answer his questions if he just gave me the chance. "I just got a card from Maggie."

"Maggie Blake? Jen, that's hardly urgent."

"You won't think so once you read it. How long will it take you to get here? Hang on, some nitwit is honking his horn outside."

I peeked out my front door to see what was going on when I saw my brother's patrol car parked in front of my shop. "Are you stalking me, big brother?"

"No, ma'am, I'm just serving and protecting the town of Rebel Forge."

I wasn't buying that, not for a second. "I don't believe that. So why are you here?"

"Hey, you called me, remember?"

I scowled at him, which worked sometimes, but not often. Luckily, it did this time. He finally admitted, "Okay, I just talked to Ethan and I wanted to see if you're satisfied with his work."

"He's top-notch and you know it, or you never would have sent him to me. By the way, I'm not letting you pay for my new lock. I won't have it, Bradford, do you hear me?"

"Fine, I was just trying to be nice," he said, a little hurt edge in his voice.

I softened mine. "Bradford, it's not that I don't appreciate the gesture, because I do, but I've got to stand on my own sometime."

He shrugged. "Have it your way. When I get the bill I'll let you know how much it was. Now, what's this about hearing from Maggie Blake?"

"Come on inside. It's on the counter." We walked

in, and before I could hand him the letter, Bradford spotted Lillian's note. I tried to grab it off the board, but he was too quick for me.

"Isn't that just like our sweet old aunt?"

I wasn't about to stand for any bashing. "Hey, she's doing me a huge favor volunteering here. Lillian's entitled to a life of her own now and then."

That mollified him some, but it was pretty apparent the two of them were still on the outs. I didn't have time to worry about their petty feud; I had more important things on my mind at the moment.

"Read this," I said as I handed him the card, tucked back inside its envelope. He took in the message printed on the back of the envelope, grunted, then took the card out. Bradford read the message twice after studying the tombstones and skeletons, then handed the card back to me.

"So what are you going to do about this?" I asked him.

"Jen, you don't honestly believe she was serious, do you? I thought you told me Maggie made all kinds of gag cards. This sounds exactly like something she would do. Only this time her timing and her taste were both off."

It was true that Maggie was known for her offbeat sense of humor, but how could I convince him that this time it was different? "Bradford, she's not joking. How else do you explain the fact that she died right after she sent it?"

"I'll admit it's a sick coincidence, but that's as far as I'm willing to go."

I'm afraid I stomped my foot, something I did only when extremely irate. "This is serious. You've got to dig deeper."

My brother ran a hand through his hair. "Jennifer, why don't you leave the police investigations to me, and I'll let you make all the cards you want. I went over that car myself. There was nothing wrong with the steering or the brakes. I told you, the road turned, but she didn't. My professional opinion is that she fell asleep at the wheel."

"Did you have an autopsy done?" I knew I was pushing him, but I didn't care. I'd lost a friend, and it had been murder, from the way things were starting to look.

"That's not my decision to make. You'll have to talk to the county coroner about that."

I wasn't about to let him derail me. "Bradford Shane, you know he'll never discuss that with me. That's why I'm asking you."

He was interrupted when the front door opened. I was in no mood to be disturbed at the moment unless a customer had an American Express Platinum Card clutched in her hand and was ready to put a serious dent in it. Not only was it not a customer, but it was my least favorite person in all of Rebel Forge: Deputy Wayne Davidson, a man who gave me the complete and utter creeps.

Bradford didn't look happy about his presence there, either. "What do you want?" he asked abruptly.

"I saw your car parked out front. I need to talk to you about something."

Bradford said, "Wait outside. I'll be there in a minute."

Wayne looked right through me, without a nod, a wave or any acknowledgment that I counted for anything. "It'll just take a second."

"I said go," my brother snapped, and Wayne left quickly.

"Why is he still working for you?" I asked Bradford. "He's a complete and utter jerk. I can't believe you are keeping him around."

"Jennifer, I can't fire the man just because you don't like him. Hold on a second," he said as he saw I was about ready to explode. "You don't have anything to worry about. I told him to steer clear of you."

So at least Bradford was willing to acknowledge that Wayne wasn't a model employee. I still didn't like him coming into my shop. "Yeah, I can see how much he listens to you. You practically had to throw him out."

It appeared that my brother wanted to say something, but then changed his mind. "It won't happen again; you can believe it."

As Bradford headed for the door, I grabbed his shoulder. "Wait a second. We're not through here."

"Jennifer, I have real work to do."

I waved the card under his nose. "So you're going to completely ignore the message Maggie sent me?"

He nodded. "You might not like it, but I don't have much choice. It was a bad joke, and even worse timing. I'm sorry she's gone, Jen, but there's nothing I can do about it. It really was an accident." He left before I could say another word. I hated when he did that. It was Bradford's way of fighting without raising his voice.

I was still fuming about my brother's reaction when Lillian walked in two hours later. As promised, she had two bags from The Lunch Box with her, but for the second time in two days, I was in no mood to eat.

When I refused the bag, she said, "My dear, I'm sorry I'm so late. I hope you can forgive me."

"Lillian, I'm not angry with you. I got a card in the mail today you should see."

As she read the note from Maggie, I discreetly pulled her note from the night before off the board, hoping she hadn't noticed it. I didn't really want to tease her anymore.

After she read it, Lillian handed it back to me and said, "Jennifer, you've got to call Bradford and show this to him."

"I already did. He wasn't all that impressed with it. In fact, he assumed it was just another one of Maggie's joke cards gone bad."

Lillian pursed her lips. "That's absolutely ridiculous.

Couldn't he see that the tone is deadly serious? It's perfectly clear that this is no joke."

"We know that, but he doesn't. The question is, what do we do about it?"

Lillian smiled grimly. "I think it's time to get out our whiteboard and make some notes about what we know and what we suspect. We can work while we eat."

It felt good having my aunt on my side. My brother was a pragmatist by nature, but sometimes it absolutely drove me crazy. He might need more proof that Maggie had been murdered, but that card was enough to convince Lillian and me that something very real had happened to her.

Chapter 5

"Should we close the shop while we eat and work this out?" Lillian asked.

"I'd rather we didn't," I said as I retrieved the marker board and set it up near our window workstation. The table where we made cards with our customers often served as our lunch table as well. In a shop as limited in space as Custom Card Creations, we were big on multitasking. "We're not really in the position to turn people away."

As Lillian cleared the table for our lunch, she said, "Now, Jennifer, the business is building, and you know it."

"I know," I said as I put placemats down. "I just wish it would build a little faster."

She looked at me critically, then said, "You need some food, young lady. I picked up your favorite burger."

I took the offered bag and saw that Lillian had added an order of onion rings. If it could be fried, Pete could do it with an artistry that brought in customers from halfway around the state. "You're spoiling me," I said. "These are going straight to my hips."

"Pooh, you deserve to splurge a little every now and then. If you're feeling guilty, you can always walk them off later."

"How far do you think I would have to go, Canada?"

As Lillian retrieved two Cokes from the refrigerator in back, she said, "Jennifer, if you don't want to eat them, set them aside."

"Like there's a chance of that ever happening," I said as I bit into one. Hot and fresh on the plate at The Lunch Box, Pete's onion rings were a clear ten. Half an hour sitting in the bag, and they'd dropped to a nine, still better than anything else I could find in our part of Virginia. I had a twinge of guilt just before I took the first bite, but after that, it was pure pleasure. I nearly forgot about my hamburger, but as soon as the onion rings were gone, I suddenly remembered it. The Lunch Box couldn't touch the ambience of Hurley's, but their hamburgers were in a dead heat, at least in my opinion.

I looked over at Lillian, who was smiling broadly at me. Before she could add her own little commentary on my eating habits, I said, "It's okay if you think it, but I don't want to hear a word, okay?"

She smiled and shrugged all at once, but I had to give her credit: she didn't say a word. We'd planned to work on Maggie's murder as we ate, but Lillian and I were both so hungry that we barely managed some small talk until both bags were empty.

"That was outstanding," I said as I cleared away the debris. "Thank you."

"It was my pleasure. That lunch was excellent. And a fine breakfast as well," she said.

I looked askance at her. "Lillian, are you trying to tell me you just woke up? Who is this mysterious stranger, anyway?"

Lillian hiked her eyebrows. "Now how ladylike would I be sharing that information? Suffice it to say that I've found another admirer."

"In a long line of them," I added.

She stared at me a moment, then asked, "Jennifer, is that a hint of jealousy in your voice? Don't worry, my dear; your time will come."

Discussing my love life—or more accurately the lack of it—with my aunt was about the last item on my list of things I wanted to do. I took a note from her style and waved the statement away with my hand. "Now let's see what we can come up with about what really happened to Maggie Blake."

I picked up a black marker and wrote her name across the top. "I'm not even sure where we should start. What questions do we need to ask?"

" 'Who killed her?' is a good place to begin," Lillian said.

I raised an eyebrow toward her as I replied, "That's kind of the point of the whole exercise, isn't it? We need to be serious if we're going to do this."

Lillian looked suitably chastened. "Very well. The first question has to be, who wanted her dead?"

"That's a fair question," I said as I wrote it on the board, then added, "Who were her friends? Did she have any enemies?"

"Jennifer, Maggie said she didn't have enemies in her card to you, remember?"

I kept that question on the board. "Lillian, everybody has people who don't like them."

She couldn't hide her smile as she asked, "So who wants to kill you?"

I really wished my aunt would take the whole thing more seriously. "Come on, you know what I mean. Who knows what someone else might take as an affront? I'm willing to bet both of us have people who wouldn't mind seeing us go."

Lillian nodded reluctantly. "I suppose you're right. Go ahead and put it down, but I'd be shocked if we found anyone that fit that description for Maggie Blake."

I thought about Maggie's death, and that led to another line of questioning. As quickly as I could, I wrote, "Where exactly was she when her car went off the road? Where was she going? Where had she been?"

Lillian must have been reading over my shoulder. As soon as I finished, she said, "How about who saw her last?"

"That's good," I said, "but we're missing something, a really important question."

"What might that be?"

Instead of answering her, I wrote it down: "Who had the most to gain from her death?"

Lillian nodded. "That *is* the most important question, isn't it? Motive is critical here."

"So how do we determine that?" I asked.

"Probably by answering all of the other questions first," Lillian said.

As she finished, the front door chimed. To my delight, it wasn't my brother, my sister or anyone else there to hound me. It appeared that we had an actual customer visiting us at Custom Card Creations.

"I'm here to spend some serious money," the woman in her early forties announced as she waved a credit card in the air. "Can one of you two help me?"

"Absolutely," I said as I turned to my aunt. "Lillian, why don't you put the marker board in back and we'll work on it more later."

"What about Maggie?" my aunt asked as she reluctantly picked up the board.

"First and foremost, we have to make a living," I said.

Our customer said, "If this is a bad time, I can always go somewhere else."

"Not at all," I said as I hurried to her. "Now what can I help you with?"

"I love greeting cards, and I've got over a thousand dollars to spend today." There was an inescapable grin on her face as she said it, and for a moment she looked more like she was nine years old.

"That sounds like you're exactly where you need to be, then," I said. "Do you mind if I ask if you won the lottery?"

The woman's smile was infectious. "Oh, no, it's much better than that. I just discovered that my husband spent that much on a new set of golf clubs after promising me he wouldn't buy anything else this year. But he just had to have them, and the bill came in this morning. Can you imagine that? Somehow he forgot that I'm the one who writes the checks. Now he's going to pay, though."

I didn't want to take advantage of this woman, but I couldn't afford to turn down a sale that large, either. I knew I should keep my mouth shut, let her have her spree, and celebrate the sale, but I couldn't do it. "I'm thrilled to help you, but all sales are final here, and I'm afraid you'll regret doing this later. Are you absolutely certain you want to do this?"

She laughed heartily. "My dear, thank you for your thoughtfulness, but this is exactly what I want to do. Don't worry; we can afford it, trust me. Last week I bought a hundred dollars' worth of material for curtains and you'd have thought I'd shot my husband when I told him. All the while, his new clubs were in the garage, hidden safely away. We can afford it, and I've always wanted to make my own cards. So can you help me or not?"

I grabbed a nearby buggy, one customers rarely used but something I found helpful when I restocked the shelves. "Oh yes, I can easily help you spend a thousand dollars here."

The woman nodded. "Now don't hold back. If we happen to go over by a few hundred dollars, well, that will be just dandy. You can explain to me what I'm buying as we go along. Don't be afraid to use your imagination; just help me put together a perfect kit."

She was the kind of customer most shopkeepers

only dreamed about, and I planned to enjoy every second of her spree.

Her purchases ultimately took two buggies. I set her up with card stocks, papers, expensive die cutters, embellishments, accessories, envelopes, specialty scissors, rubber stamps, cutouts, stickers, stencils, pressed flowers and more. I'd also included a good selection of books, and the store's phone number. "Call me if you have any trouble, and I'll walk you through whatever you're doing," I said as I handed her one of my business cards. I'd made them myself, shunning the printers and creating each one individually. I couldn't give out a lot of them, but so far their creation had more than kept up with the demand.

She took the card, then asked, "Now, is there anything else we're missing?"

"I can't imagine what it might be," I said in complete and utter honesty.

"Neither can I. This looks perfect." She glanced at the clock over the register. "Is that right? Is it really that late?"

I checked and saw that we'd been shopping together over two hours. Time truly did fly with fun. "I'm sorry I've kept you so long."

"No, that's fine—this has been absolutely joyous—but I've got to get home so I can set things up before Lee gets there. I can't wait to see the expression on his face."

"Sybil, don't give him a heart attack." We'd gone to first names early on, and not just because of how much money she was spending. Sybil was my kind of gal, a free spirit who embraced life.

"Jennifer, he's as stout as a horse. Besides, he could use a good shock to his system."

She signed the credit card charge slip with a flourish, then said, "I feel like I should tip you; you've been so helpful."

"Nonsense," I said as I slid the deposit in the drawer. "It's been great fun."

"It has, hasn't it? I may come back for more later."

"I'll be here." If she created and sent cards to everyone in the state of Virginia, then she might need more supplies, but I couldn't imagine her running out until then. "Come by and tell me how you're doing."

"I will," she said. "Now how am I going to ever get this all to my car?"

"I'll help. Lillian, could you watch the front? I'm going to help Sybil with her bags."

My aunt looked up from the worktable where she'd been brainstorming on new card ideas for her own section of the store. I'd given her an area to display and sell her acerbic cards, and she'd reveled in the opportunity. Her cards were full of zingers, put-downs, sarcasms and innuendos, perfect for the cynical souls who walked among us. "I'd be delighted," she said. "Hurry back, though. It's nearly closing time."

"Do you have another big date tonight?" I asked. Where did the woman get her energy? I knew I couldn't keep up with her if I was aided by a quart of coffee and a dozen PowerBars.

"No, I'm staying in tonight," she admitted as she stifled a yawn.

"Don't worry. We won't be long," I said as I grabbed several of the heavier bags.

Sybil took the rest, then held the door for me. It was drizzling slightly outside, but I'd double-bagged her purchases, so they would be safe from the weather. By the time we got to her car, my arms were ready to fall off. She opened the trunk and I gratefully put the bags inside. That's when I had the chance to look more closely at her transportation. It was a shiny black Mercedes, a big one at that, and all doubts about Sybil being able to afford my bill vanished. "That's a lovely car you've got," I said.

"I'd rather drive something a little more austere, but Lee has to have his symbols." She turned to me and said, "Jennifer, I've had the best afternoon in I don't know how long. Thank you."

"You're most welcome," I said. "Now don't be a stranger."

"Oh, I won't," she said. "I can't wait to get home and get started."

I watched her drive away, and wondered what the scene at her house would be tonight when her husband came home. Sybil could handle it; I had no doubt about that.

I was still smiling about the thought as I walked back to the shop, and I was nearly at my front door when I heard a familiar voice calling to me.

"Jennifer, wait up. I need to talk to you."

It was Greg Langston, my ex-fiancé times two. I thought about ignoring the summons, then I remembered that card he'd sent me so long ago and I stopped.

"Hi, Greg, how are you?"

From his expression, it was pretty obvious he wasn't expecting a cordial greeting, and I really couldn't blame him. I hadn't been at my nicest with Greg lately, something I really needed to remedy. Truly, all he'd done was express concern over my welfare, and no matter how aggravating I found it when people tried to protect me, I knew he acted like he did because he still cared.

"I'm fine," he said. "Listen, there's something I'd like to ask you."

"Fire away, but you'll have to make it quick. It's closing time, and Lillian's in a hurry to get home."

Greg wasn't classically handsome, but I never could resist him. He had a boyish charm that melted my heart, and a pair of deep brown eyes that lit up everywhere else. "Well, what I've been meaning to do, what

I wanted to ask—blast it all, this shouldn't be this hard. Jennifer, would you like to have dinner with me tomorrow night?"

He'd asked me out on a dozen times since we'd broken our engagement the last time, and I'd never failed to turn him down. Before I could overanalyze the ramifications of my answer like I always did, I said, "That sounds like fun. Where did you have in mind?"

I don't know who was more surprised by my answer. "I'm not sure yet—I didn't think . . . I'll let you know later. Thanks. I'll pick you up tomorrow at seven. Bye." He hurried away, no doubt before I could change my mind. Now what was I thinking? Greg Langston was the one man in all of Rebel Forge I shouldn't be having dinner with. For some odd reason, to me he was like catnip was to my roommates; I found it extremely difficult to say no to him, including the times he'd asked me to marry him. I was having some serious second and third thoughts when Lillian walked out the door. "I've turned off all the lights, so we're ready to lock up and go home." She stared after Greg's fleeing form and asked, "What did he want?"

"Greg asked me out to dinner tomorrow night."

Lillian frowned. "No wonder he bolted away so quickly. Jennifer, you can't keep saying no to him forever."

"Evidently not," I admitted. "I just agreed to go out with him again."

Lillian's face lit up. "Why how delightful. I'm so pleased." Then she studied my face. "Aren't you?"

"I'm not sure yet. Ask me in a few days."

Lillian hugged me. "You'll have a delightful time, I'm sure of it."

"That's what I'm afraid of," I said, wondering what I'd gotten myself into this time.

"Well, if you'll excuse me, dear, I need to go," Lillian said.

"You didn't change your mind about staying in, did

you? Please don't tell me you're going out again," I said, not able to believe that my aunt had more energy than I did.

"Child, I'm driving straight home, where I plan to enjoy a hot bath, then go straight to sleep. If you need me, don't call, as I'll have the ringer turned off. We can brainstorm about Maggie's demise tomorrow."

"Good night," I said as I locked the front door and walked to my car. I'd been ready to leave the shop, and I was exhausted myself, though I hadn't done anything exceptional all day. The thought of going back to my new place wasn't as appealing as it should have been, and if it hadn't been for Oggie and Nash, I probably would have delayed returning even longer, but my roommates hadn't asked to move, and I wasn't going to abandon them just because I was starting to get a little jittery about my new domicile. I picked up a pizza on the way home, an extra large that would probably end up being breakfast, too. I didn't care if it wasn't the best dietary choice. That was one of the joys of living alone; I didn't have to worry about what anyone else thought about what I did or didn't eat.

The commute to my new home was a lot quicker than to my old place, even with the stop for pizza, so I was there before I wanted to be. I walked upstairs and was trying to fit my key in the lock while balancing the pizza when I heard someone tear up the steps behind me.

When I turned, I nearly dropped the pizza. It was Deputy Wayne Davidson, my brother's employee and my own worst nightmare.

"Go away, Wayne," I said as I fumbled with the key. Why wouldn't it go in the lock, especially when I was in such a hurry?

"Now Jennifer, is that any way to act?" I could smell his breath, and it didn't take a sobriety test to tell me he was drunk.

"Go home and sober up," I snapped. Why wasn't the blasted key working?

"Why can't you be friendlier to me? You like me; I know you do."

He was close enough that I could feel the heat coming off him now. I was going to have to throw the pizza in his face and run downstairs, since I couldn't get my key to work.

"Jennifer, you're late," another voice said from below. There was no way there was room for three of us on that tiny landing, but I didn't care. My new neighbor Barrett was climbing the steps at a good clip. "We're eating in my apartment tonight; did you forget?"

Wayne said, "Sorry, she's already got plans, bub."

"You're right, and they're with me." He reached past Wayne, plucked the pizza out of my hands and said, "We don't want this to get cold. I've got the wine all ready, and I picked up a movie on the way home."

As I slid past Wayne, Barrett said, "Sorry, my friend, but there's just enough for two. Have a good evening."

I followed Barrett into his apartment, waiting for Wayne to protest, but when I glanced back as the door was closing, I saw him frowning at us but apparently unable to come up with a reason to stop us. With the door locked, I said, "Barrett, you're a lifesaver. How did you know I needed help?"

My new building mate shrugged. "He wasn't exactly keeping his voice down, and in all honesty, I was just going out to grab a bite myself when I heard him."

"Your timing couldn't have been better. After I make a quick telephone call, you're more than welcome to share my pizza."

He laughed. "Jennifer, you're certainly under no obligation to share your food with me. I didn't do all that much."

He'd done more than he'd ever know. "Considering

the fact that I was about ready to slam the box into his face and run, I disagree. What do you say?"

"I'd be delighted," he said. "Let me open a bottle of wine and we'll eat."

"What, no movie?" I asked, joking.

"I have a healthy selection of DVDs to choose from. I'm sure we can find something we both like."

I took my jacket off, then said, "You've got a deal. Let me call my brother and then we can eat."

He looked at me carefully. "Do you have to get permission before dating strange men? He's awfully protective of you, isn't he?"

I shook my head. "He's that, all right, but he's also the sheriff, and that man outside my door is one of his deputies."

Barrett just nodded, then said, "I'll get the wine."

I dialed Bradford's cell phone and he picked up on the third ring. "Shane here."

"Bradford, Wayne Davidson just accosted me on my doorstep, and he's been drinking again. He was close enough for me to smell it on his breath."

My brother isn't prone to foul language, but he ripped a few choice words off at that news. "I'll take care of it. Are you okay?"

"One of my neighbors stepped in before I had to defend myself, but just barely. He's a real menace. Bradford, you can't keep covering for him."

There was a long pause, then my brother said, "Okay, you're right. I've had a blind spot about him for a while. We had a talk today, and I told him if he came within a half mile of you, I was going to fire him."

"So are you?" I asked. "Or do I have to go over your head and make a formal complaint to the state police?"

"He's gone, Jennifer, as soon as I can find him. You might not want to go back to your apartment just yet. Why don't you wait there and I'll send Jim over?"

Barrett glanced over at me, and I held up one finger. "That's not necessary. I'm having pizza with my new neighbor. Find him before he hurts someone, Bradford."

"I will," he said, then hung up.

Barrett asked, "Is everything all right?"

"It will be, thanks. Are you ready to eat?"

"Absolutely," he said. As Barrett led me into his dining area, I got my first good look at his apartment. It was furnished beautifully, with elegant Queen Anne furniture and lush rugs throughout. The art on the walls was magnificent as well. I'd felt that my apartment was well furnished, but compared to his place, it suddenly felt like the attic it was.

"How much of this is your taste, and how much of it is the owner's?" I asked a little more abruptly than I probably should have as we ate.

"It's more Mrs. Thomas's than it is mine. To be honest with you, I prefer your apartment. I'm more into simple lines than all this ornamentation."

"So you've been to my place?" I asked as I served us both more pizza.

He topped off our wineglasses, then said, "Frances and I were friends, not just neighbors."

So he'd known the former tenant. "What was she like, or is it too painful to talk about?"

Barrett took a sip of wine, then said, "She was comfortable, you know? Like a pair of slippers you've worn for years, or a ratty old bathrobe. No, that's not fair to her. You must think I'm awful speaking of the dead so callously."

I felt myself gazing into his eyes. "Barrett, I think that's a wonderful way to describe a friend. I just lost one myself, and I'm having a hard time with it."

He stared at me a moment, then said, "Did you know Maggie Blake too?"

I nearly dropped my wineglass. "She was in my card-crafting club at Custom Card Creations."

He nodded. "So you're a card maker too?"

"It's my shop," I said. "But I never realized Maggie knew Frances."

"Oh yes. They were great friends," he said, "And I got to know her in passing. Jennifer, take care of yourself, would you promise me that? I don't have many people I like left in this world, and I'm hoping we can get closer as time goes on."

I suddenly realized that there was more to his body language and the tone of his voice than the words coming out of his mouth. Was he actually making a pass at me over pizza? And more importantly, how did I feel about it? I'd agreed to have dinner with Greg tomorrow night, but was that really going anywhere again?

Barrett leaned in toward me, and I could swear he was going to try to kiss me. It normally took me a lot longer to warm up to a man, but there was something about him, some kind of charm, that held me in place. At the last second I pulled back, and all I could manage was to smile as cryptically as I could. I was struggling to come up with something to say when there was a pounding on his front door. Was it Bradford coming to check on me, or had Wayne decided to invite himself to dinner anyway?

Either way, I didn't want Barrett to answer the door.

Chapter 6

I heard a woman's voice call out, "Barrett, I know you're in there. I saw your car. Let me in. We need to talk."

He looked at me like someone had just slapped him. Grimly, he said, "We can try to ignore her, but I know from experience that Penny's not going away. It's better if I just deal with her right now."

"Go ahead and talk to her," I said. "It's fine with me."

Barrett clamped his jaw so tightly that for a moment I was afraid he was going to break a tooth; then he opened the door. Standing there was a petite blonde in her midtwenties. If she hadn't been scowling so hard, I was willing to bet she'd have been one of the prettiest women I'd ever seen. She was exactly the type of woman who had always intimidated me. I'm brunette, tall and a little overweight, and while I'm not unattractive, no one had ever told me I was beautiful, at least not believably enough for me.

She was ready to unload on Barrett when she saw me standing just behind him. "Who's this? Don't tell me you've replaced me already."

"Penny, this is Jennifer. She just moved into Frances's apartment."

The girl frowned. "It didn't take you long to move in on this one, did it?" She turned to me and chilled my blood with her glare. "Don't waste your time. You don't have a chance with him."

Barrett snapped, "Penny, that's enough. Why are you here?"

"You're going to talk to me, and I'm not leaving until you do."

Barrett barely glanced at me as he told her, "I've got company."

"She can stay if she wants to," Penny said as she brushed past us both and came in uninvited. "In fact, she probably should. It will give her some idea of what kind of man she's dealing with."

Barrett turned to me and said, "Jennifer, I'm sorry about this."

As I slipped out the door, I said, "No, that's fine. We were finished here anyway. Good night."

He whispered, "I'll come up later and explain."

"It's really not necessary. Listen, I've had a long day." I hurried up the stairs to my apartment, for the moment not caring if Wayne was still lurking around or not. As I tried my key in the lock, I realized why I hadn't been able to get in when Wayne had been there. In my rush to get inside, I'd been trying to use the key to the shop instead. I took a deep breath, found the right key on my ring and opened my apartment door. Once I was inside, I threw the deadbolt in place, happy that Bradford had arranged to have my lock changed. I'd actually found myself intrigued by Barrett's pale green eyes and his dark good looks. Maybe I should make Penny a thank-you card for getting there before I could make a fool of myself. If he'd tried just a little harder, it was difficult to say what might have happened.

I turned on a light and finally looked around the apartment. It appeared that someone had done his level best to wreck the place. If I hadn't just had the locks changed, I would have sworn that I'd had a visitor.

Then I found both the cats curled up on my pillow, sound asleep, no doubt from their energetic day. "Time to get up," I said, but neither one of them budged. I knew the wrecked apartment was their sincerest form of protest over our relocation, and I decided that they'd been at least partially justified in their display of disapproval. There wasn't anything else I could do, so I started cleaning up after my insane roommates.

After an hour, I had most of it straightened up and just about everything put away except my carton of books. Oddly enough, there weren't any bookshelves in the apartment. I knew space was at a premium in my would-be loft, but that was going to have to be corrected immediately. I don't just love to read books—though I do desperately—but I also like to see them out in the open with their spines reminding me of stories I treasured. I'd pick up a few boards and some bricks tomorrow to make a temporary bookshelf until I could manage something better. I'd done it in college, and it didn't make a bad-looking display, though I doubted it would fit in with the furniture I had. That was too bad. It was my apartment now, and just because Frances hadn't enjoyed reading didn't mean that I was going to shove my books back into a box and jam them all under my bed. It was barely past ten when I opened two cans of food for Oggie and Nash. The rascals came running at the sound of the opener, and I chatted with them as they ate. It was too early for bed but too late to do much of anything else. I grabbed one of my favorite books out of the box—a well-read copy of *The Mysterious Affair at Styles* by Agatha Christie—and started to read, but it couldn't hold my attention. After ten minutes, I decided to give up the battle and go to bed.

There was someone waiting for me the next morning when I opened the shop. I was surprised to find Hilda Bunting there, my inaugural member of the

Crafty Cut-Ups Club, and the woman responsible for recruiting most of the rest of our group. I started to offer her a hug, and Hilda, in her usual stern manner, stepped back and said, "Yes, I know, it's a terrible thing. Jennifer, we need to talk."

"Of course," I said as I unlocked the front door.

She watched me go from lock to lock with a curious expression on her face. "Security is important to you, isn't it?"

I shrugged. "What can I say? My brother's the sheriff, and he believes in preventative measures."

Hilda smiled slightly. "Are there attack dogs roaming around inside as well?"

I laughed. "No, but I have a couple of insane cats back at my apartment. I'd bring them with me, but they both love to shred paper, and I don't have to tell you what a disaster that would be." I locked the door back behind us and put my things down on the crafting table in the window.

"Then perhaps it's better you leave them right where they are."

It was pretty obvious she had something she wanted to say, but Hilda was having a tough time getting it out, something that was completely out of character for her. Finally I couldn't stand it anymore. "You mentioned there was something you wanted to talk about."

Instead of speaking, she nodded and handed me an envelope. I didn't have to look at the return address to see who it was from. It appeared that Maggie had chosen to speak to someone else beyond the grave besides me.

I pulled the card out and saw a clock on the front with its lightning-bolt hands set to seven thirty. In jagged letters, the message read, "You Are Cordially Invited to My Wake." Inside, Maggie had written,

Hilda, don't cancel the next meeting for the Crafty Cut-Ups Club. Instead, do it in my memory. Love, Maggie.

Hilda met my gaze as I looked up, and she said, "You see why we've got to convene, don't you? It was Maggie's last request."

Maggie's last requests were becoming more common than falling leaves in October, but I could hardly say no. "If you can get everyone here, we'll do as she asks."

Hilda nodded firmly. "They'll be here, all right." She took a breath, then said, "All but Dot."

Now that was interesting. "Why won't she be here?"

"Her daughter's having a baby in North Carolina, and she went to visit her."

It was difficult to imagine Dot killing anyone, but I had to pursue it. That woman dearly loved all ten of her grandchildren, and it was a ritual at every meeting we'd had so far that she'd pass a new collection of photos around. "Did she leave today?"

"No, she left right after one of our meetings last month. I expect her back in a few weeks, but I don't have any way to contact her now. She'll be sorry she missed it."

"She'll understand," I said, striking Dot off my list of suspects. "But everyone else will be here, right?" I'd been dreading interviewing my witnesses away from the store, and Maggie had unwittingly helped me in trying to solve her murder. Or was it accidental? Knowing Maggie, she'd probably planned this foray to allow me access to everyone in the club without going door-to-door. If that were true, then it meant that she suspected a member herself.

Hilda nodded. "If I have to hog-tie each and every one of them myself, the club members will all be here tonight."

I held on to the card. "May I keep this?"

"I guess you could until tonight, but I want it back after the meeting."

"That's fine," I said, wondering why Hilda would

want to keep it. She didn't strike me as all that sentimental, but who really knows what goes on in someone else's heart?

Lillian showed up ten minutes after Hilda was gone.
She was breezing in later and later to work, but I
couldn't say anything, especially since we rarely had
customers that early. It would also be indelicate of me
to say anything, since Lillian wasn't exactly being paid,
though she was using card stock at a prodigious pace.

"Sorry I'm late; I slept in," she offered as she
walked in. "I trust I didn't miss anything."

"Just another message from Maggie," I said casually.

As Lillian took off her jacket, she said, "Jennifer,
while I normally appreciate your sense of humor,
that's a little over the line, even by my standards."

I walked over to the card corner where we sold
Lillian's creations. "That's coming from the woman
who made this card?"

I pushed one on her, and she studied it a moment
before commenting. The card in question had a tombstone with an "RIP" engraved on it. The tombstone
was on a spring and would dance at the slightest provo-
cation. That wasn't the worst part, though. Inside, she'd
inscribed, "Wish you were there instead of here."

"Tell me it's a sentiment you've never entertained.
I'd considered another greeting for this one. Would
you like to hear it?"

"Do I have a choice?" I asked.

She ignored my comment and said, "Perhaps I
should make another one that says, 'Do us all a favor
and make the world a better place.' What do you
think?"

"I think you're a sick puppy."

Lillian frowned. "I'm not the one claiming actual
dead people are communicating from beyond the
grave."

"I'm not making it up," I said as I showed her Maggie's card.

She read it, then said, "Jennifer, I apologize. Maggie is certainly trying to make our quest easier, isn't she?"

"So you agree that she thinks one of our group killed her?"

Lillian said, "No, I believe she wants us to eliminate her friends first before we start our search in earnest."

That was an approach I hadn't even considered. "Either way, we need to interview them at the meeting tonight. But how are we going to do it without making them suspicious?"

Lillian paced around the room. "I don't have a clue, but there's got to be some way to approach them."

While it was bad for business, our lack of customers did give us time to think. Lillian took up the seat at our display worktable facing the window, while I paced through the aisles of the shop. Custom Card Creations was a fine size for selling cards, but it didn't leave a lot of room to pace. I was straightening cards as I walked, just because I had a tough time seeing any of my creations askew, when my glance caught the title of the section I was working in. I'd created the most sympathetic sympathy cards I could manage. Staring at the heading gave me a sudden idea. "I've got it."

"What is it?" Lillian asked. Had she been dozing off? It didn't matter, but I could swear she'd been taking a catnap instead of brainstorming with me.

"We make a sympathy book for Maggie's long lost cousin, sharing her life with him."

Lillian said, "Everyone knows Maggie didn't have any family, Jennifer."

"That's where we get creative. He was a black sheep, so Maggie never talked about him, but they'd reconciled recently."

Lillian frowned a moment, then said, "I suppose it could work, but where is this mystery man?"

"Let me think." I considered the possibilities, then said, "Okay, here's what we'll say. Maggie wanted to meet him again at a neutral place, so she rendezvoused with him here at the card shop a few weeks ago. I called to tell him about Maggie and he asked me to gather this information for him, since he couldn't get back in time for her funeral. Do you think they'll buy it?"

She grinned. "And why not? After all, she was his last living relative."

"Lillian, you know we're making him up, don't you?"

My aunt favored me with one of her driest looks and said, "I'm not batty yet, child, but we need to give them some excuse why he's not here."

"Well, why don't we say he's burying his wife in England, and he can't show up."

Lillian eyed me carefully before saying, "And you claim I'm the one with the dark side. Jennifer, I'd hate to visit one of your nightmares."

I brushed that off. "But would it work?"

"Yes, I think it will. Double tragedies would explain his absence and still garner sympathy. By the way, what's his name?"

"Again, we're making him up. What would you like his name to be?"

Lillian stroked her nose, then said, "I've always been partial to 'Timothy.'"

"Then 'Timothy' it is," I said. "Now we need to make a booklet for their memories."

"Oh, let me. It sounds like fun."

I looked askance at my aunt, then said, "You do remember why we're doing this, don't you?"

"Jennifer, if anyone in this world or the next would want us to get some joy out of this, it would be Maggie herself. Wouldn't you agree?"

I chose a blank memory book for my aunt. "I can't disagree with that. Just keep it in good taste, will you?"

"I can be tasteful when the situation calls for it," she said with a sniff.

"I know you can, but will you?"

Lillian said, "Dear girl, I promise you, you'll be amazed."

And I would be if my aunt actually did what she said she was going to do. I could always throw something together later if Lillian's efforts weren't up to my standards. I couldn't wait until the meeting so I could start digging into Maggie's murder, but I had no choice. In the meantime, I had a shop to run, and bills to pay.

Lillian was still working on the front of the memory book for the fictitious Timothy when a man in his thirties walked into the shop. He had a furtive look about him, and I wondered if I was going to have trouble with another shoplifter. It amazed me that some people would rather steal than pay for their goods, but if I caught them doing it, my brother was just a phone call away.

"May I help you?" I asked politely, trying to give him the benefit of the doubt.

"I'm just browsing," he mumbled, another sign that I was about to be hit. I had a technique I'd learned from Sara Lynn about dealing with suspected shoplifters. I'd follow him around the store closer than his own shadow, offering helpful suggestions as we "browsed" together.

"If you could tell me what you're looking for, I can be of more assistance," I said.

He glanced over at Lillian, around the otherwise empty shop, then back at me. "Okay, but you have to promise not to laugh."

That wasn't exactly the reaction I'd expected. "I'm not in the habit of laughing at my customers. It tends to drive off potential business."

"I'm serious," he insisted.

"I promise," I said, wondering what kind of revelation he was about to share.

"I'm a stay-at-home dad," he said in a lowered

voice, "and I started wondering what to do with all
the pictures of my daughter I'd been taking. One of
the mothers at the preschool started talking about
scrapbooking, and it sounded perfect."

"I don't handle scrapbooking supplies, but I can
recommend Forever Memories. It's just down the
block."

He nodded. "I know all about that place. The thing
is, I really like doing it, but now I've got the bug and
I want to do more. Your sister told me I should talk
to you about card making. By the way, my name's
Daniel."

"I'm Jennifer," I said, then added, "I think it's wonderful you're interested in cardmaking." I said, "I
have lots of men who come here for supplies. In fact,
there's even one in my card-making club." I thought
about inviting him to our meeting tonight, but I
doubted we'd be making many cards, and besides, I
didn't want any distractions while I grilled my club
members.

"So you don't think it's odd I enjoy doing this kind
of thing?" he asked.

"I think your wife's lucky to have you," I said sincerely. "Raising children is one of the most honorable
things you can do with your life, in my opinion."

A partial smile started to show on his face. "I think
so too, but sometimes it's tough being a man doing it
in the South."

"I imagine it's hard for anybody. Let's see, you
should already have most of the supplies and tools
you need. Where should we get started?"

"I'd like to make an anniversary card for my wife,"
he said. "Could you help me make something nice?"

"I'd be honored," I said. "Lillian, could we have
that space? You can work in back, and I'll call you if
I need you."

"Certainly," Lillian said as she gathered her supplies and moved to the workroom. She'd learned early

on that our customers came first. After all, they were the ones who were keeping us afloat.

"Now let's see," I said. "What kind of card did you have in mind?"

"I honestly don't know," he said. "I was hoping you'd be able to help me."

I led him to the section of anniversary cards I'd made myself, showing him a few examples as we went. Finally, he said, "These are all nice, but I was kind of hoping to do one myself."

"I understand perfectly. I just thought this might give you an idea of what can be done. We're just looking for inspiration right now."

He nodded, then chose an off-white card with an embossed border and a bouquet inside. "Something like this would be perfect. Is it hard to make?"

"You're going to be amazed how easy it is," I said as I grabbed some card stock and the embosser Lillian and I had been playing with earlier. "Let's get started."

I showed him the basic technique of embossing, and in no time at all he was working on a card of his own. The man had a real gift for card making, and I was willing to bet his scrapbooking sheets were beautifully done, too.

"You're good at this," I said.

"It's fun," he admitted reluctantly.

I had to make this man feel good about his new hobby. "You know, Rosie Grier knits, and he used to play pro football."

"Yeah, but can he make a greeting card?" Daniel asked with a smile.

"I'm sure he can if he wants to," I admitted. "I certainly wouldn't try to stop him."

Daniel's card was beautiful, and by the time he was finished and ready to leave, I'd sold him several new tools and a healthy supply of card stock, including some sheets of paper I'd made myself.

"Now call if you have any questions, and come back anytime."

"I will," he said.

Lillian was still in back when my sister came in. "I just helped one of your customers," I said. "Thanks for the referral."

"I know; I saw Daniel in here, so I decided to wait outside. He's quite gifted, you know."

"I don't doubt it," I agreed. "So what brings you here during regular business hours?"

"Can't one sister take another one to lunch without a reason?" Sara Lynn asked.

"Probably not if you're one of the sisters," I said, trying and failing to hide my smile.

Sara Lynn tried to look stern, but she couldn't manage it. "Let's go eat, unless you've got other plans."

"If you're buying, I'm all yours," I said.

"I'm inviting you, so of course I'll pick up the check," Sara Lynn said sternly.

"Can Lillian come too? She's working in back."

After she glanced around the shop, Sara Lynn asked, "Are you planning to leave your store untended again?"

I knew my sister meant well, but it was my shop, and my decision alone whether we closed it or not. "Honestly, I doubt we'll miss a single customer."

Sara Lynn shook her head. "If you don't mind, I'd like it to be just the two of us."

"I don't mind, but who knows how Lillian's going to react?"

Sara Lynn said, "Don't worry. I'll take care of her." She called out, "Lillian, I need some time with my sister. Would you mind watching the store?"

Our aunt came out smiling. "I'd be delighted. You two have fun."

I was feeling guilty just abandoning her like that. "Can we bring you back something?"

"No, I'm fine. Just be back by two if you could."

"Why, do you have a hot date?" I asked.

"Wouldn't you like to know," Lillian replied.

Once Sara Lynn and I were outside, she said, "Is she serious? Is that woman ever going to slow down?"

"If she does, I for one will be disappointed in her. She gives me fresh hope every day. So, where are we going?"

Sara Lynn appeared to think about it for a moment, then said, "I haven't been to Hurley's in a while. How does that sound?"

"Outstanding. Now I'm glad I skipped breakfast."

"Jennifer, you really should . . . oh, never mind, you won't listen to me anyway."

"That's one of things I love about you, Sara Lynn. You know how to choose your battles."

Chapter 7

After we'd placed our orders, Sara Lynn smiled at me. "What is it?" I asked her.

"We've been together ten minutes and you haven't once asked me what we're doing here."

"I figured you'd tell me when you were ready," I said as I ate one of the warm rolls with some honey butter Jack Hurley had brought us personally. Jack owns Hurley's, and he's a longtime friend of the family's. In fact, he dated Sara Lynn at one time, and I wondered if the special treatment was for me or for my big sister. Sara Lynn had been married to Bailey for what must have felt like forever, while Jack seemed like he had more kids than Baskin-Robbins had flavors. Still, there was a secret smile the two of them had shared when he'd brought the rolls, and I felt like I was twelve years old again—in other words, completely invisible.

Sara Lynn reached for another roll, then pulled her hand back. "I'd better not if I'm going to have room for my lunch."

I grabbed the one she'd ignored. "I'll find a way to make room. These are too good to just leave."

As I ate, Sara Lynn asked, "So how's business?"

"It's fine. How's yours?"

"Forever Memories is on stable ground, as always." She took a deep breath, let half of it out, then said,

"I've been hearing rumors that you're not doing as well."

I dropped the half-eaten roll on my plate. "And who did you hear these rumors from?"

"That's not important," Sara Lynn said. "What matters is—"

I rarely interrupt my sister, but I wasn't about to let that go. "It might not matter to you, but it does to me. Now tell me who's saying I'm in trouble."

She looked primly at me as she said, "Jennifer, I'm not going to betray a confidence."

"Then you shouldn't have brought it up. Sara Lynn, nobody knows how I'm doing, and that includes Lillian."

Sara Lynn's gaze dropped down for just a moment, but it was enough. "Oh my word. You're saying that our aunt is telling the world I'm failing?" I couldn't believe it. Lillian was more than just my aunt, more than my only employee. In a very real way, I considered her a partner in my business. The revelation that she believed I was failing hammered me between the eyes.

I stood up and threw my napkin on the table.

"Where are you going?" Sara Lynn asked.

"I'm going to set Lillian straight."

"She didn't say anything," Sara Lynn snapped.

"Don't lie to me, Sis. You're lousy at it."

Sara Lynn snapped, "If you'd give me a moment to explain before you go off like a firecracker, I'd appreciate it."

I wouldn't sit back down, but I didn't head for the door either. "So talk."

Sara Lynn looked around us, obviously caring about what other people at the restaurant thought. As for me, they could all kiss the wind if they didn't like the way I acted. Finally, my sister said, "All right, Lillian didn't say anything, at least not directly. I happened to ask if she was on any kind of salary yet, and she joked that she was taking her pay in supplies."

"I can afford to pay her," I said levelly, and I could, if I stopped eating and cut back on a few other nonessentials like that. "Did it ever occur to you that getting supplies instead of cash was her idea?" While Lillian hadn't asked for that arrangement, it was working out fine for me.

"My mistake then," Sara Lynn said in a soft, humble voice that made me repent my latest outburst. I picked up my napkin, put it back in my lap and said, "Listen, I'm sorry. I'm the first one to admit that I'm a little touchy when it comes to my shop. If I thought Aunt Lillian was unhappy with our arrangement for a second, I'd work something out with her. Sara Lynn, I'm not making a fortune, but between special orders and my walk-in trade, I'm doing okay."

Sara Lynn looked honestly repentant. "I wasn't trying to pry, Jennifer." I let that go, which I thought all in all was pretty big of me. She continued. "I just worry about you so."

"Sis, if I fail spectacularly or if I end up running a dozen stores, this is exactly what I want to be doing with my life, okay? You know I don't believe in regrets. I'm giving Custom Card Creations all I've got, so no matter what happens, in the end I can look back and feel well pleased that I did my best."

Jack put our plates down and said, "I don't know whether to applaud or salute. That was some speech, Jennifer. Are you running for office?"

"I'd throw a roll at you, but they're too good to waste," I said.

Sara Lynn added, "My little sister was just reasserting her independence."

"When doesn't she?" Jack asked. Then he stepped back out of the way in case I changed my mind and threw something at him after all. "Is there anything else?" he asked.

"This all looks wonderful," Sara Lynn told him. I took a healthy bite of my hamburger, then watched my sister spear an errant cucumber in her salad.

"I can't believe you call that lunch."

"Wait until you hit your midforties; then we'll have this conversation again."

I waved a steak fry in the air. "It's never going to happen. My metabolism just burns it right up." That was a lie and we both knew it, but my sister was too gracious to call me on it. I'd expected to lose weight when I'd opened my shop. Heck, that had been one of the entries in the plus column, but to my dismay I was gaining. If I kept packing in calories at the rate I was now, I wasn't going to be anybody's little anything anymore. There was a trail around the lake, and now that I had easy access to it, I'd lost my last excuse to not start exercising again.

We were nearly through with our meal when lo and behold, our brother Bradford came strolling into Hurley's. He took off his sheriff's hat, then said, "If I'd known we were all getting together for lunch, I wouldn't have been late. Oh, wait a second—that's right—nobody invited me."

I scooted over. "Don't let that stop you. Sit down and join us."

Sara Lynn nodded her approval, but Bradford wouldn't sit. "This isn't a coincidence. Jennifer, Lillian told me where you'd be. I need to talk to you."

"So talk," I said, eating the last fry I'd had every intention of leaving on my plate.

"Maybe we should do this later," he said.

Sara Lynn snapped, "Bradford Shane, if you think you're going to hide anything from me, you've lost what little you have left of your mind."

He sighed, and I knew that sound too well. My brother wasn't stupid; he knew when he was beaten. "It's about Wayne Davidson," Bradford said, his words weary and tired.

"What about him?" I asked. "You're not going to say you didn't fire him, are you?"

Sara Lynn asked, "What about your deputy?"

"Shh," I said to her, "I'll tell you about it later. Bradford, I'm waiting."

"I fired him all right. The only problem is, it looks like he's not going to give up that easily. You need to watch your step, Jennifer."

I could tell Sara Lynn was dying to ask what it was about, but she was going to have to wait. "Bradford, do you think he's going to do something?"

"When he's sober, he's as good a cop as I've ever seen, but when that boy starts drinking, I can't predict his behavior. Wayne won't leave town—he told me that point-blank—but I put a scare into him. If you so much as see his shadow or smell his cologne, call me. None of this 'brave single woman against the world' crap, do you hear me?"

"I do," I said. I didn't know if my brother was trying to scare me, but he was doing a bang-up job of it anyway. "Now if you ladies will excuse me, I'm late for lunch with my wife."

Sara Lynn said, "Give Cindy our love."

"I will," he said before he left.

My sister said, "Tell me about it."

"We both need to get back to our shops," I said, not wanting to dredge up the past again.

"Jennifer, family is above everything else. I'm waiting."

So I told her, everything from Wayne's stalking me at my business and my apartment to the crude passes he'd made in the past. By the time I was finished, Sara Lynn was livid. I added, "Listen, there was nothing I could do about it. I didn't ask for his attention."

"I'm not angry with you," Sara Lynn said. "Our brother is a thickheaded clod."

I couldn't help myself; I started defending Bradford. "He couldn't fire him just on my say-so. You shouldn't be mad at Bradford. He was just trying to be fair."

Sara Lynn paid the check, barely nodding to Jack as she led me outside. "Fair is fine, but his first job is to watch over us. That's what family is about."

At least she was off my back. "Be nice to him, Sara Lynn. He's doing the best he can."

As she stormed off in the direction of the library to head Bradford off before he picked Cindy up, Sara Lynn snapped, "Then his best isn't going to be good enough for me."

I walked back to Custom Card Creations alone, glad to have a little time to myself. I hated it when Sara Lynn and Bradford fought, especially when I was in the middle of it, but we were all grown-ups, at least in theory, and if two of us were going to be battling, I was just glad to be on the sidelines for once.

I was nearly back to the shop when I heard someone call my name. "Hey, Jen, wait up."

It was Gail, and she had a perplexed look on her face as she approached me.

"What's up?" I asked.

"Jennifer, are we good? Is there something going on I should know about? If I've done something, you'd give me the chance to make it right, wouldn't you?"

I took her arm. "What on earth are you talking about?" I'd never seen Gail act that way.

"I just need to know if we're in trouble."

I hugged her and said, "We've never been better. What in the world has upset you?"

She pulled away and said, "I dropped by your place last night, but you weren't there. I couldn't believe you'd move without telling me."

Oh, no, I'd completely forgotten to let her know. No wonder her feelings had been hurt. "A new place just kind of dropped in my lap, and I couldn't say no." I told her all about my new apartment, leaving out the part about Frances haunting it. "You've got to come by. We'll have a housewarming party, okay?"

"That sounds great. I can't wait to see it." It was clear by the clarity in her blue eyes that we were on solid ground again.

I had a sudden thought. "Would you like to come over tonight? I can make us something," I said.

She grinned. "I'd love to, but I've got a hot date."

"Tell me about it," I said.

She nearly skipped away as she said, "I can't. I don't want to jinx it. I'll call you tomorrow." She stopped, then said, "Your phone number's still the same, isn't it?"

"I wouldn't change that," I said. "Have fun tonight."

"I'm going to do my best," she replied.

By the time Gail was gone, I suddenly remembered I wouldn't have been able to have dinner with her after all or meet Greg, either. My card club was meeting, and I had suspects to interview. There were too many things to juggle at the moment, but I was going to have to manage somehow.

Lillian wasn't alone when I walked up to the card shop and glanced in the window, but she wasn't talking to a customer. I couldn't be sure how I knew the man, since I could only see his back, but I did nonetheless.

As I walked in the door, I heard him say, "I'm not going to ask you again. When will she be back?"

"I'm right here," I said.

"I need to talk to you," Barrett said, turning his back on Lillian.

My aunt said coldly, "Jennifer, he's been most insistent. Should I call your brother?"

"No, it's fine. Barrett's my new neighbor."

It was clear Lillian didn't like anything about him. She stood there glaring at him, and I could tell it was making Barrett uncomfortable.

After what had happened the night before, I wasn't his biggest fan either, but he had helped me with Wayne. "Lillian, will you check that order that came in this morning? Last week they shorted us three sets of stickers and an expensive stamp. I think the shipper's hired his cousin again."

Lillian looked as if she wanted to refuse, but I signaled her to go in back. "Call me if you need me," she said as she glared at Barrett.

Once she was gone, he turned to me and said, "Thanks, she was making me a little nervous."

"My aunt is just looking out for my well-being. What can I do for you?"

He bit his lower lip a second, then said, "I'd like to take you to dinner tonight."

"Sorry, I'm busy," I said. Even if my card group wasn't meeting, or if I hadn't tried to make plans with Gail, even if I hadn't said yes to Greg's dinner invitation—discounting all of that, I still wouldn't have gone out with him. His ex-girlfriend Penny looked like she wasn't going to accept the "ex" part of their arrangement, and I had no earthly desire to get in the middle of that. My life had enough complications without my going out of my way to add any more, thank you very much.

But Barrett wasn't going to give up that easily. "Then how about lunch tomorrow?"

"No, again. I'm busy."

He looked like he was going to snap. "You have to eat sometime, Jennifer."

I'd let him dangle long enough. "I'm not going out with you, Barrett, so you can stop asking me, okay?"

"How am I going to explain what happened last night if you won't at least hear me out?"

I nudged him gently toward the door. "You don't

owe me any explanations. We shared some wine and most of a pizza. Just because I was willing to eat with you once doesn't mean I'm in any hurry to repeat it."

That killed his last ounce of effort at niceties. "I can't help it if my ex-girlfriend is stalking me."

Enough was enough. "What you don't understand is that it's not my problem if I don't choose to let it be. You seem like you can be nice enough when you're not scowling, and you're not totally repulsive, but believe me when I tell you that you're not that nice and you're certainly not good-looking enough to make it worth my while to take your problems on, too. Believe me, I've got enough of my own."

"You can't let Penny get away with this," he said.

We were at the door, and I reached over and opened it for him. "It's got nothing to do with me," I said. "I'm not going to be a part of this."

Barrett walked outside, but before I could close the door, he said, "I'm going to keep asking you out until you say yes."

"I've got a feeling you'll give up before I cave in to that particular request," I said.

Lillian was out of the storeroom before the door shut. "I don't like him, Jennifer. Good for you for not letting him bully you into dating him."

"That approach didn't work on me in the seventh grade; there's no way it's going to work now." I raised an eyebrow and asked, "How's that inventory coming?"

"You know perfectly well that I was eavesdropping," Lillian admitted.

"I knew it, but I wasn't sure you'd admit it."

She waved a finger in the air toward me. "I realize you think you're completely autonomous, but there are times when even the strongest of us needs someone else."

"What exactly are you implying?"

Lillian frowned. "Jennifer, don't be any more difficult than you already are. You know perfectly well what I'm talking about. I'm not saying you need a man in your life; I'm saying you need your family, no matter how much we tend to grate on your nerves."

I wasn't about to admit that she was right, though I knew that on some levels she was. Needing my clan was one thing, but admitting it to any of them was something else entirely.

"Let's jump on that inventory," I said. "Did you at least get the invoice out of the box?"

"It's still there, and it can wait until I go to lunch myself. I wasn't included in your little tête-à-tête, now was I? When I get back, I think we should discuss our questions before your group gathers tonight, don't you?"

"We're still running a business here, you know," I said. "Our profit is every bit as important as finding out what really happened to Maggie Blake."

"I'm not denying that, but our investigation is critical, too. We can't forget that."

I took my aunt's hands in mine. "Lillian, I'm just as eager to uncover the truth as you are. Tell you what, we can talk about the questions on the board as we check the shipment's bill against the actual inventory, okay?"

"I suppose it will have to be good enough," she said as she squeezed my hands gently in hers.

"That's the spirit," I said. "Have a nice lunch, and take your time. Things are dreadfully slow around here, aren't they?"

"We're doing fine, Jennifer."

After she was gone, to my surprise I waited on several customers, adding nicely to our day's receipts. Lillian took me up on my offer, because by the time she got back, it was an hour till closing.

I said, "We've just got time to finish this. Would

you like the invoice or would you like to do the actual inventory?"

"And rob you of the chance to muck about with your accessories? Give me the sheet." She took the invoice from me, but before she'd let me get started, Lillian said, "I'm going to set the marker board up where we can see it. Don't worry. I'll make certain no one will be able to spot it from the sales floor."

I wanted to protest that we had enough to do without worrying about Maggie at the moment, but Lillian was right. I was just going to have to find the time to look into her death while I ran the card shop, got settled into my new apartment and watched my back with the former deputy Wayne on the loose in Rebel Forge. It was just about more than a gal should have to deal with, but I was going to manage it if it didn't kill me first. Man, I was glad I hadn't said that out loud.

"Jennifer, what's a can stamp number two? Is it actually a stamp in the shape of a can?"

I took the sheet from her and looked. "No, the invoice is smeared. Let me think. I know." I dived into the box and came out with a fancy stamp of a candle in its stand. "Here it is. I ordered this for Nancy Klein. She's got a distant cousin in the candlemaking business, and she wanted me to get her something festive. I can't imagine how tough it must be to run a candleshop."

"No harder than a card shop, I'd say," Lillian said.

"I certainly wouldn't trade places with him," I said.

"I doubt he'd ask. Now, what's a roll of heart sticks? That sounds ghastly."

"They're heart-shaped stickers. Honestly, Lillian, perhaps we should trade jobs after all."

Lillian handed me the list, and I said quickly, "Okay, I saw this and this and this" as I checked the items off.

Lillian said, "It might help me know what to pull before you check them off the list. I swear, Jennifer, this would be faster if you just did it yourself."

"I don't want you to feel left out," I said, though I agreed with her.

"You've got to be kidding; you won't hurt my feelings. While you do this, I'll focus on our other list."

I couldn't help wondering if Lillian's incompetence was feigned or real, but it didn't really matter. She was right; I was much happier doing the job on my own. By the time I finished, I'd seen that every item listed on the invoice had been in the box. At least this time, it appeared that the order had been filled properly.

"All done?" Lillian asked.

"I am. So why am I a little disappointed everything was there?" I asked her.

She laughed. "I can answer that, my dear. It's because you bristle with competence, and you accept nothing less from the world around you. Think how fun it would have been to catch them with their knickers around their knees."

I grabbed one of the stools we kept in back. "Lillian, am I impossible?"

She put an arm around me, and for just a moment I remembered what she'd been like when my parents had died, loving and supportive, always there for me. "My dear, I think you're just about perfect."

A few errant tears crept down my cheeks, and I wiped them quickly away. I swear, sometimes my emotions get the best of me when I least expect it.

To divert my aunt's attention from my behavior, I asked, "So do you have any other ideas about what we should ask tonight?"

Lillian stared at the board a few moments, then said, "No, I'm afraid much of it is going to have to be spontaneous. The last thing we want is for anyone to suspect we're looking into Maggie's murder."

As I studied the board, I asked, "Why, don't you want to be tarred as an amateur investigator?"

"Jennifer, one of the people coming tonight could very well have killed Maggie, if our theories are correct. Do you honestly think it's a good idea to warn them that we're suspicious, when even the police are ruling her death an accident? This killer is very good, so we don't want to give any reasons to set their sights on us, now, do we?"

That surely took the fun out of it. "You're right, of course. So how do we ask questions without it sounding like we're grilling them?"

Lillian smiled. "Follow my lead, dear child. I've been doing it for more years than I care to admit. If there's any advantage in being married to as many different men as I have in my life, it's learning early on how to spot a lie."

"So you think it's some kind of acquired ESP that came with your vows?" I asked.

Instead of laughing at my jab, Lillian looked at me with a serious expression. "Don't scoff. Being able to separate the truth from the fiction made me a very rich woman."

I didn't even know how to comment on that, but I didn't have to. The front door chimed, and I walked up to see who was visiting. Greg Langston was there, and after a quick glance at the clock, it looked like he wanted to start our date early. The poor dear even had a bouquet of daisies in his hand.

Too bad I was going to have to dash his hopes yet again.

HANDCRAFTED CARD TIP

While precise, sharply cut edges are perfect for many cards, sometimes I like to tear the edges of additions to the cards I'm making. This rough border gives a much more informal tone to the card, and while I wouldn't use it on a wedding invitation, it's perfect for any card that just says hello to an old friend.

Chapter 8

"Greg, I can't go out with you."

He looked at me like I'd stabbed him in the heart. "Jennifer, I'm not going to let you get cold feet. We're going, and that's final."

"You don't understand," I explained. "I've got a meeting here tonight, and I need to prepare for it. It won't be over till ten, and I know how you hate to eat that late. I do too, for that matter, but it can't be helped. I really am sorry."

Greg paused a second, then said, "No, I'm not willing to accept that. I think a late dinner would be perfect."

"We can do it tomorrow, I promise." Honestly, he was as stubborn as ever, though I didn't mind it nearly as much as I had when Barrett had been so insistent earlier.

Greg smiled as he said, "If we can do it tomorrow, we can do it tonight. Ten o'clock sounds great."

Before I could say another word, he was gone.

Lillian had obviously been eavesdropping again in the back room. "I knew there was something I liked about that young man. He's persistent, isn't he?"

"A little too much for my taste," I said. "Now my schedule's going to be all out of whack eating that late. Blast it, I forgot! I have to go home and feed the cats."

Lillian glanced at her watch. "So go feed them.

You've got plenty of time; just don't dawdle. I'll start getting things ready here."

"Thanks," I said as I hurried out the door. I knew if I waited till midnight to feed Oggie and Nash, there would be an open cat rebellion, and I wasn't in the mood for shredded paper towels and toilet tissue all over the apartment, their favored method of showing their displeasure.

I raced back to my new place, intent on making the round trip in minimum time. It wasn't that I didn't trust Lillian to get things in order, but it was my shop, and ultimately, everything that happened there reflected on me. I might be preparing to grill some of my best customers, but that didn't mean I wasn't going to do right by them in everything else. I'd ordered two extra embossing kits so my group could play with them. If the club members liked the equipment, I offered the ones we used at a healthy discount, but still allowed myself enough of a profit to make it worth my while. It was something I'd wanted to try at Sara Lynn's shop, but she'd always vetoed it, hating to give anyone a discount on anything. I believed that it encouraged more spending, not less. After all, what fun was it to have a new tool or technique and nothing to practice it on?

Both of the doors in the building's foyer were shut, which was fine with me. I was in no mood to deal with either one of my fellow tenants. When I got to my door, there was a bouquet of flowers leaning against it. Barrett just wouldn't get the hint! What was I going to have to do to convince him I wasn't interested, smack his hand with a ruler? Without giving it a second thought, I grabbed the bouquet and marched down the steps. Barrett answered after my third knock.

"Hey, what's the problem—is there a fire? Oh, hi, Jennifer. Listen, I'm sorry, but if you came by to take me up on dinner, I've already made other plans."

"You arrogant son of a snot," I said, "How dare you? I wouldn't date you if there was bonus money at the end of the evening, do you understand? Here. I don't want these." I slammed the flowers into his chest, but instead of looking miffed, he just smiled.

"What's so funny?" I asked, ready to blast him again.

"I don't want them either," he said.

"So take them back to the flea-bitten florist where you bought them and try to get your money back."

"Jennifer, I'm afraid you're mistaken. I didn't send you flowers, and I won't ever in the future, not if this is the way you react to them."

That stopped me. "What do you mean you didn't send them? If they weren't from you, who are they from?"

Barrett reached into the crumpled bouquet and snatched out a card. "I'm willing to wager the name of your admirer is in here. Shall I read it to you?"

I snatched the card out of his hand; then after a moment's hesitation, I collected the flowers, too. "Sorry. It was an honest mistake."

"I'd love to stand out here in the hallway and chat, but I've got company."

I rolled my eyes. "Tell Penny I said hi."

I was halfway up the stairs when I heard him say, "It's not Penny."

"Don't brag about your conquests to me," I said just as an older man stepped through Barrett's door.

"Jennifer, say hello to my father."

"Hi," I said as I ducked around the corner. The older gentleman looked amused by the display, and as I fumbled with my door key, I heard him ask Barrett, "Is that the one you were telling me about?"

"Charming, isn't she?"

Why wouldn't my stupid key fit into the stupid lock?

I finally got it, then bolted inside just in time to hear the elder say, "Well, she's got fire, I'll say that for her."

I tried not to slam the door, but I couldn't help myself. After all, I might as well live up to the reputation. Ten seconds later something pounded on my floor, and I could hear my downstairs neighbor, the thoroughly unpleasant Mr. Wallace, shout, "Quiet! You're disturbing my peace."

I wanted to shout something back at him, but he was right. I hadn't been much of a new neighbor, even if he had started things off on the wrong foot. I made myself a promise to try to be quieter and see if I could at least get along with one of my fellow tenants. Barrett was hopeless. His smug expression was still in my mind when my roommates sashayed up to me. "Hi, you felons. What have you two been up to today?"

Oggie rubbed against my legs and I picked him up, stroking his fur. Though Nash loved attention too, he wouldn't deign to offer such an overt expression of affection for me. I played with both of them for a few minutes, fed them, then headed back for the door. That's when I remembered the flowers. Several of the daisies were broken, hanging precariously by their stems, while most of the baby's breath and ferns were most likely still on Barrett's doorstep. I worked with them a few seconds trying to salvage something, but they were hopeless. I owed whoever had sent them an apology. I dug the card out of my jacket pocket and read the note. It said, "From Your Not So Secret Admirer," but that wasn't what creeped me out. It was signed "WD," and there was only one person in all of Rebel Forge I knew with those initials: Wayne Davidson, the deputy who wouldn't go away. I thought about calling Bradford, but that would lead to a conversation I didn't have time for just then. I'd tell him later, but for the moment I had other things to do that needed my full attention. I grabbed the flowers and threw them in the trash cans outside, thought about adding the card but changed my mind. I might need it as evidence if Wayne's behavior escalated. Hopefully he'd gotten it out of his system, but I wasn't taking any bets. I planned to take Bradford's advice and watch my back until the situation was resolved, hopefully by Wayne leaving Virginia altogether.

I was still a little shook up by the time I got back to the card shop, and Lillian could tell the second I walked in the door that something was wrong.

"What happened, Jennifer?"

I didn't want to tell her; I didn't want to talk about it to anyone. Talking somehow made it real. But I had no choice. "There were flowers waiting for me when I got to my apartment."

"How delightful," she said.

"Read the card." I handed it to her and watched her expression. Her smile vanished quickly. "What does Bradford think you should do?"

"I don't know, because I'm not telling him, and neither are you. Not tonight, anyway."

Lillian frowned. "Jennifer, you know I'm not your brother's biggest fan—we've had plenty of differences in the past—but he is the sheriff."

I took the card back from her and tucked it in my pocket, then thought better of it. I didn't want that thing in physical contact with me if I could help it. I pinned it to the board in back of the register so I could deal with it later. "Lillian, we're not going to talk about this right now. Do you understand?"

She neatened a stack of paper on the worktable. "I understand, but I don't agree. He might be more dangerous than you realize."

"Lillian, I said drop it." The last thing I needed was a vision of Wayne Davidson lurking in the shadows while I was trying to find Maggie's killer and run a shop, too. I'd meant it. I would tell my brother soon, but not right away.

To my surprise, my aunt didn't say another word, though I knew she had to be burning inside to talk about it. It was funny, but our relationship had started to change since she'd come to work at Custom Card Creations. She treated me more and more as an equal than a young foal in need of protection. I liked it, and wasn't about to go back to the way things had been before. "Now let's get ready for our meeting. Where should we hide the board?"

"I don't think we should hide it at all," Lillian said. "I've been thinking since you were gone. If we leave it out where everyone can see it, our questions will be a perfect way to open the inquiry. What do you think?"

I took the whiteboard and slid it behind the counter where no one could see it. "We don't want to alert the killer if we can help it, remember? Tonight calls for subtlety."

"Never my strong suit," Lillian said. "I'm a woman of action, direct and intense."

I laughed, despite the cares on my shoulders. "I wouldn't recognize you if you were any other way. Though it might work in your love life, it's not going to do us much good tonight."

"You'd be amazed by how productive a direct question can be, Jennifer. You should try it sometime."

"I'm normally a big fan of straight talking myself, but not tonight." I glanced over at the papers and the two embossers Lillian had laid out. "Do you want a little practice before the club gets here?"

"Goodness no, I've mastered it. After all, it's not that difficult, is it?"

"No, ma'am," I said, happy that my aunt's confidence in her card-making skills had grown since she'd been working at the shop. "Would you like to lead the demonstration tonight?" We always started with a demo of the new tool or technique, then everyone else had a chance to try whatever we were doing.

"Are you out of your mind? I get stage fright when there are more than two people in the room. No, I'll let you handle that."

Speaking in public had never bothered me, for some odd reason. I could remember leading the Pledge of Allegiance at school when I'd been in first grade in the auditorium, and I'd had so much fun, I'd begged Mrs. Ashire to let me do it again on the spot.

"I wonder if Hilda's still bringing the snacks tonight. I forgot to ask her." We rotated our snack provider among members, since I was supplying the tools and papers.

Lillian spoke curtly. "Can you honestly imagine her forgetting? Hilda is a model of efficiency."

I knew the two women didn't get along, one of those dreaded personality conflicts that no one could explain or understand. "Why don't you leave questioning her to me?" I said.

"I'd be happy to. Since Dot is out of town, I'll take the dynamic duo." That was our secret name for Howard and Betty Hudson, a long-married couple that acted as if they were one person instead of two, to the point of interrupting each other in midconversation and taking over without missing a single beat.

"That would be great," I said just as there was a knock at the door. Hilda was standing outside, a tray of something in her hands. Though she was never a fashion plate, Hilda's stocky form was dressed in black, and I wondered if I should have changed when I'd been home. Oh well, it was too late now.

I opened the door and said, "Come in. Can I help you with that?"

She shoved the platter into my hands. "That would be great. I've got two more trips. We shouldn't go hungry tonight, should we?"

I waited for Lillian to offer to help, but when I realized she wasn't going to, I shoved the platter into her hands and said, "We'll be right back."

I followed Hilda outside, and when the shop door was closed, she said, "I know she doesn't much care for me."

"Lillian is a hard woman to read," I said, struggling for something to say that wasn't a direct confirmation of Hilda's on-target assessment.

She laughed. "Come on, Jennifer, I know she's your aunt. I wasn't expecting you to agree with me."

"Believe me, I'm the first to admit that Lillian can be an acquired taste," I said carefully.

"Can't we all? You know, there are some women on this earth I just have a tough time getting along with. I've always been fiercely independent, even when Karl was alive, but I would have stayed with that man forever. I've never been able to understand women who go from one husband to another as if they're collecting trophies along the way."

I stopped for a second, and Hilda looked at me with concern. "Jennifer, I'm sorry. That was out of line, and I apologize. Blast my mouth, I've grown too used to saying what's on my mind."

"There's something you should understand about my aunt," I said. "She was deeply in love with her first husband. I can still remember them holding hands after twenty years of marriage. When he had a heart attack, we all wondered if it would have been kinder to bury Lillian with him; she was that lost. Hilda, since then, she's been trying to replace him, and failing at it. You've been strong enough to go on alone, but my aunt has never been the type of woman who could do that. I'm not saying it's a flaw, mind you; it's just the way she's wired. So take it easy on her, okay?"

Hilda mumbled something and started walking again. Wonderful, Jennifer, you've managed to step in it again. If I took half the time I spent trying to make the world get along better and devoted it to my own life, I'd be the most successful woman in all of Virginia. As we loaded up our arms at Hilda's car and walked back to the shop, I tried half a dozen times to make light conversation, but my card-making friend wasn't having any of it. If I ran her off, I'd never be able to forgive myself. As we neared the shop, I tried one last time. "Hilda, sometimes I have a big mouth, too."

Great. I'd planned it better in my head, but then I blurted out the backhanded apology.

Hilda just shook her head sadly, and I knew in my heart that I'd failed. I pounded at the door with my foot, and Betty Hudson let me in. Betty was a slight, petite woman with a full head of gray hair and a steady smile on her face, though it was gone tonight. From the look of her eyes, I could tell that she'd been crying. I hadn't realized that she and Maggie had been that close. I saw her husband, Howard, in deep conversation with Lillian. He wore a bright knit sweater over his rotund form that made me feel better about my own clothing choices.

"Let me help you with that," she said as she took the large Tupperware container from me. I held the door so Hilda could come in, then locked it behind her. I'd been trying to add on to the club, and Daniel might join later, but for now, I just wanted to deal with the original members. Flipping the sign to CLOSED, I joined the rest of them at the card table where Lillian had set up the first tray. I always found it ironic that we ate at the card table and made cards on the other table, but I refrained yet again from commenting on it. Instead, I said, "What a lovely sweater, Howard."

His cheeks reddened slightly as he said, "Maggie made it for me for my birthday. I can't believe she's gone."

At that, Betty mumbled, "Excuse me," and bolted for the bathroom in back.

Howard looked at us all apologetically. "She's been like that since we got the news. I don't know what to do."

I started to go back to the bathroom when Lillian said, "I'll talk to her."

Hilda surprised us all when she said, "I'll go with you."

Lillian certainly didn't know how to react. "Perhaps it would be better if you dealt with her yourself. After all, you've been friends a great deal longer than I've known either one of you."

Hilda locked her arm in Lillian's. "Nonsense. You're a part of this group, too."

Lillian had no choice but to be dragged into the back. I didn't know what Hilda was up to, but at least it didn't look like I'd driven her away. If the circumstances for our meeting hadn't been so dire, I would have had a tough time not laughing aloud at the sight of my aunt doing anything in this world she didn't want to do.

That left Howard and me standing by the food. He looked over the opened trays, then said, "I know we probably should wait, but I haven't had much to eat lately."

Before I could stop myself, I blurted out, "Are you on one of those new diets?"

He patted his stomach, and if Howard took offense by my abrupt question, he didn't show it. "No, it's not that, but I never really learned to cook, and Betty seems to have lost interest in it altogether."

"She's really taking it hard, isn't she? I didn't realize you-all were that close."

He bit his upper lip for a moment, then said, "Closer than you might think. Jennifer, I need a bit of air. Do you mind?"

"Of course not," I said. "I'll join you. It's a beautiful night." It was chilly out, but I'd never minded the cold. Despite living in the South, we got our share of snow, being so close to the mountains, and I always reveled in the change of seasons.

"If you don't mind, I'd rather be alone."

That was plain enough. I unlocked the door and Howard could barely wait to bolt through it. The three women walked back in as I was securing the door again.

"Where's Howard?" Betty asked.

"He said he needed some air," I explained.

"He's not running away from this," Betty said firmly. "Stay by the door. I'll be right back."

I felt like the doorman at the Sherman Arms Hotel as I let her out, too. I wanted to discuss Howard's odd comments with Lillian, but Hilda was entrenched beside her. I wasn't sure what she was up to, but she was certainly being earnest about it. We could all hear Betty calling to her husband, and there was a whip in her voice I'd never suspected. In two minutes, we were gathered together again.

I met each of their gazes, then said, "Thank you all for coming. I was surprised when Hilda insisted we have our regular meeting tonight, but now that we're gathered here, I believe it was the right thing to do." I wasn't about to mention Maggie's card to Hilda to the group, let alone the one I'd received myself.

Hilda did it for me. "They all know about my card, Jennifer. It's how I got them here." She looked sideways at Howard, which caught me by surprise. If anyone had needed convincing to show up, I would have bet my next-to-last dime that it would have been Betty.

It was time to get started. "I've got a demonstration set up, if you-all would like to make some cards, or we could just eat instead."

Betty spoke up, her voice strong and clear. "I don't think we should change anything," she said, and no one else was about to disagree with her.

I moved to the table and picked up one of the embossers. "We just got these in, and Lillian and I have been having a lot of fun playing with them." As I explained the layering and pinning procedures, I tried my best to be enthusiastic, but it was tough with Maggie's ghostly laughter hanging in the air around us. She'd embraced our little card-making sessions even more than I did, gleefully making mistakes and learning as she kept us all entertained with her wild and outlandish stories.

I embossed a sample vine pattern on a sheet of smooth card stock and handed it around. "Isn't it lovely?"

Hilda took the sheet after everyone else had seen it and said, "I used to do this for my scrapbook pages. Jennifer, do you mind if I show you another trick?"

"Be my guest," I said. It was our custom to dive in if any of us had something to add, and I'd easily learned as much from the club as I'd managed to teach them myself.

She walked over to one of the aisles and grabbed a fine paintbrush and some gold paint. "It just takes a light touch, so I won't use much."

"You're the teacher," I said.

Hilda put a little paint on a paper towel, then lightly touched her brush to it. "You need a gentle hand for this." She stroked the paintbrush across the top of the card, barely touching it. When she showed us the results, I could see that the embossed areas were highlighted with the gold, while the brown stock I'd chosen remained untouched.

"That's beautiful," I said.

Everyone had to try their hands at it after that, and soon we were chattering away again. It was almost as if Maggie's spirit was with us, urging us to have fun in her memory instead of waste a single second mourning her.

By the time we were ready to eat, the tension in

the air had nearly dissipated, and I almost hated to ruin it by grilling any of my friends, but I'd made a promise to Maggie, even though it had been after her death, and I was going to follow through on it.

Chapter 9

"It's hard to believe Maggie's gone," I said to Howard as we nibbled on the crab puffs Hilda had brought. I'd been trying to get started with my interrogations, but it was hard to get any one member alone.

"I can barely believe it myself. I've known her for years," he said.

"So did Betty know her equally well?" I asked, hoping to come up with some way to focus the conversation on my investigation.

He shrugged, trying to dismiss my line of questioning, but I couldn't stop there.

"Were you surprised when you heard it was an accident?" I watched his reaction, hoping for something that would tell me what was on his mind. He was too good at masking his emotions, though.

Howard stared at me so hard I thought he was going to slap me. "What are you doing, Jennifer?"

"I'm making conversation, that's all," I protested, lying.

He wouldn't avert his gaze. "I think there's more to it than that."

If he was going to accuse me of being too direct, I might as well take advantage of it. "Did you see Maggie the day she died?"

Howard snapped, "Are you asking me for an alibi?"

"Why, do you need one?" I shot the question right

back at him. Why was he acting so strange? I hadn't even zinged him with a good question yet.

Howard must have realized he was talking louder than he should have. "You don't know what you're getting yourself into."

"That sounds like a threat," I said. I couldn't believe this normally mild-mannered man had turned on me.

"However you want to think of it, that's fine by me."

He blew past me before I could say another word, but before he could get to the door, Betty was after him. "Where are you going?"

"I'm leaving. Get your coat."

Her head jumped back as if he'd slapped her, but she held her ground. "What are you going to do if I say no?"

"Tell you to get a ride home. Do what you want. I'm leaving."

His exit would have been a great deal smoother if he hadn't had to stop and unlock the door, but he was gone quickly enough, and if my front door had been capable of slamming, Howard would have knocked it off its hinges.

Instead of going after him, Betty stormed toward me. "What did you say to him to set him off like that?"

I said, "I was just making conversation about Maggie's death."

Betty wasn't buying it. "There's more to it than that. I've been married to that man most of my life. What else did you say, Jennifer?"

She was backing me up against the wall. Had everyone in my club gone suddenly and utterly mad? "I asked him where he was when she died. I wasn't accusing him of anything, I swear it. I've just been wondering where Maggie was going when she died."

Betty's face went pale, and her voice was suddenly so low I could barely hear her. "If you must know, she was leaving our house and heading for home when it happened."

I certainly hadn't expected that. "What was she doing there?"

Betty's expression went dead. "Once upon a time we were friends. I didn't need her kind of friendship anymore though, and she wouldn't get the message."

I felt my knees start to buckle. "Betty, tell me you didn't do anything to Maggie."

"I threw her out of my house," Betty said shrilly. "And I'd do it again. I caught her making a pass at my husband during our last meeting here, and I had to protect my marriage."

"So you killed her?" I asked, my own voice growing weaker by the moment.

"I didn't hurt her!" Betty's shout of denial nearly blew my hair back. "She was fine when she left our place."

Lillian approached and put a hand on Betty's shoulder. "Are you certain of what you saw?"

"You knew Maggie; she'd flirt with anything wearing pants! Well, she wasn't running off with my husband."

Lillian said softly, "No dear, it appears he's running off all by himself."

Betty said, "Not if I can help it."

After she was gone, I looked at Hilda, and then at Lillian. "I swear I didn't know."

Hilda said, "Don't blame yourself, Jennifer. Betty even accused me once of making a pass at Howard. As if I ever would. She's been feeling threatened for the last six months."

"Does she have a reason to?" Lillian asked.

Hilda shrugged. "All I can say is that he never made a pass at me."

"But that's not all you suspect, is it?" Lillian pushed.

Hilda sighed. "It's common enough knowledge if you move in the right circles around Rebel Forge. I suspect Betty's paranoia wasn't completely irrational, but I doubt Maggie was the one in his life."

"But you don't know," I said.

"No," Hilda admitted. "It's all just idle speculation, isn't it?" She surveyed the food, still plentiful after our abbreviated meeting. "I'll be eating leftovers for weeks unless you both help me with some of this."

"I'd be delighted," I said.

To my surprise, Lillian added, "I'll take a few crab puffs home with me."

Hilda snapped the container shut that held them. "Take them all."

"I couldn't," Lillian protested.

"Honestly, I insist." I wanted some for myself, but if it would seal the rift between Hilda and my aunt, I supposed I could give the puffs up, as delightful as they were.

Lillian acquiesced. "Very well. At least let me help you carry these other trays back to your car."

"I'd be honored," Hilda said. Man, was she ever laying it on thick.

"Lillian, can I speak to you for a second?"

Hilda took the hint. "I'm down that way. I'll meet you there."

After she was gone, I asked my aunt, "Did you say anything about Timothy?"

A look of horror crossed her face. "Jennifer, I completely forgot! Everything happened so quickly. I'm so sorry."

"Don't be," I said. "I forgot all about the mysterious cousin myself. It's just as well neither one of us brought him up." I gestured toward Hilda. "What's going on with her?"

"I wish I knew," she said as she headed off in Hilda's direction. After she was gone, I shut the lights off, locked the door behind me and walked in the other direction. I couldn't get my mind off Howard's reaction as I drove home. What could have possibly set him off like that? Could Betty's suspicions have been on the money? Why else would Howard react so strongly? He could have felt guilty about the last time he saw Maggie, but unless he'd had an affair with her after all, would he be so outraged by my fairly innocent questioning? I wasn't any closer to the truth when I got back to my apartment. Thankfully there were no notes or flowers waiting for me, but there was a message on my answering machine.

The second I hit the PLAY button, I felt my heart twinge. It was Greg's voice, and he was more hurt than I could ever remember hearing him. "Hi, Jennifer. Guess you changed your mind. I just went by the card shop and the lights were all off. You should have had the decency to tell me to my face. Bye."

Oh, no. I'd forgotten all about our late dinner date. I looked Greg's pottery shop up in the phone book and dialed the number, but there was no answer. I tried his home number, and the machine kicked in before it could ring a third time. "Greg? Are you there? Pick up. I didn't stand you up, I swear it. At least not on purpose. I'm sorry, something happened at the meeting tonight. No, that's no excuse. Call me, Greg. I'm sorry."

It was a pitiful apology, but until the next day, I wasn't going to be able to give him a real one. I even thought about driving over to his apartment, but Sara Lynn had told me he'd moved recently, so I didn't even know where to look. There was a chance she might know, but I realized that if I called my sister after eleven, she'd have a heart attack or, worse yet, give me one. Patching things up with Greg would just have to wait until tomorrow.

For the moment, all I could do was go to bed and hope the nightmare of a day I'd had would fade away once my head hit the pillow.

No such luck. I was haunted again in my dreams, with Maggie frowning at me in disappointment.

I didn't blame her. So far, I'd bungled things up pretty well, but I decided to take a page from Scarlett O'Hara. Tomorrow was indeed a new opportunity to muck things up even more.

I was walking downstairs the next morning when I saw the renter below me open his door. My first reaction was to bolt for the front door, but I knew I was going to have to make peace with this man whether I liked it or not, since he was my neighbor. All I knew him as was "J. Wallace," and that was from his mail slot instead of any formal introduction. He was dressed in a stuffy suit and very conservative tie, and I half expected him to have a bowler hat perched on his head.

In a rush of words, I said, "I'm really sorry about the other night. I can assure you that I'm normally not like that."

He didn't want to talk to me any more than I wanted to talk to him, but I was standing too close for the man to ignore me. "That's fine," he said, trying to brush me off, but I wouldn't hear of it.

"I've been meaning to thank you for your concern about me renting the place," I said. "I wish I'd had all the information I needed before I took it."

"I felt it was the least I could do," he said. Was the glacier in his voice actually warming up some?

"Well, it was more than neighborly. It was the right thing to do. Did you know Frances well?"

"We had a passing acquaintance," he said. "Not much more than that. If you want to know anything about her, I suggest you ask him." The last bit was said with a gesture toward Barrett's door.

"Are you two friends?" I asked.

"Hardly. I can't think of a single thing we have in common."

"Except addresses," I said, trying to be light and cheerful. He wasn't making it any easier on me. "By the way, we didn't have a chance to really meet before. My name's Jennifer Shane." The way I put my hand out to him, he would have had to knock it away to move anywhere but backward, and I intended to follow him inside his apartment if that was what it took to get the man's first name out of him.

He studied it a moment longer than I would have liked, then took my hand gingerly in his. "My name is Jeffrey Wallace."

"Mr. Wallace, it's a pleasure to meet you." I considered for a moment calling him Jeffrey, but I was afraid he would bolt for sure if I did that.

"Ms. Shane," he said with an air of formality.

I was dying to ask him what he did for a living, but I ultimately decided to let it go for the moment. We'd made great progress so far, and I didn't want to ruin it.

"Well, it was nice meeting you, Mr. Wallace. I hope we have the chance to chat more another time."

"Yes," he said, "that would be fine."

To my surprise, he followed me out the front door. As we walked to the parking pad for our cars, he said, "Ms. Shane, I shouldn't say this, but I'd be careful in my dealings with Barrett if I were you."

"Why is that?" I asked.

Mr. Wallace looked around before he spoke. "He entertains a fairly wide range of young women in that apartment of his. I'd hate to see him take advantage of you."

I touched his arm lightly, and could feel him tense up. Obviously Jeffrey Wallace was not a big fan of body contact in any guise. "Thank you for your concern, but nobody's taken advantage of me since the second grade. You might want to warn him about me, though."

Was that a smile that broke through his stern countenance for a moment? "Perhaps we'll let him discover that for himself, shall we?"

"It's a lot more fun that way," I said as I unlocked my Gremlin. Mr. Wallace was driving a Mercedes, but not a new shiny one as I'd suspected. This one was at least twenty years old, and though he'd obviously done his best to keep it up, the signs of wear and age were pretty obvious.

"That's an interesting vehicle you've got there," he said.

"I like a car with character," I said. "I like yours, too."

He nodded, then got into his Mercedes and drove away. I sat there a minute wondering what had brought three such different people together to live under the same roof. It was funny. I usually knew right off the bat if I liked someone or not, but I'd met Jeffrey Wallace twice and I still didn't have a clue how I felt about him.

As I drove through town to the card shop, I stopped at the bakery and picked up a couple of bear claws for the store and then decided to grab an apple fritter for Greg. Flowers or balloons might have been more appropriate for an apology, but I knew Greg's weakness for the confections, and I needed every advantage I could get to make up for last night. I parked in the lot near the store, then bypassed my front door and walked to his pottery shop. He had some pieces with a beautiful green glaze displayed in the window, and I could swear they shimmered as I walked past them. Greg was a decent potter, but it was his wonderful glazes that set his work apart. I could see a light on in his back room, so I was pretty sure he was there.

I banged on the door, then heard him shout, "We're not open for an hour."

"I'm not here to buy anything," I shouted right back.

He opened the door suddenly. "Jennifer, I'm surprised to see you here." Greg wore an apron over his blue jeans and T-shirt, and his dark hair was more disheveled than usual. I had to wonder if he'd slept at his shop again, but now wasn't the time to bring it up.

It was time to plunge in with my apology. "Listen, I'm so sorry about last night."

"I am too," he said. "If that's it, I'm working."

Boy, he really was miffed. I held up one of the bags from the bakery. "I brought you a present. Can I come in?"

He seemed to think about it, then reluctantly stepped aside. "Fine, but just for a second. I'm trying something new in back."

"Can I see it?" I knew how reluctant Greg was to share his unfinished work with anyone, but I was hoping if I showed enough interest, it might help break the chunky block of ice between us.

"Sorry, it's not ready for the world yet."

While it was a denial, I could see that Greg appreciated the attempt. I could read that man's face like a paperback. And why shouldn't I? We'd been together for a long time. Maybe that was part of the problem.

"So what did you bring me?" he asked, gesturing to the bag.

"What do you think?"

He rubbed his chin, then said, "If there's not an apple fritter in there, you're going to have to go back." A slight hint of playfulness danced in his brown eyes, a very good sign indeed.

"I've got two bear claws," I said, and saw the light dim a moment, "but those are for the shop. The apple fritter's all yours."

He grabbed the bag I held out to him, opened it and tore off a chunk of the pastry. "Man, that's good. All I've had this morning is coffee, and that's from yesterday."

"I'm sorry; I should have brought you some fresh this morning. Tell you what, I'll brew a pot when I get to the shop and bring it back to you."

He took another bite, then said, "Don't bother, Jen, I've got one brewing in back myself. Listen, I appreciate the gesture, but I really do have to get back to work."

"So all is forgiven?" I searched his eyes, hoping he could see the sincerity in mine.

After a moment's hesitation, he said, "I guess so."

That wasn't the most convincing acceptance I'd ever heard in my life. "So do you want to try again tonight?" I shocked myself saying it, but it was already out and there was nothing I could do about it now.

"Thanks, but maybe we should just forget it."

In the past six months, Greg Langston had asked me out a dozen times. I couldn't believe he was saying no when I was finally willing to go. "So you're still upset about last night," I said.

"That's not it—at least not all of it."

"So what is?" I asked.

I didn't think he was going to tell me, but finally, reluctantly, he said, "Jennifer, I understand you were distracted last night, but you forgot about me altogether. I'm beginning to think you were right to say no all along. Maybe our last chance is gone and it's time to finally move on, for both of our sakes."

"Greg, you're reading an awful lot into one momentary slip," I said. "One of my crafters died, didn't you hear?"

He took a deep breath, then said, "Of course I heard. Rebel Forge isn't all that big. You still had your meeting last night, though."

I wasn't about to admit to him that Lillian and I were digging into what we thought was a case of murder. "We were holding kind of a wake last night. It turned out to be a mistake, though."

"I'm sorry," Greg said.

"It's not your fault," I replied a little too abruptly. "So that's it, then? We're finally calling it quits?"

He just shrugged. "I know, it's hard, isn't it? Thanks again for breakfast."

I left his pottery shop a little in shock. Even though I'd been holding him at arm's length for half a year, I still wasn't ready for the finality of his pronouncement. Sometimes it was just nice to be wanted, especially by someone I used to love. I was going to have a hard time wrapping my head around this new development, and knowing me, I'd probably stew, pace, overanalyze the entire conversation until there wasn't a shred of it untouched in my thoughts.

I hated to admit it, but a part of me mourned my loss, whether it was real or imagined.

Lillian was late again, and after I ate the bear claw I'd bought for myself, I nearly started on hers. I was sad and depressed and irritable, a bad combination when there was any kind of treats around. I'd finally decided to yield to temptation when the front door opened. I don't think I would have been more shocked if the queen of England herself had walked in when I saw Howard and Betty come in. Neither one of them looked like they'd gotten a bit of sleep, and I didn't doubt that was true. I thought I'd had a rough night, but from the look of them, I'd had a night at the Ritz.

"Good morning," I said, trying to put a smile on my face, though I was hardly in the mood for it.

Betty nudged Howard, a subtle thing that I would have missed if I hadn't been watching them closely.

He said, "Jennifer, I owe you an apology for storming out of here last night. I'm sorry."

"You don't have to apologize," I said. "Emotions were running high last night."

"Still, I was wrong. I overreacted."

"It's fine. Honestly it is." I didn't know if Betty had been hammering away at him all night, but the man who stood before me bore no resemblance to the cold fellow who'd stormed out of my shop. He was so contrite I would have just about forgiven him anything. Anything except killing Maggie Blake. "How are you two doing?"

Betty said, "We're not doing all that well, to be honest with you, but we'll get there." She frowned, then added, "We're going into counseling, so we'll see what happens."

I didn't have the heart to ask them about Maggie, but Betty brought her name up instead. "We wanted to come by to speak with you before the funeral. You're coming, aren't you?"

"I hadn't heard about it," I admitted. "When is it?"

"It will be at noon. It's a graveside service only. That was Maggie's request. I know you're busy here, but it would have meant a lot to her."

"I'll be there," I said, wondering how I was going to manage to get home, change clothes and attend the service without shutting my shop down for the afternoon.

Betty turned to her husband. "Howard, why don't you go wait by the car? I want to talk to Jennifer a moment."

He obeyed without a word or glance in my direction, and I wondered if we'd ever see him at a meeting again.

Once he was gone, Betty said, "I should thank you, but after the night I had last night, I won't be able to just yet. Your questions were the catalyst we needed to clear the air between us."

"I'm sorry," I said as sincerely as I could manage. I hadn't meant to drive a wedge between them with my line of questioning.

"Don't be," Betty said. "We'll work through it. I wanted to talk to you about Maggie."

Just then the front door opened and Lillian came in. "Hello, all. It's a beautifully crisp morning out there, isn't it?"

She instantly took in the somber expressions on our faces and her smile quickly faded. "Jennifer, I need to work on that inventory in back. If you two will excuse me, I'll get right to it."

After Lillian was safely ensconced in back, I said, "Honestly Betty, you don't have to talk about it if you're not comfortable."

"No, there's something you should know. She and Howard were not having an affair. I'm sure of that now. But that doesn't mean she wasn't seeing anyone. There was a man I saw her with recently, an older gentleman who lives in town. From the looks of it, they were quite close. If you're going to look into what happened to Maggie, you should talk to him about her."

"Betty, what makes you think I'm doing anything of the sort?"

Her expression lightened for a moment. "Jennifer, I worked as a secretary for the Charlottesville police for twenty-five years. It's true I mostly just typed and filed, but I've been around enough investigations to know one when I see it. Be careful; it can be dangerous."

I wasn't going to admit what I was doing, even if she did already suspect it. "Just out of curiosity, who is this fellow you saw her with?"

Betty shook her head. "I don't know, but I'm sure he'll be at the funeral. I'll point him out to you."

"Did you happen to catch his name?" It would be a big help if I knew who we were talking about, since

I was acquainted with just about everyone in Rebel Forge.

"I didn't know it at the time, but I asked around. His name is Jeffrey Wallace."

Chapter 10

"Are you sure that's his name?" I asked. It was hard to imagine my straitlaced neighbor being with Maggie, a woman who was so vibrant and full of life.

"I'm positive," she said. "Jennifer, I know your brother thinks that what happened to Maggie was an accident, despite that card you got in the mail from her, but I don't believe it."

"How did you know about the card?" I hadn't told anyone but Bradford and Lillian, and I couldn't imagine they'd shared the information with anyone else.

"We all got them," Betty said simply. "I can't imagine Maggie leaving you out."

"What did yours say?" I asked. Why hadn't Maggie done more to prevent her death than just make cards? If she'd come to me earlier, I would have done something more to help her than just try to find her killer. Could I have saved her? Maybe I could have, or maybe she would have died anyway, but at least I would have had the chance.

Betty looked down at her hands. "I tore mine up and threw it away without even reading it," she admitted, tears creeping down her cheeks. "I was jealous; I didn't want to have anything to do with her. I hate the way I've been acting lately."

I offered her a hug, trying to console her. Then the strangest thought jumped into my head while I had my arms around Betty. Was she really feeling guilty over not reading Maggie's card, or was it possible her guilt went deeper than that? She admitted herself that she'd been acting irrational. If Betty had truly believed that Maggie was having an affair with her husband, could she have killed her competition? How about Howard, then? Now that Maggie was gone, his wife had only his word that he hadn't been fooling around with Maggie. I was suddenly very happy I wasn't a member of that particular household. If either one of them acknowledged the thoughts I was having, it would shatter what was left of their marriage. I didn't see how either one of them could live with the other if they suspected their spouse was capable of murder.

That gave me another question. I pulled away from Betty and asked, "What about Howard? Was the card addressed to both of you, or did he get one himself?"

Betty scratched her cheek hard enough to leave white streaks. "I don't believe I even saw how it was addressed. I recognized her handwriting the instant I saw the back of the envelope. If Howard got one too, he didn't volunteer the information. I'm going to assume she didn't write him unless I learn otherwise." Her gaze was darting all around the shop as she spoke, and I wondered again about her state of mind.

I had to talk to Howard, and this time, it had to be without his wife hovering nearby. "Lillian, could you come here for a second?"

She came out so quickly I was certain she'd been listening to every word. That was okay; after I started getting more suspicious of Betty's behavior, it was good to have some kind of backup. "Is there something I can do for you?"

"Yes, I need you to show Betty that new computer program we got in the other day." Betty started to protest, but I cut her off. "Would you do me a favor and look at it? You're a lot better with those things than I am. I'm not at all sure it's worth what we paid for it. Would you mind?"

Betty looked startled by the suggestion, but I was just glad she couldn't see Lillian's face. My aunt must have thought I was nuts, but it was the only way I could think of to occupy Betty's time while I hunted down her husband. I knew that Betty considered herself a computer expert, but I had a suspicion I'd be lucky if mine even worked after she was finished with it. "Is this the time for that, Jennifer? I'd be happy to come by tomorrow and look at it if you'd like."

I shook my head. "Sorry, tomorrow will be too late. We have to send it back by five p.m. or we'll lose our chance. I know it's a terrible imposition, but would you mind?"

"Anything to help. After all, you've been so kind to me. Let me just step into the powder room and then I'll have a look."

After she was gone, Lillian whispered, "Have you lost your mind, Jennifer? What's this program, and why does she need to evaluate it?"

"Find some way to keep her occupied. Take one of the new card-making programs and ask her opinion about it. I need to talk to her husband without Betty hovering nearby."

Lillian laughed, then cut it off when she realized how loud she was being. "I can see you inherited my devious streak. I'm delighted, I must say. I was beginning to wonder if any of you would step forward."

"So you'll do it?" I asked as I grabbed my coat.

"I'll ask her so many inane questions she'll be hoarse in an hour."

I patted her hand. "I don't need that long. Give me twenty minutes."

Lillian flicked a stray strand of hennaed hair out of her face. "Let's leave it open-ended, shall we? This is going to be fun."

"Try not to torture her too much," I said as I walked out.

"Now what fun would that be?"

I left Betty to Lillian's devices, and didn't envy either one of them the upcoming session. I couldn't worry about that, though. I had to find Howard and talk to him while I had them separated.

I found him leaning against their car smoking a cigarette. "I didn't know you smoked," I said as I approached him.

"I quit twenty years ago," he said, the evidence of his lie dangling from his fingertips. "Okay," he added, "every now and then I sneak one, but not many, and not often."

"Just in times of stress, maybe?" I asked.

Howard dropped the cigarette to the curb and snuffed it out with his shoe. "Who knows why any of us do what we do?" He looked behind me. "Where's Betty?"

"She's helping Lillian with something at my request. I hope you don't mind."

"Why should I mind?" Howard asked, still looking back toward the shop. It appeared he was going to bolt any second, so I had to act quickly. "She told me about the card you got from Maggie. Do you still have it?"

The color drained from his face, and his hand went back to his pocket, no doubt reaching for another cigarette. "How did she know about it?"

"She got one, too," I said, watching his reaction. It wasn't good. I swear, the man got physically ill just thinking about the prospect. In a halting voice, he asked, "What did hers say? Did she tell you?"

I thought about toying with him a little more, but I didn't have the stomach for it. "She tore it up before she read it. So what did yours say?"

The relief that swept over him was palpable. "What? It was nothing, just a regular card she made." He paused, then added, "She was trying out her Christmas cards and asked me my opinion."

Now I've told some lies in my life, from little white

ones to huge and utter whoppers, but I could swear I saw his nose grow as he told me that.

Trying my best to hide my incredulity, I asked, "Do you still have it? I'd love to see it."

He couldn't resist the lure of his cigarettes any longer. As he lit another one, he shook his head. "No, I threw it out. After all, she didn't need my input anymore, did she?"

It was clear Howard was hiding something, but what? I was about to press him when I heard Betty's voice behind me. "Howard Hudson!" she shouted. "Put that out this instant."

He looked guilty as he stubbed it out. "Sorry," he muttered.

"Sorry won't cut it. You promised."

Not able to hide the exasperation in his voice, Howard said, "It was one cigarette, Betty."

She approached us and pointed to the curb at his feet. I noticed four butts there at the same time Betty must have. "Get in the car, Howard; we'll talk about this later."

I could see he wanted to protest, but he got in docilely without looking at me again.

Betty said, "Why were you out here talking to my husband? Haven't you done enough already?"

"I was just getting some fresh air," I lied. "I'd forgotten he was out here waiting on you. So what do you think of the new program? You didn't take long to look at it."

"It's worthless," she said. "I didn't need long to determine that. I'd send it back while you have the chance." She lowered her voice, then added, "Your aunt seems to have some trouble with her basic computer skills. You should send her to the class at the library. Your sister-in-law is a good teacher, and believe me, Lillian could use the lessons."

They drove off, and I was left there staring after them. I glanced over at Greg's pottery shop, saw a sudden movement, and wondered if he'd been watching me. I wished I had the time to make things right with him again, but I had a funeral to get ready for. Besides, I didn't have a clue what I could say to him to change his mind. I wasn't even sure that I wanted him to.

Lillian was waiting for me just inside the door. "Jennifer, I'm so sorry. She was determined to leave, and the only way I could have kept her was with the dead bolt."

"Don't worry about it; you did fine. I heard everything I was going to hear."

That perked her up. "So what did his card say?"

"Now, how did you know that?" I asked. "Oh, that's right; you were eavesdropping again when I talked to Betty."

"Jennifer, I prefer to think of it as being able to confirm your account of the conversation if you ever need it. I was doing you a service, young lady."

"And I greatly appreciate it," I said, fighting to hide my smile. There were days when my aunt was the only bright spot around, and this one was shaping up as one of those times.

"Don't keep me in suspense. What did it say?"

"I don't think we'll ever know," I said as I took off my coat. "He made up a quick lie about her trying out Christmas cards on him. It wasn't the slightest bit credible, but I couldn't shake him."

Lillian frowned. "Jennifer, perhaps he's telling the truth."

"What do you mean?"

Lillian paced around the shop. "You know as well as I do that Maggie liked to experiment with her card making. Is it that unreasonable that she wanted to field-test a few of them? She could have mailed the card to Howard before she decided to mail the ones to you and Hilda. I'm wondering about something, though."

"What's that?"

Lillian bit her lip, then said, "I don't mean to sound petty, but it appears that everyone in the club got a card but me."

"That is odd," I said. "You and Maggie got along, didn't you?"

"As far as I was aware," she said.

"Don't worry about it, Lillian," I said. "I'm sure she wasn't in her right state of mind when she sent those cards. I'm going to break one of our rules, if you don't mind."

Lillian perked up. "I'm always up for rebellion, you know that. What did you have in mind?"

I flipped the sign from OPEN to CLOSED. "We're shutting the shop down so we can both go to Maggie's memorial service."

"I don't mind staying behind," Lillian said. There was a tinge of hurt in her voice.

I took her hands in mine. "Listen, I'm sure she didn't mean to slight you. Besides, I need you there to catch anything I might miss. I loved Maggie, but I'm not going to this thing for her. I want to see who else shows up, and how they act."

Lillian nodded suddenly. "I'll go with you, then. It did surprise me that you were willing to attend, given how you feel about funerals in general."

I pinched the bridge of my nose, fighting the tears before they could develop. "It's no secret how I despise them," I said, trying to fight off the images of my parents after they were dead, laid out in finery some stranger had chosen for them. "We'll say our proper good-byes to Maggie after we figure out what happened to her."

"I'd be honored to do just that," she said. "I hope you have something more appropriate to wear than what you had on last night."

I thought about my closet and tried to come up with

something I could wear. "I've got a charcoal gray dress; it's close enough to pass for black," I protested.

"Jennifer, Jennifer, you simply must let me buy you a basic black dress. It's the answer for so many different social occasions."

As we walked back outside, I said, "We'll worry about my fashion sense later, if it's just the same to you. Right now I have to get home and change. If we both don't hurry, we're going to be late as it is."

Lillian said, "You drive home. I'll change as well, then meet you back here. That way we can go together. Fifteen minutes, Jennifer."

"I'll make it if you can," I said, knowing my aunt's penchant for trying on a dozen outfits before finding one that worked.

"Count on it," she said.

Back at my apartment, I was tempted to have a conversation with Jeffrey Wallace, but there wasn't time if I was going to make my deadline. I changed as quickly as I could, sparing a few minutes to say hello to Oggie and Nash, then dashed back out. Despite my tight schedule, I rapped on Jeffrey's door, but he didn't come out.

Barrett opened his, though.

He looked startled to see me there. "Jennifer, are you going to Maggie's memorial?"

"I am," I said. "I was just checking on Jeffrey."

"So you're on a first-name basis with both of us already," he said with that slightly smug smile of his.

"I do my best to get along with the people around me," I said a little too stuffily, even for my taste. For some reason, Barrett brought it out in me. "Will your girlfriend be attending with you?"

That got him, and I secretly celebrated the point. "I told you, Penny's not my girlfriend."

"That's right; you did say that, didn't you? If you'll excuse me, I'm late."

I heard a man chuckling inside Barrett's apartment, and realized that his father was taking great joy from my zingers. Him I could get along with.

I couldn't believe it, but Lillian was waiting for me in front of the card shop, dressed in an elegant black number that probably cost more than my monthly rent at Custom Card Creations. "Don't you look lovely?" I said.

"As do you," Lillian said. "Shall we?"

"We shall," I said as I got into the passenger seat of her Mustang. There was never any question about who drove when Lillian and I went anywhere together. She wouldn't be seen in my Gremlin, while I enjoyed being squired around in her vintage sports car.

As we drove to the grave site for the service, I said, "I bumped into my neighbor Barrett outside his door."

"You're collecting admirers like some people collect stamps," Lillian said.

"I'd hardly call him an admirer," I said. "Who else are you talking about?"

"Greg, of course. He came out to keep me company while I was waiting for you."

"What did he say?" I asked, trying not to hold my breath as I waited for her reply.

"He's troubled," she said. "Jennifer, you know I don't like to meddle."

She broke off as I laughed out loud. After I managed to contain it to a dull whoop, Lillian asked, "Are you quite finished?"

"I'm just glad I wasn't drinking a Coke," I said.

"I believe I'll keep my advice to myself," Lillian said.

"If you can manage that, I'll be more stunned than you will be," I said.

She wanted to be mad; I could tell by the firm way my aunt grabbed the steering wheel.

There was just one thing that might work. I pushed

harder. "Come on, you've got to admit that butting out would be completely out of character for you."

She sniffed once, then said, "How can I stand idly by while people I love are constantly making mistakes? Isn't it my obligation to help them find their way?"

"I know you mean well," I said, ducking the question altogether.

"It's true; I'm simply misunderstood."

She drove a few minutes more, and we were almost to the cemetery when I asked her, "So what's your advice?"

She hesitated, then replied, "No, you're right. I do have a tendency to meddle in your life, don't I? I'm going to make a resolution to do better, starting right now. How you live your life is going to be up to you from now on, Jennifer."

I could barely believe what I was hearing. "Does that mean you won't give me advice if I ask for it?"

She frowned. "Of course not. Don't be a nit. But you'll have to ask for it from now on."

She parked among several other cars and started to get out when I touched her arm lightly. "Okay, I'm asking. What advice do you have for me?"

"Do you really want to know what I think?"

"I do," I said.

"Very well. Jennifer, I know Greg has made more than his share of mistakes in the past, but you either need to forgive him once and for all or move on. It's not fair to him this way, and it's not fair to you."

I started to protest when she held up a hand. "Don't talk; just think about what I've said. My, my, we've got an interesting crowd gathering already."

I was about to say something about her earlier advice when I noticed someone standing in the shadows. Bradford had shown up for the memorial, and I wondered if he was there in his official capacity. His squad car wasn't around; then I spotted it tucked behind the

trees and out of sight. I started to walk toward him
when Lillian grabbed my arm. "Where do you think
you're going, young lady?"

"I spotted my brother, and I want to talk to him."

"You'll do no such thing," Lillian said, her voice
suddenly a firm line. "It took bribery and begging to
get him to show up, and I won't let you ruin it."

"You called him?" I asked.

"I did. Jennifer, what does it cost him to be here?
He can claim he showed up for crowd control if he
has to, but I want our suspects to squirm a little. When
they see Bradford attending dressed in his uniform, the
guilty party might do something stupid to give themselves away."

"You're absolutely brilliant," I said. "Now why
didn't I think of that myself?"

"That's why there are two of us, my dear," Lillian
said, unable to hide the pleasure she was feeling.

"I just hope it works." I caught my brother's glance,
offered a quick smile of thanks and received a nod
acknowledging it, all accomplished without a word.

As Lillian and I walked forward to the grave site,
I noticed that the service was being held in the crema-
tion area. That didn't surprise me; Maggie could always be counted on for doing the unexpected.

There were two faces in the group gathered there
that I didn't recognize, but I knew everyone else present. Barrett had beaten me there, but he was standing
as far from Jeffrey Wallace as he could manage and
still hear the service. Hilda was there, as were Betty
and Howard, though none of them looked particularly
happy to be there. To my surprise, Hester Taylor was
there as well.

I whispered to Lillian, "Did you see that Hester's
here?"

My aunt looked in the direction I gestured, then
said, "That surprises me, I admit. Don't worry, I'll
speak to her later to see her connection with Maggie."

As we stood near the interment site, close enough to hear but far enough back to watch everyone else, I asked Lillian, "So what did you have to do to bribe Bradford?"

"I had to promise to make him a double batch of banana pudding."

From her voice, I could tell that wasn't all. "And what else?"

"Why must there be anything else?"

"Because I know the two of you better than just about anybody else on the planet," I said, "including Sara Lynn." It was true, too. Since I'd opened my card shop, working side by side with Lillian every day had let me get to know her better than I ever had growing up. She'd become much more than a wacky aunt to me; to my surprise, Lillian had also become my friend.

"If you must know," she said with distaste thick in her voice, "I have to watch him eat it, every single bite, and not have the least spoonful of it myself. Your brother is an odd man; you know that, don't you?"

I put my arm around Lillian and hugged her. "Of course I do. It runs in the family." The two of them had been feuding over a bowl of banana pudding from our past, and I was hoping this episode would end the spat forever, but I sincerely doubted it. I wasn't quite sure if Bradford or Lillian would know how to act toward each other without a hint of the resentment they'd shared over the years.

A large woman dressed in a brightly dyed muumuu and sandals walked up to join us, an urn tucked safely in her arms. There were a few whispers in the crowd, and she waited for us all to quiet down before she started.

In a light, tinkling voice that didn't match her physical appearance at all, she said, "Friends and loved ones, we're here not for farewells, but to say 'until we meet again' to Maggie Blake. She was a free spirit, alive with the essence that is in each of us. By her request, I want to read this to you."

From the folds of her outfit she produced a letter, the urn never wavering. "She mailed this card the day she died, sending her voice into the wind from the great beyond. Let me share it with you all now." I'll say this for Maggie: she had certainly embraced card making in her last days.

Samerena, share with those I love, and all those gathered together, that the truth is all that matters, and it will see the light of day soon.

She closed the card, then said, "Maggie obviously wanted to share a sense of her spiritual enlightenment with you all. She was devoted to our yoga classes at the Y, and I'm honored she chose me to share this message with you."

I heard a snort of derision and saw Jeffrey Wallace stomping off. I'd have to speak to him later about his reaction, but Samerena wasn't finished. She opened the urn, took a pinch of the ashes within it and scattered them into the air. Thank goodness there wasn't any breeze to speak of. The last thing I wanted was some of Maggie's ashes on me. Samerena took another pinch and sprinkled it on the ground, then took a final pinch and spread it over a birdbath reservoir inset into the ground. "To the sky, to the sea, to the land," she said, and I felt a chill run through me. After a moment of silence, she put the urn into the ground, nearly stumbling as a fold of clothing tightened, but she managed to right herself.

"She wanted each of us to say good-bye in our own way." Then she shoveled a small portion of dirt over the hole and handed the trowel to Hilda, who had been standing closest to her.

Lillian asked me in a whisper, "Have you seen enough, or do you want to shovel, too?"

"Let's pull back," I agreed. I had no desire to participate in the ritual, suspecting that Samerena had made it up herself on the spot. "Did you hear that message?"

"That woman is certifiable," Lillian said. "I don't get this New Age mumbo jumbo."

"I'm not talking about that," I said. "I mean what Maggie wrote her. It didn't have anything to do with spiritual enlightenment. Maggie knew whoever killed her would be at the service. The truth she was talking about was a lot more concrete than Samerena thinks. Maggie was warning whoever killed her that they weren't going to get away with it. I just wish I had as much confidence in us as she had."

"Just what do you think you're doing?" Barrett's voice behind me froze my blood. There was real animosity in it, but I was tired of having him push.

It was time to push back.

HANDCRAFTED CARD TIP

If you're at all handy with a paintbrush, you can embellish your cards with everything from autumn leaves to shining stars, but I've found a way that everyone can add a touch of color to their offerings. An inexpensive watercolor kit can do wonders to give a handcrafted card that distinctive touch. By adding washes of different colors to your paper—simply diluting some of the pigment into water until the desired effect is achieved and then brushing it onto your card—you can make each of your efforts a truly unique gift.

Chapter 11

"I'm saying good-bye to an old friend, not that it's any of your business," I said.

Lillian took a few steps back, pretending to give us privacy while hanging on every word. I didn't care who our audience was. It was time to put Barrett in his place.

He said abruptly, "She was my friend, too, but that's not what I'm talking about. I know you're up to something, Jennifer. Is that why you took Frances's apartment, to snoop around?"

"What on earth are you talking about?" The man was positively daft.

He stepped into me, close enough for me to smell his aftershave. "Don't play games with me. It was a suicide. Nobody killed Frances, and nobody killed Maggie, either. One was a mistake, and the other was a tragic accident."

I took a step back. "Have you lost your mind? I didn't even know Frances, and I wouldn't have suspected she knew Maggie if you hadn't told me yourself."

That seemed to shake him. "I just thought . . . I assumed . . . you've been . . ."

"Enough," I said. "I'm not in the mood for your prattle." I turned to Lillian. "Let's go."

"Jennifer, wait a second. Let me explain," Barrett said to my back.

"I'm not interested in your explanations," I said. "Call Penny if you want someone to talk to. I'm sure she'd be delighted to hear from you."

Once we were out of Barrett's earshot, Lillian asked, "Would you like to tell me what that was all about?"

I kept moving toward the main part of the crowd. "He's delusional, what can I say? We need to find out Hester's connection with Maggie. Do you want to ask her, or should I?"

Lillian said, "Why don't you wait here? She'll talk to me, but other people make her nervous. To be honest with you, I'm surprised she's here."

"Go talk to her before she gets away, then," I said, slightly miffed that I couldn't question her myself.

I waited until Lillian approached Hester, then got closer so I could overhear their conversation. As I neared, I heard Hester say, "Before long, I'll be the only one left." Was there a hint of amusement in the woman's voice? Lillian had said she was an odd bird, but Hester's comment was beyond the norm, even for her.

I could feel someone's presence behind me and turned, ready to blast into Barrett again, when I saw that it was only Hilda.

"Nice turnout," she said as she surveyed the dozen people milling around.

"I suppose," I said, still mad at Barrett.

"So what was that all about?" she asked as she gestured to Barrett.

"We're having a communication problem," I said.

"How do you know him? Is he a boyfriend?"

I shook my head. "He wishes. No, I live in the same house he does. It's not like it sounds. The place is divided up into three apartments. It's called Whispering Oak. Have you ever heard of it?"

Hilda thought about it a moment, then said, "It doesn't sound familiar. Where is it?"

"Over by the lake, but it's a tough place to find. Hilda, did you know that nearly everyone else in our card group got letters from Maggie just before she died?"

Hilda looked honestly surprised by the news. "I didn't have a clue. Actually, I thought it was just the two of us."

"So did I, but Betty told me otherwise."

Hilda asked, "So what did hers say?"

I shrugged as I caught sight of Lillian trying to catch my attention. "I'm sorry, but my aunt needs me."

"That's fine; I'll talk to you later. I need to come by the shop to pick up a few things. Will you be open later?"

"I'll be there," I said as I left her to see what my aunt wanted.

Lillian said, "Jennifer, are you quite finished socializing? I need to speak with you."

I shrugged. "You know me, I'm a social butterfly. What's so important?"

"Hester Taylor just told me something fairly interesting. Did you realize that there was another tenant in your apartment after Frances died?"

"No, but it doesn't surprise me," I said as I watched the other people head for their cars. "Can we continue this conversation in the car? I'd like to get the shop opened back up if I could."

"Yes, of course we can. One second, don't you want to see if Bradford learned anything this afternoon?"

I looked for my brother, but he was gone, and so was his car. "If he wants me to know something, I'm sure he'll tell me. Let's go."

As we drove back to the shop, Lillian asked, "Did you want to go home and change first?"

"No, I don't want to take the time right now." I wasn't sure if I was avoiding the change of clothes, or if I didn't want to see Barrett any time soon. I did want to talk with Jeffrey Wallace, especially now that

I had new information about his relationship with Maggie, but it was going to have to wait. "So tell me about this interim tenant."

"I didn't get the name," Lillian said. "Apparently, the woman only stayed one night. Hester was so eager to leave that I barely got that much out of her. I just thought it was significant," she added lamely.

"It might be," I said. "After all, it just makes sense."

As she pulled up in front of the shop, she asked, "And why do you say that?"

With my hand on the door latch, I said, "Think about it. Why else would they think the place was haunted, unless someone else was living there?"

Lillian said, "They could have heard about it from Mr. Wallace and your friend Barrett."

"Believe me, Barrett is no friend of mine. So they based it all on bumps in the night they heard upstairs?"

As I unlocked our shop door, Lillian said, "No, from what I heard, it was substantially more than that. According to Hester, your downstairs neighbor claimed it sounded like someone was wrecking the place. He even called the police once, so your brother should know about it."

"Let me guess," I said as I flipped the CLOSED sign to OPEN. "He didn't find anything there."

"On the contrary. He made Hester come out one night to see if anything was missing. According to her, the place was a wreck, but there were no signs of forced entry at all."

"No wonder Bradford insisted I get the locks changed," I said. "I've got a feeling we're not dealing with ghosts. Could it be that Frances left something behind that someone else wanted?"

"Jennifer Shane, don't we have enough to do finding out what happened to Maggie to worry about Frances?"

It was funny, but that was the first time I'd thought

of the two of them together in death. Barrett's scolding had triggered something in my head. "Maybe they're related," I said.

"Nonsense. I knew all of Frances's family, and Maggie was nowhere in her family tree."

"I'm not saying they were blood family; I'm wondering if their deaths were somehow connected, though."

Lillian scoffed. "Jennifer, Frances killed herself. We know that."

"No, we don't," I said. "That's what the world thinks, but they also think that Maggie died by accident. What if neither death was what it appeared to be?"

Lillian's complexion paled. "Do you honestly think that one person killed them both and then staged them to look like anything *but* murder? What possible reason would someone have to murder those two women?"

"I'm not sure," I said. "But I think it's something worth exploring, don't you?"

Lillian appeared to think about it for nearly a minute before she said, "Absolutely, and I know just how we can begin."

"I'm waiting," I said, not at all sure I wanted to hear what my aunt had in mind.

"It's good you have on dark clothing," she said. "How do you feel about a little breaking and entering tonight?"

"I'd rather get the flu," I said. "Exactly where are we breaking and entering into?"

Lillian took off her coat and said, "Maggie's house, of course. If there's anything tying her together with Frances, we may be able to find it at her house."

I looked down at my nice outfit. "If I'm going to jail, I don't plan to do it in one of my best dresses. I've got some dark pants I can wear, though."

Lillian laughed. "Jennifer, sometimes you let yourself get bogged down in the minutiae of life. Loosen up."

I was about to protest when Hilda walked into the shop. "Is this a bad time?" she asked.

"No, we were just planning a little felony together," Lillian said, laughing a little too loudly.

Hilda obviously didn't know how to take that. I tried to lighten the tone of things when I added, "It's more of a misdemeanor, I think. So what can I help you with?"

Hilda shrugged and said, "I'd like one of those new embossing kits we tried out last night. It didn't seem appropriate to buy one then."

I nodded. "Would you like one of the demo units, at the same discount of course? Or I could sell you a new one still in the box."

Hilda said, "I'll take one of the demos. And some paper, too."

As I started to help her, she turned to Lillian and said, "I hear you got a card from Maggie, too. What did yours say?"

Lillian looked miffed by the question. "I wouldn't know anything about that," she said, then walked to the back room.

Hilda looked at me. "Sorry, was it something I said?"

"She's just a little high-strung today," I admitted, which was true most days. "Now let's get you fixed up."

It was pretty obvious that Hilda wanted to talk more about Maggie, but I couldn't bring myself to respond to any of her comments, and she soon gave up trying. After we settled her bill and Hilda was gone, I called out to Lillian, "It's safe to come out now."

She poked her head out of the back room. "What on earth are you talking about?"

"It was pretty obvious you were ignoring her. Lillian, we can't afford to be rude to our best customers."

"Jennifer, I don't need a lecture from you on customer service. I just wasn't in the mood to discuss it with Hilda. If you're unhappy with my work here, you always have the option of firing me."

My aunt was in a mood, and if I wasn't careful, I was going to lose her. There was a tone in her voice that was full of finality. "How could I do that? I can't afford to replace you." Okay, I'd tried a light response, which didn't go over with her at all. So instead, trying to salvage the situation, I hugged her and added, "Besides, no one could replace you at any salary."

I felt her tension ease, and in a minute I stepped back. "I really do need you here; you know that, don't you?"

It was obvious the declaration, while needed, made her feel a little uncomfortable. "You don't need my help, not really."

"I'm not saying I couldn't do it by myself," I admitted, "but it wouldn't be nearly as much fun."

"I won't argue with that," she said, adding a smile. Lillian glanced at her watch, then said, "Any chance we could close the shop early? I know what your sister would say, but now that we've decided to explore Maggie's house, I'd like to do it before it gets dark."

That surprised me. "You want to break in there in broad daylight? Have you lost your mind?"

"Think about it, Jennifer. If we go there at night, we'll be stumbling around in the dark with flashlights, barely seeing a thing and risking getting caught. But if we go over in the daytime, we can say the door was unlocked, and that we were helping get Maggie's affairs in order."

"Do you honestly think Bradford's going to believe that?" I asked. "He'll check—you know it—and then we'll both be in jail."

Lillian frowned a moment. "Yes, he is determined,

isn't he? Let me make a few telephone calls and see what I can do."

She disappeared in back, and there was nothing left for me to do but wait on customers until my aunt deigned to tell me what she was up to. I was ready to flip the sign to CLOSED when Daniel, my stay-at-home dad and brand-new card maker, came in with a brief-case tucked under one arm.

I had to give him credit. Though he did look around briefly before he spoke, Daniel didn't whisper when he addressed me. "Jennifer, I owe you."

"We settled our bill," I said.

"I'm not talking about money," he said. "I love making cards. They are so much fun." He pulled a few samples out of his briefcase and handed them to me. "What do you think?"

I looked at the crisply folded edges, the clean cuts, and the nice balance of accessories to each of the cards. "I'd say you've got the knack for it. These are wonderful."

He smiled brightly. "They're a start. Listen, do you have time for a quick lesson?"

I waved his cards at him. "I suppose so. I'm always willing to learn something new."

He laughed at that. "Come on, we both know you're a lot better at this than I am. There's one thing I'm having trouble with, and I was kind of hoping you could point me in the right direction."

"I'll help if I can," I said. "What is it?"

He retrieved a Baggie from his case and held the contents out to me. "I am having a miserable time making flowers, see?"

I studied his teardrop petal flowers and was de-lighted that the problem was something I could help him with. "Okay, first off, your paper is too wide; a tenth of an inch is perfect for a greeting card. Another thing is that your coils are too loose. Here, let me show you." I grabbed a precut paper ribbon about eight inches long and twisted it tightly around a paper-quilling needle. I coiled the paper into a tight circle first; then I loosened it gently, allowing a little bit to uncoil at a time until I had a dimensional size I was happy with.

He said, "Okay, I was going about that the wrong way, but what do you do now? How do I get a tear-drop shape for my petal?"

"Hold it in the middle," I said, demonstrating as I worked, "and pinch one end like this. After that, all you have to do is pinch the opposite side and secure it with a dab of clear glue. Make five more and you've got a flower. Oh, and don't forget to add a tight circle to the middle. Here, let me show you what I mean." I retrieved a card I made covered in teardrop flowers, and handed it to him. "It's a little gaudy, but you get the idea."

He studied it, then said, "I'll take it, along with a needle and a stack of ribbon papers. I've been cutting them myself."

"You can always do that," I said, despite the fact that I made more money off the ribbons.

"No, I want the best materials I can buy."

As I rang up his purchases, I said, "You really seem to be enjoying the process."

"It's fun," he admitted. "You should have seen my wife's reaction when I gave her an anniversary card I made myself. She couldn't believe it."

"That's great," I said, for a moment envious that I didn't have anyone in my life at the moment to make special cards for. It really did mean more when it came from the heart.

Lillian came out of the back as Daniel left. She had a smug smile on her face.

I studied her expression a few seconds, then asked, "Okay, whose canary did you just eat?"

"Jennifer, how would you like a job?"

I ran a hand through my hair. "Gee, I'm kind of busy getting my shop off the ground. What did you have in mind?"

Lillian laughed. "You're going to love this, and it won't interfere with your card-making vocation. I'm happy to report that Patrick Benson has offered to pay us to go through and sort Maggie Blake's things for the estate. We're to hold aside the valuables for her heir, then sort the rest of it for the Salvation Army, and get rid of what's left."

"How in the world did you manage to pull that off?" I asked, again in awe of my aunt.

"There are only so many lawyers in Rebel Forge. Who else would be Maggie's executor? Once I got Patrick to admit that he was handling the will, it was simple to convince him to hire us." I wasn't sure if I even wanted to know how she'd persuaded him to give us the assignment. Still, I couldn't contain my grin. "So let me get this straight. Not only have you gotten us access to Maggie's house so we can snoop around to our hearts' content, but we're going to get paid for it, too?"

She nodded, that smile still present. "We do actually have to do the work, you know, but yes, I managed to secure us a small stipend for our trouble."

"When do we get started?" I asked.

"I'm afraid it's going to have to be tonight. We have to be finished by this weekend. That's the only way I could get Patrick to agree to canceling the professionals he'd already hired. If you've got plans, I'm sorry, but you'll have to change them."

"Sadly, I'm free," I admitted. "How about you?"

She waved a hand in the air. "Hearts will be broken and tears will be shed, but what can I do? Patience will have to be a virtue once again. Now if you'll excuse me, I'm going to go buy a load of boxes to make our job easier. I'll be back by closing so we can change, eat a bite, then get started."

"That sounds like a plan," I said.

Ten seconds after Lillian was gone, I regretted not closing the card shop down so I could join her. The only thing holding me back was the fact that I'd already closed the place up for Maggie's service, and I knew that if I wanted to continue operating the card shop as a business, I actually had to have my door open to the public. Working for Sara Lynn had been a wonderful apprenticeship in many ways, but I sometimes wished I hadn't acquired her work ethic. It would be marvelous to own a business I could shut down whenever I pleased, but I couldn't imagine what type of place it would have to be. Cards were my vocation and my avocation, and if I wanted to stay in business, I was going to have to be more dedicated.

After giving myself that speech, I was ready to help make the world a better place through custom-crafted greeting cards.

And of course, no one else came in for the rest of the day.

However, I did manage to make a few cards to sell and added them to my inventory. I was feeling a little sad about being alone in the shop and in my life, so I browsed through the cards my aunt made for sale. Before long I was smiling again, and I even laughed out loud a couple of times. I could make a sympathy card that would bring tears, or create a birthday card that smelled like cake and candles, but while I had a light touch of subtle humor in my cards, Lillian's were like sledgehammers. There was nothing droll or dry about them; Lillian's were little explosions on paper, and I envied her the touch. There wasn't any future in that, though. I might as well envy a petite blonde like Penny just because I happened to be a well-rounded tall brunette, but that was the path to madness. I'd embraced my physical attributes for what they were, and I'd learned to enjoy my own humor, however subtle.

That was the thing about working in an empty store all by myself. It certainly left me with plenty of time for introspection. A little of that went a long way, though. I was more interested in doing anything other than thinking about my place in the world, and I couldn't wait for closing time so I could start looking into Maggie's life.

It would be a welcome change from examining mine under the microscope.

Chapter 12

Lillian was late, and by the time she showed up, I was sitting on the bench outside, the shop closed up for the night.

"Sorry, I didn't mean to keep you waiting," she said. "I had a little unexpected difficulty."

"Were the boxes that hard to find?" I asked, seeing a stack of them in the backseat of her car.

She sighed, then said, "No, it wasn't that. My date was reluctant to let me cancel tonight."

I stood. "Lillian, we can always do this tomorrow, or even later tonight, if you'd like."

She said, "Nonsense, it will do him good to wait. Let's go get something to eat and then we can get started." She looked at my fancy attire, then said, "But first let's take you home to change. The one day your regular store outfit would be perfect for after hours and you show up in a dress." Lillian had changed into blue jeans, but they were nothing like my well-worn Levi's. Instead, she had a designer's name embroidered across a back pocket and sported a neat collared shirt. At least she'd abandoned her high heels for a pair of brand-new tennis shoes.

I got into the Mustang. "You're still more dressed up than I am, and I haven't even changed yet."

"Jennifer, this is as casual as I care to get. You could use a sense of . . ."

As she searched for the right word, I interrupted.

"Let's say we drop this particular conversation right now. So where would you like to eat?"

"I was thinking we could go by Hurley's," Lillian said. "I'm in the mood for a salad."

"You're always in the mood for salad," I protested. "How about The Lunch Box instead?"

"Surely you're kidding. I'm not going to let Savannah see me like this. She'd never let me hear the end of it."

"You look great," I said, "and you know it."

Lillian started the car. "The only way I'll agree to The Lunch Box is if you get our food to go."

"Fine," I said. "But I still think you're over-reacting."

Lillian quickly pulled up in front of my place. "And I'll ask you to tend to your own knitting. Why don't I wait here while you change?"

"You don't want to come upstairs and say hello to my roommates?" I asked. While Lillian had made her peace with Oggie and Nash, they weren't the best of friends. I thought it had more to do with Lillian's choice of perfumes—they invariably made Oggie sneeze—but Lillian claimed it was deeper than that.

"Thank you, but I've got a few telephone calls to make while you're changing," she said as she pulled out her cell phone.

"Coward," I called out as I hurried inside.

To my surprise, Jeffrey Wallace's door was open when I walked into the foyer.

"Jennifer, I was hoping to speak to you," he said, still dressed in the same clothes he'd worn to the service.

My first reaction was to blow on past him, because I really wanted to start digging into Maggie's life, but I caught myself. Wasn't that what this could be, if I just played it right?

"Fine," I said, stepping into his apartment before he had the chance to meet me in the hallway. Jeffrey looked at me, then the door, and finally decided to close it behind us. Could he be afraid of being alone with me? I couldn't see how, though I was taller than him and would admit—only under oath or at gunpoint—that I probably outweighed him too.

"That was an abrupt exit you made today," I said bluntly. There wasn't time to dance around the issue, and besides, I couldn't help wondering if a more direct approach than I'd been taking up to now might be more helpful.

"It was a pitiful excuse for a memorial," he said, slumping down into a nearby chair. On a table beside it, I saw a photograph of Maggie. Whoever had snapped it had captured her essence, as far as I was concerned. The laughter was on her lips, and in her eyes as well. I reached over and picked it up. "This is remarkable. Did you take it?"

"I did," he said. "I don't know if you're aware of it, but Maggie and I were special friends."

"I heard," I said, wanting to add that I'd heard they'd been a lot more than that, but I didn't know how to do it delicately.

Jeffrey said, "Why am I not surprised? There's not much that goes on in this town that everyone doesn't know about two seconds after it happens."

He reached for the photograph, but I took a step back. "Jeffrey, is there any way I could get a copy of this?"

He snatched it out of my hands. "Why on earth would you want one?"

I shrugged. "I lost her too, and this is the way I'd like to remember her. It's exactly how I'll picture her from now on."

Jeffrey offered it to me. "Keep it. I've got others."

"I couldn't," I said. "I'd just like a copy."

He pushed it on me. "I insist. Jennifer, your request just now was more of a memorial than she had out there on the lawn. Can you imagine such nonsense?"

I had to ask. I just had to. "Jeffrey, when's the last time you saw her? I'm not asking for alibis, just memories."

He looked at me a moment, then said, "So you think it's murder too?"

That surprised me. "What makes you say that?"

"Come, Jennifer, I haven't known you long, but you seem fairly intelligent. What is the police's theory, that Maggie fell asleep driving and missed her turn? In the middle of the afternoon? I don't think so."

He'd certainly captured my attention. "So what do you think really happened?"

Jeffrey stood and paced around the room. "Don't you think I've been tearing my hair out trying to figure that out? Maggie was a special woman, the most alive person I ever knew. When she agreed to pursue a relationship with me, a man twenty years her senior, I actually tried to talk her out of it! Can you imagine that? I didn't want to hold her back, but she'd have none of it. Three months might not seem like a long time, but it was the best part of my life, those days I had with her."

Though there wasn't a single tear on his face, I could tell he was destroyed inside, fighting to keep hold of his emotions.

There was only one thing I could say after hearing that. "Okay, I admit it. I'm trying to discover what happened to her. You're right; I don't believe it was an accident, either. Jeffrey, did she send you a card in the mail?"

"Are you kidding me? She sent dozens. Maggie loved making them, and they were great fun to get. Follow me."

We walked into a room that turned out to be a spare bedroom. On a card table, I saw quite a few handcrafted cards, all with Maggie's distinct touch. Beside me, he said, "She had a real knack for it, didn't she?"

"No doubt about it," I said. "Do you happen to remember the last one she sent you?"

He frowned, scratched his chin a second, then grabbed one and handed it to me. Maggie had added a few real oak and maple leaves to the front, their stems crossed like swords. They were pressed under contact paper, and I knew they'd stay like that forever. I opened the card, and saw in Maggie's distinct script, "I'd Fall for You All Over Again."

"This was the last one? You're sure?"

He nodded, then took it from me and placed it back on the table in his makeshift shrine. "Why are you so adamant about it?"

Should I tell him about the other messages from the grave, and let him know that she'd skipped him? What purpose would it serve, to break his heart for no reason? I just couldn't bring myself to do it.

"I just wondered about it," I said.

I wasn't absolutely certain he bought it, but if he didn't, it was pretty obvious he was going to let it slide. "So why do you think anyone would kill her?" I asked.

He shook his head. "It doesn't make sense. Believe me, I haven't been able to think about anything else."

The poor man looked as if the tears were about to fly. I had to change the subject, and quickly, if I was going to get anything else out of him. "How did you two happen to meet?"

He hesitated for a moment, then said, "It's ironic, but Frances introduced us. They were best friends, and I happened to run into them outside one day. I was smitten with Maggie instantly; she had that effect on me from the start. I asked Frances to introduce us formally, and I started courting her soon after."

"Tell me a little about Frances," I said, trying to acquire more information that might prove to me one way or the other if the two friends' deaths could be related.

"She was gruff, stubborn, a real pain at times," Jeffrey said, contradicting his word choices with a great amount of love in his voice. "We were cut from the same cloth, so it was natural that we became friends the second day she moved into Whispering Oak."

"I heard she was rich," I said.

Jeffrey snorted. "Hardly. Her parents were—I knew that—but Frances lived on a pretty modest pension from them. When they died, they left her a rock, a pair of doorstops, a batch of other worthless things and a note chastising her for her choices in life. From what I understand, the rock was symbolic of their entire relationship."

"So if she didn't get their money when they died, do you know who did?"

He laughed. "Anyone who knew Frances was well aware of that. There's a trust fund set up now in Rebel Forge for neutering stray cats and dogs, and from the size of the account, there won't be an unwanted pet in this entire part of Virginia. She thought it was a wonderful idea, and never made a squawk about not getting anything from them."

So that ruled out money as the reason for her death. "Did she have any enemies that you knew of?"

"Frances? She had scores of them. As I said, she wasn't an easy woman to get along with." He paused, then added, "Jennifer, I thought you were looking into Maggie's death. Why the sudden interest in Frances?"

I started to stammer out some lame excuse when he said, "It's pretty obvious, isn't it? Forget I asked. It's perfectly natural for you to want to find out what happened to the woman who once lived in your apartment." He led me out of the bedroom and to the door. "Listen, if there's anything I can do to help you in your investigation, I trust you won't hesitate to call on me. Day or night, I mean it."

"Thanks," I said at the door. "I just might take you up on that."

"Please do," he urged me.

Barrett must have come out of his apartment at the sound of my voice. He'd been listening to the last bit of my conversation with Jeffrey, but how much had he really heard? He stared at me cryptically a few moments, then said, "It didn't take you long to make friends, did it?"

"I respond well to civil behavior," I said as I turned my back to him and hurried upstairs to my apartment. After I changed into my most comfortable pair of jeans and an old shirt, I decided to feed my roommates before I left, just in case I didn't get back until late. If they noticed the change in their dining schedule, neither one of them commented on it.

I was all ready to blast Barrett again when I went downstairs, but his door was shut, as was Jeffrey's. Lillian was outside her car, leaning against it and staring off into space.

She studied me closely, then said, "Jennifer, it took you all that time to choose that to wear?"

"Just get in the car and start driving to The Lunch Box. I'm starving."

She did as I asked, so I explained, "I only took a minute to change."

"I can't tell you what a relief that is to hear," she said.

"Do you want me to tell you what happened or not?"

Lillian bit her upper lip. "Of course I do. Not another word from me, I promise."

I didn't see how I could possibly hold her to that, but it was a step in the right direction. "I spent most of my time talking to one of my fellow tenants."

Lillian sighed, then said, "Jennifer, if you're going to tell me you had a quick dalliance with Barrett, please spare me the details."

I flicked her arm, not enough to sting but enough

to show my displeasure with her assumption. "I was with Jeffrey Wallace, if you must know."

"Far be it from me to criticize, but isn't he a tad old for you?"

"Lillian, get your mind out of the gutter. We were talking about Maggie. You'll never believe this. He thinks she was murdered, too. They were in love."

Lillian nearly swerved off the narrow path. "So it is true? He was dating Maggie?"

"He confirmed it, and there were a dozen cards on display that she'd made him. The one I read inside certainly indicated that they had some kind of relationship."

"You just never know, do you? So what else did you discover in your impromptu interview?"

"Nothing," I said, "but he offered to help."

Lillian glanced at me quickly. "And what else did he offer you, Jennifer?"

"What do you mean by that?" I asked as we finally neared The Lunch Box.

"Did it occur to you that his offer might be to see what we discover, and not out of some altruistic motive?"

I unbuckled my seat belt. "I'm not following you."

"If he killed her, wouldn't he want to know if we were getting close to him? He could have murdered Frances too, for that matter. After all, who else had better access to her apartment than he did?"

What was my aunt talking about? "How about Barrett? He lives there, too."

Lillian studied me a moment before speaking. "Jennifer, are you suggesting that Barrett had something to do with both murders? I hope you've got more proof than an honest dislike for the man."

"That's the trouble, isn't it? We don't have much proof of anything yet, just a few cards and some suspicions."

"Perhaps that's about to change," she said as she handed me a twenty.

I took the bill, then asked her, "What's this for, my superior detective work?"

Lillian grimaced. "Don't flatter yourself; it's for the food I ordered while you were inside. Knowing Savannah, it's ready and waiting for us."

"I can't let you buy dinner for me, too," I protested. "You pay for too many of my meals as it is."

"Think of it as a business expense for our new venture. As far as I'm concerned, Patrick Benson can pick this one up. After all, we're doing him a tremendous favor on rather short notice."

"Is that how you've spun it in your mind?" I asked. "He hired us under unusual circumstances at your request so we could have some legitimacy for our snooping. So now you're going to stick him for our dinner?"

Lillian laughed. "Why not? He's got more money than he knows what to do with."

I opened the car door and asked, "So what did you order for me?"

"It's a surprise," she said. "If you're that curious, ask Savannah yourself."

"Thanks, but I'll pass. I'm sure whatever it is will be fine, as long as it's not anything healthy."

Lillian averted her gaze.

"Are you telling me you ordered me a salad too? Lillian, you've got to be kidding."

"I never said anything like that. Stop jumping to conclusions."

I walked into the restaurant, and the second Savannah saw me, she called back to her husband, "Pete, Jennifer's here."

He handed her two bags, and as I gave her Lillian's twenty, I said, "So what are we having tonight?"

"I'm having brown beans, spinach and corn bread," she said.

"You know what I mean," I said.

"If I had to guess," she said as she handed me my change, "Lillian's having a salad and you're having a barbeque sandwich and onion rings, but I could be wrong. I might have that mixed up."

"I'm willing to bet you got it dead-on. Thanks, Savannah."

"You're most welcome, girl. If you don't mind my saying so, you could use a few more pounds to help take the sharp edges off that figure of yours."

"Savannah, if I gain much more, I won't have any edges left at all. See you later."

"Bye, Jennifer. You behave yourself now, you hear?"

"Now what fun would that be?" I asked as I walked back out to the car. As I handed Lillian her change, I said, "Just be glad there really weren't two salads in there."

"I never claimed there were," she said. "Should we wait until we get to Maggie's to eat?"

I looked at one of the picnic tables in front. "I know it's a little chilly out, but I'd rather eat before we start working if it's all the same to you."

"I understand and agree. Let's dine outside, shall we?"

We'd hardly sat down at the table when the front door of The Lunch Box opened. Savannah stared at us for a second, then asked, "What are you two trying to do, freeze to death?"

"We find the brisk weather invigorating," Lillian said frostily.

"Well, when you've had enough invigorating, come on in. I've got fresh coffee that will take that right out of you."

Lillian shook her head, then gathered up her food. "Come on, Jennifer, I knew this wouldn't work."

I protested, "Hey, where are we going?"

"Inside, where we don't have to freeze to death,"

she whispered to me as we walked in past Savannah. Lillian paused, then told her friend, "Not one word, do you hear me?"

Savannah stared at her a second, then both of them started laughing. They had the oddest friendship I'd ever seen, and I envied them both every ounce of it.

We took a spot at the serpentine counter, and Savannah delivered two fresh cups of hot coffee. As she finished pouring Lillian's, she said, "Now if I was going to comment on your outfit, which I won't because you've asked me nicely and I respect your request, I'd have to say I think you look mighty fine. But I'm not talking about it."

Lillian said, "It's a good thing, or I wouldn't have a chance to eat because I'd be sitting here all night listening to you."

Pete rang his little bell in back from the kitchen to let Savannah know another order was up. The restaurateur said, "You, dear girl, have been saved by the bell."

"It's not the first time," Lillian said, and again the two shared a private joke that nobody else in the world got. The diner was half full, but it was late for their usual crowd. I knew Savannah; her husband, Pete; and their daughter, Charlie, did most of their business at noon, feeding everyone from factory workers to judges, but they liked to stay open for the early-dinner crowds, something I heartily endorsed. Charlie wasn't around, no doubt off working on her degree. I knew that neither Savannah nor Pete had gone to college—though they were both extremely bright—and it was their one stone-cold rule that Charlie was going to get the best education she could.

After Savannah delivered a hamburger plate to a lone diner, she came back over to us. "What brings you two out together in the evening? And why aren't there lines of men clamoring to get your attentions?"

I started to answer when Lillian said, "It was all we

could do to avoid the crowds, but we denied them all. We heard the cuisine was better here at night."

Savannah leaned forward. "And what's your verdict?" There was no jesting in her voice, and I hoped Lillian didn't get us banned from the place with an ill-timed joke.

"I can't imagine there's anything in the world that could beat your lunchtime fare. Honestly, I think they're both great."

Savannah whooped and slammed the counter with her spatula. "Now, that's what I'm talking about. Now are you ready to answer my real question?"

Lillian said softly, "If you'd lower your voice, perhaps I would."

"I can speak softer than you can," Savannah said in a near whisper that still seemed to carry across the room. "Now what are you two really up to?"

"We're helping clean Maggie Blake's house. Did you know her?"

Savannah nodded, and her ever present smile faded for a few moments. "She used to come in here now and then before she got all health craze nuts on me. It's a real shame what happened to that girl."

Lillian leaned forward and said, "And what exactly did happen to her?"

Savannah looked startled by the comment. "You mean you think something happened to her?"

"Keep your voice down," Lillian snapped.

Savannah actually looked contrite. "Sorry, that surprised me, that's all." She appeared to think about it a few seconds, then turned to me and said, "What do you think?"

"You're asking me?" I said after I finished my bite.

"I trust your instincts, Jennifer; I always have. You know that."

I searched her face for a hint of a smile, but she was deadly serious. "I agree with Lillian. Something's not right."

Savannah nodded, then said in a loud voice, "Did anybody here know Maggie Blake?"

I thought Lillian was going to kill her on the spot, but I was surprised when an older woman raised her hand. "I knew her fairly well," she volunteered.

"Then get right over here," Savannah said. "If you can add anything to the conversation, I'll give you a slice of lemon meringue pie on the house."

That got the attention of everyone in the diner. Savannah was famous for her pies, and she charged accordingly.

"I know her, too," the diner with the hamburger plate called out.

"Heck, we used to go out," a man in his thirties yelled.

"I'm her godfather," another old man said.

"We're sisters," a woman barely out of her teens added.

Savannah slammed her spatula down on the counter, and that ended the chorus. "Funny, you all are riots, every last one of you. Now eat your food before I charge you double."

There were a few grumbles but mostly laughs as the crowd went back to their food. Savannah could do that, kid and cajole a group of strangers and make them feel like they all belonged to the same family. She was an artist at it, and I wished I could do the same with my customers.

The original woman who'd spoken joined us at the bend in the bar. "I'm afraid there's not much I can tell you about Maggie. She was a friend of mine, but I never got as close as I would have liked. She was fun, you know? Always a real joy to be around."

Savannah looked at her steadily and asked, "Do you think she fell asleep at the wheel in the middle of the day?"

The woman looked startled by the suggestion. "Is that how she died? I hadn't heard." She paused, then added, "I can't imagine it. We drove to Richmond once for a quilt show, and she was the safest driver I ever rode with. Unless she changed dramatically, there's no way she would have taken the chance. That's one of the reasons we drifted apart. Maggie wouldn't ride with anyone else, she didn't trust them behind the wheel, and I got tired of always riding with her. It's a shame," she added. "I've missed her, and now I've lost my chance to be her friend again."

Savannah reached over and patted the woman's hand. "Tillie Matthews, I'm sure you were a fine friend to her. People drift in and out of our lives all the time. Now let me get you that pie."

As Savannah left to grab the promised dessert, Tillie told us, "I don't believe those other rumors I've been hearing, either."

"What have you heard?" Lillian asked.

Tillie looked down at her hands, then said, "I hate to speak ill of the dead."

"What if you could help her? Would you do it?"

"Of course I would," Tillie said.

"So tell us what you've heard," I urged her gently.

Tillie looked around, then said softly, "I heard she'd had an affair."

Lillian said, "We've heard that ourselves."

"I don't care if she and Frances were close. That's how rumors like that get started."

"Are you talking about Frances Coolridge?" I asked.

Tillie nodded. "She even put her in her will, the way I heard it."

I'd heard they were friends, but this was not really any new information. "Maggie put Frances in her will? I wonder who inherited her stuff instead?"

"No, you misunderstood me," Tillie said. "From what I heard, when Frances died, Maggie got everything she had. Honestly, I think that's what started the rumors."

Savannah returned with Tillie's pie. The older woman said, "You don't have to give this to me on the house."

"I'm a woman of my word," Savannah said. "Enjoy it, girl." Instead of sliding it in front of her, Savannah walked it back down to where Tillie had been sitting before. It was a clever way to get our privacy back.

As we finished our meals, Savannah came by again with two Styrofoam cups. "Here's some coffee for the road. Sorry I couldn't help with Maggie."

"You did fine," Lillian said as she slid a few dollars under her plate.

"You already paid for your food," Savannah said as she tried to hand the bills back to Lillian.

"But not for the coffee," my aunt said, refusing the money.

"Are you saying I can't treat a couple of my best friends to a cup of coffee when I please?"

We were starting to attract attention again. "Put it in the college fund jar," I prompted. There was a glass jar near the counter that used to hold pickles but now housed money for Charlie's college tuition. I knew Savannah and Pete were doing okay at their restaurant, but their income wasn't always enough, no matter how popular the spot was.

"That I can do," Savannah said. "And we thank you for the contribution."

Once we were outside, Lillian said, "I don't believe that rumor for a second. Maggie and Frances together? I just don't see it."

"I know what you mean. Maggie was a big fan of men; there was never any doubt about that. I wonder if the other part is true, though."

"It should be easy enough to find out. When we get to Maggie's place, I'll call Patrick back."

I glanced at my watch. "There's no way he'll still be in the office, Lillian. We'll just have to find out tomorrow."

My aunt smiled as she unlocked her car. "We won't have to wait. I've got his home number, and I'm willing to bet that if he handled Maggie's business affairs, he'll know if Tillie was right."

As she drove, I asked, "How do you happen to have a lawyer's home telephone number memorized?"

"Patrick's much more than just a lawyer," Lillian said cryptically.

"Don't tell me you dated him, too."

Lillian said, "And what would be wrong if I had? He's not that much younger than I am, and some men find sophisticated older women a refreshing breeze from the banality of youth."

When it came to my aunt, I didn't doubt that for a second. "So you two used to go out."

"I never said that," Lillian said. "You just assumed it."

I swear, sometimes she could drive me crazy. "So we're back to our original question. How do you have his home number?"

Lillian waved a hand in the air. "The truth is so mundane, it barely needs to be repeated."

When I realized that was all the answer I was going to get out of her, I gave up. My aunt liked to think of herself as mysterious, and I wasn't about to try to dissuade her of that opinion. She more than made up for my intermittent frustrations with her, with an air that made her exciting to be around.

We pulled into Maggie's driveway, a neat cottage with a well-kept garden in front and a white picket fence.

I stared at it with longing in my heart. "Why can't I find a place like this to live?"

Lillian asked, "Are you unhappy with your current accommodations?"

"No, I guess it's fine, but there are a few things I'm not exactly thrilled about."

As Lillian started retrieving folded boxes from the

trunk, she said, "Honestly, get over what happened in the bathroom. People die every day."

"You know, I'd forgotten to even put that on my list," I said.

Lillian didn't look like she believed me, but it was true. I didn't associate Frances's demise with my new apartment, even with the rumors of her haunting the place. To be perfectly honest, I wasn't spending enough time there to know if it was haunted or not. Oggie and Nash could have given a more informed opinion about it than I could have.

Lillian shrugged, then asked me, "So what's on your bad list, if a suicide doesn't even make the cut?"

I grabbed the rest of the boxes she'd brought and said, "I'm not crazy about my neighbors. No, that's not true. I'm actually starting to like one of them."

"I was afraid you'd start to feel that way," Lillian said. "That Barrett is a handsome man, isn't he?"

"If you like him, then you can have him," I said. "I was talking about Jeffrey Wallace."

Lillian put her boxes down and retrieved a key. That would certainly make it easier than our original plan to somehow break in so we could snoop around the place. "What in the world could the two of you have in common? He's quite a bit older than you, you know."

"There's no age limit on friendship," I said. "Besides, what were you saying before about a man wanting a little sophistication sometimes?"

Lillian's eyebrows shot up. "Dear child, it's one thing for a man to crave the wisdom and experience of an older woman, but the reverse is completely unacceptable. I suggest you find a man more your own age. I always thought Greg was a good match for you."

"Why don't you open the door and we can talk inside?" I swear, sometimes the only way I could get my aunt to change the subject was with a sledgehammer.

Lillian gave me one of her famous looks. Then she opened the door and we stepped inside. The boxes were forgotten on the porch for now.

It was time to snoop around and see if we could figure out what had really happened to Maggie Blake.

Chapter 13

The first thing that hit me when I stepped inside was the mixed scents of a dozen different candles and pot-pourris. It appeared that Maggie was an aroma freak, and she didn't mind in the least mixing lavender with cinnamon or apple spice with sage. I started to open a window, but Lillian protested, "Jennifer, we'll freeze to death."

"It's better than being asphyxiated," I said, ignoring her complaints as I went around the place flinging open every window I could find.

"If you insist on doing that, then I'm turning the furnace on," she said.

"That's fine by me. I wonder if there's a fan somewhere in here."

She frowned at me and said, "Honestly, I think you're overreacting."

I grabbed a trash bag from the kitchen and started gathering up candles. "And I think your sense of smell must be on the blink. You know what this stuff does to my allergies."

"I think it's delightful," she said as she sniffed the air.

"Then you can take all of this stuff home with you." I finally got everything I could find that had any aroma to it at all and tied the bag tightly before putting it out on the porch. The air was definitely starting to clear, but I wasn't in any hurry to close the place back up just yet.

"I'm still chilly," Lillian complained.

"So grab one of Maggie's sweaters," I said.

"Who realized you could be so thoughtless?" Lillian snipped at me.

I wasn't about to take that from her. "What can I say, it runs in the family."

That was a risk. It would either snap her out of her little snit or she'd be impossible to work with the rest of the night. Either way, though, I wasn't about to back off. After all, it wasn't that cold inside. We weren't even officially in autumn yet, and though we were near the mountains, Rebel Forge was still blessed with moderate temperatures most of the year.

Lillian paused a little longer than I would have liked, then chuckled. "Sometimes you are exactly like your grandfather." It was the highest praise she could give anyone, and I knew it.

"Thank you kindly. So now that we've got the place aired out, what say we get started?"

Lillian retrieved one of Maggie's jackets from the front hall closet and put it on, then said, "I'm ready if you are. Jennifer, should we put the boxes together and pack as we search? That way we can eliminate some of the clutter and still manage to explore."

"That sounds like a good plan," I said as I collected the boxes from outside.

"I'll fold them, and you tape the bottoms," Lillian commanded.

Ordinarily I might have fought her out of sheer stubbornness, but I'd already pushed her hard enough for one night, and besides, I loved duct tape.

After we had our containers ready, it was time to start in earnest. "What room should we tackle first?" I asked.

Lillian thought about it, then said, "Let's leave the

public spaces for last. Why don't we start with her bedroom? That way we'll get the hardest room out of the way first."

"Do you really think it will be the hardest to search?" I asked.

She shook her head. "It's the most intimate spot here. Jennifer, if we can disassociate this place from Maggie, it will make all of this a great deal easier on both of us. Think of it as a job and try not to remember her laughter, or the way she smiled."

I really wished Lillian hadn't said that. Up to that point, I had somehow managed to forget why we were really there. Now that was impossible, though. Maggie was everywhere. I took a few deep breaths, catching more than a hint of the banished candles and potpourris. That helped. If I dwelled on the smells, I might be able to forget about my lost friend.

The house was as neat inside as I expected it to be. Lillian had been joking when she'd claimed that the place was cluttered. Maggie had been nuts for organization, and like many other scrapbookers who had gone into card making, I knew she'd enjoyed using many of the same tools she'd used to create lasting memory books to personalize her own greeting cards. As Lillian and I walked to the back bedroom, I looked around for the scrapbooks Maggie must have made over the years. Sure enough, there were a stack of them on the shelves in the living room, but I did see an odd-looking empty space with no dust on it toward one end. "Come here," I said to Lillian as I got a closer look.

My aunt glanced at me. "What am I looking at, Maggie's scrapbooks? Jennifer, we're here to look for clues."

"Don't you get it?" I asked. "I'm willing to bet she kept her most recent scrapbook here where there's an empty space."

Lillian frowned at the shelf. "For all we know, that's where she kept her diary."

"That might be a good read too, but I can't imagine it being here. Look, there's no dust on the shelf at all. That means the missing books haven't been gone very long." I picked up the last one in line. "This one is dated two years ago. There have to be at least two more missing, from the look of things. You and I both know she got involved in card making because of her scrapbooking, and I'm willing to bet that she didn't just stop making her scrapbooks."

"I honestly don't know," Lillian said. "Do you think it's important?"

Suddenly I was sure of it. "Think about it. What kind of memories has she had lately that someone doesn't want us to know about? I'm willing to bet whoever killed her stole those last few books. That probably means that whoever killed her was in her life over the past couple of years and not before then."

Lillian sighed. "Jennifer, for all we know she gave up scrapbooking when she started making cards, no matter what your theory is. She was doing them long before you opened your shop. Maybe she just got tired of it."

"I know one way to find out," I said as I picked up the telephone.

"Who are you calling?"

I stopped dialing as I explained. "Where would Maggie get her supplies if she was still scrapbooking?" I finished dialing. Then before it could ring more than once, my sister picked up on the other end.

"Sara Lynn, hey, it's Jennifer. I need to ask you something."

She was short with me, even testier than usual. "Can it wait? I'm just putting dinner on the table."

I glanced at my watch. "My, you're eating awfully late, aren't you?"

She huffed into the telephone. "If you must know, Bailey's still out of town."

"I thought he was supposed to come back this morning." That was odd. My sister's husband was normally as reliable as an engineer's watch.

Sara Lynn snapped, "As did I, but I don't control his schedule. I will call you back after I eat."

She hung up before I could say another word, so I hit the REDIAL button.

"Hello," she said tensely. It sounded like something was definitely wrong in her paradise, and I wondered if I was interrupting more than her dinner.

"Sorry, it's me again. Listen, I'm not home. Call me at this number when you get the chance." I rattled off Maggie's number, conveniently printed in script and taped to the phone in the slot meant for it. It was just one more example of the woman's eye for detail, which I sorely lacked.

"Where are you?" Sara Lynn asked abruptly.

"I'm at Maggie Blake's place," I said, then hung up.

Lillian asked, "What in the world did you do that for?"

I grinned, held up my fingers and started to count. Before I could get my third finger in the air, the phone rang. "Hi, Sara Lynn."

"Sorry?" a man's voice asked.

"Oh, excuse me. Hello." Who on earth was telephoning Maggie's house?

"Is Lillian there?"

"One moment, please. May I tell her who's calling?"

Instead of supplying the information, a reasonable request as far as I was concerned, he said, "Just put her on, please."

I handed the phone to my aunt. Lillian asked, "Who is it?"

"He wouldn't say, but whoever it is, he's in a pretty foul mood."

"We'll just see about that." She took the phone from me. "Hello? Patrick, why are you calling?"

She held the phone away from her ear so I could hear, too. "I want to be sure you're not overstepping your bounds there."

"And whatever gave you the idea that I might?" Lillian asked in a saccharine sweet voice that set my teeth on edge.

"Don't do it, woman. I don't know what you're up to, but you wheedled that job out of me, and I expect you to perform, do you hear me?"

"Of course," she said, dismissing his complaint. "While I've got you on the telephone, would you mind telling me if it's true that Maggie Blake inherited everything that Frances Coolridge owned?"

The attorney exploded again. "I can't tell you that! Don't even ask me, do you hear?"

"They're both dead, so don't bore me with that attorney-client privilege nonsense. I was once married to a lawyer, if you recall."

"That didn't make you one, any more than sitting in a garage makes you a car."

Lillian's voice had a steel edge to it the next time she spoke. "Patrick, are you certain you want to poke this particular bear? The world might be fascinated to hear about your trip to Las Vegas three years ago."

There was a sudden intake of breath on the other end. "You wouldn't," he said. "No, strike that. You'd tell for the fun of it, wouldn't you?"

Lillian said, "I'm going to ask you this one last time. Did she or did she not inherit everything Frances owned?"

With obvious reluctance, the lawyer admitted, "There wasn't much, but whatever Frances had went straight to Maggie. As I recall, there were a few books, some property in the middle of nowhere that no one in their right mind would want, and a box of personal things like paperweights and rocks, if you can believe that. I drew all of the wills up at the same time, so there were no real surprises."

"And what was the nature of their relationship?" Lillian asked.

"Come on, do you really expect me to answer that?"

"I do," Lillian said, and then she simply waited. I thought for sure he'd hang up on her, but after nearly a minute, Patrick said, "Maggie and Frances were friends, no more and no less. The way it was explained to me was that neither of them ever had children, had no close relatives at all, and they wanted their things to be handled with respect in the end."

"And there wasn't anything more to their relationship than that?" Lillian asked.

"I'm certain of it, and that's the bottom line. I've heard the rumors too, but sometimes folks in this town need something else to talk about, you know? When the truth runs out, they start making things up as they go along. Can I go now?"

"You did a fine job, Patrick. And don't worry; your secret is safe with me."

"Until you need something else," he grumbled before he hung up.

Lillian smiled at me. "There, that wasn't all that difficult, was it?"

"Do I even want to know what you've got on him?" I asked my aunt.

"Now, Jennifer, you just heard me pledge my silence to him. I'm not going to say another word about it."

I was ready to pump her for more—I could tell Lillian wanted to share—but suddenly the front door opened and Sara Lynn stormed inside.

"That was cute, Jennifer, calling me and then keeping the telephone off the hook so I'd have to drive over. Now that you've got me here, what do you want?"

I'd nearly forgotten about calling my sister. "Sara Lynn, I swear it was just an accident."

"What, you just happened to hang up after giving me this number?" She looked around at the boxes, then asked, "What are you two doing here, anyway?"

Lillian said, "We're working. Jennifer's telling the truth. Someone else called as soon as she got off the line."

Sara Lynn sat on the couch. "I don't see any card-making supplies around. What kind of work are you doing?"

Before Lillian could say anything, I chimed in. "Maggie's attorney needed somebody to clean the place up, and we took the job to supplement our income." Well, most of it was true, though I'd left out parts of the rationales behind our actions.

It didn't look like Sara Lynn was buying it, though. "Don't bother to embellish any more. You two are snooping around again. I can't say I'm shocked, but I'd be lying if I said I wasn't disappointed."

Lillian said, "Then perhaps you should leave."

"You called me, remember? What was so urgent that it couldn't wait?"

Lillian said, "You know what? Perhaps it's not important after all. Sorry we bothered you at home. Why don't you get back to your dinner? I'm sure it's getting cold by now."

Sara Lynn's voice faltered, then she said, "That's not all that's getting cold. I've lost my appetite lately for eating alone."

That softened Lillian immediately. "Child, every marriage has troubled times."

"Coming from you, I'd say that qualifies as expert testimony," Sara Lynn snapped.

Before things could escalate, I said, "The reason I called you was for some information. Did Maggie quit scrapbooking cold turkey a few years ago?"

"What? Of course not. She started making cards

around then, but she was still buying supplies at For-ever Memories right up until she died."

Lillian asked, "When was the last time she was in your shop?"

"Why do you two want to know?" Sara Lynn asked.

"Please, just humor us, okay?" I asked. "Do you need to check your receipts before you answer?"

"Would you have to?" Sara Lynn asked me. "Two weeks ago she bought a new scrapbook and some stickers. She said she wanted to make a present for a new friend."

"It wasn't for a man, was it?" I asked.

"Do you mean a boyfriend? No, I was fairly sure it was a woman, given the cover she chose. Honestly, at what age does it cease being 'boyfriend' and 'girl-friend'? Surely we can come up with a more dignified set of labels for later in life."

"I prefer 'paramour' myself," Lillian said.

"Okay, maybe I spoke too soon," Sara Lynn said. " 'Boyfriend' might not be so bad after all."

"You didn't happen to get a name, did you?" I asked.

"No, sorry. Let me look at her books a second and I can tell you immediately. There they are."

It only took my sister two seconds to notice some-thing was wrong. "At least two are missing, do you realize that?"

I was glad to have some independent confirmation. "That's what we've been trying to figure out. It's a lot harder to tell what happened by what's missing than what's there, isn't it?"

"So what do we do now?" Sara Lynn asked.

Lillian wasn't having any of that. " 'We' aren't doing anything. You are going to go home while Jennifer and I stay here and work."

Sara Lynn shook her head. "I believe I'll stay here with you, if I'm welcome. Right now the last thing I need to do is rattle around in that house alone, and to be honest with you, I could use something productive to do."

I could tell from the set of Lillian's jaw that she was about to throw Sara Lynn out despite my sister's plea, but I could tell she needed me, and I didn't have the heart to say no to her. "Of course you can help us. We'll even cut you in on our earnings."

My sister nodded. "Thank you, but I'm willing to do this for an old friend."

That touched me. "I think of you as a friend, too," I said as I put an arm around my petite sister.

She pulled instantly away. "I was referring to Maggie. You will always be my baby sister."

"I knew that," I said, trying to hide my frown. It didn't help matters that Lillian had found the display amusing and wasn't trying to hide her delight in any way.

"Enough talk," I said, ready to move on. "Let's get to work."

Sara Lynn said, "The first thing we need to do is close the windows. Are you two trying to heat all of Rebel Forge?"

"Talk to your sister. She's the one with the fresh-air fetish," Lillian said.

Great. I'd reached out to my sister in her time of need, and I'd ended up being on the wrong end of a majority vote. Sometimes it just didn't pay to be nice.

"Let's do this in an organized fashion," Sara Lynn said, stepping into her usual role of leader/director/ president. "We'll mark boxes 'Personal,' 'Charity' and 'Trash.' Any objections?"

"No, that sounds fine," Lillian said, smiling behind Sara Lynn's back but holding it long enough for me to see. It wasn't mocking, just an acceptance of how my sister worked.

"What room were you two going to do first?" she asked.

"We'd thought about starting with the bedroom," I admitted. "Where would you like to begin?"

"The bedroom's fine," she said. "Ladies, we all knew Maggie and cared about her, so it's perfectly fine to shed a tear along the way."

That was another side of Sara Lynn, an emotional woman to balance the efficiency in her. I didn't doubt she was a hard person to live with; hadn't I experienced that myself? I just always thought of her marriage to Bailey as a goal I hoped to achieve someday. Hearing about their problems was not a part of my fantasy, and I was sad to hear that it was a part of her reality.

"Let's do the clothes first, shall we?" Lillian suggested. "They're always the hardest for me."

Sara Lynn nodded her agreement. I didn't care where we began, just as long as I could look for clues about what had really happened to Maggie.

Sara Lynn asked, "Who is *her* main beneficiary? Does anyone know?"

"I could always call Patrick back," Lillian said.

"No, let's leave him alone tonight unless we really need him," I said. I couldn't bear the thought of Lillian making him squirm again. "We'll just do the best we can."

Sara Lynn said, "I'm not just being nosy; it's an important question. Who knows why one person holds something as sentimental? You'd be amazed at the things I've kept over the years."

"Like what?" Lillian asked, clearly intrigued as she opened the closet door.

Sara Lynn started neatly folding the first dress after she put the hanger in a box she'd already labeled "Hangers." "I've got an entire box this size full of cocktail napkins, matchbook covers, silly fluff like that that wouldn't mean a thing to anyone else in the world."

"If it was important to Maggie, she'll have it tucked safely away as well," I said.

"True," Sara Lynn said as she gently laid the first dress in the bottom of another box. "Tell you what, I'll start on these. Lillian, why don't you work on the chest of drawers, and Jennifer, you can pack away the knickknacks and photographs. They're everywhere, aren't they?"

I agreed. "It looks like Maggie enjoyed being surrounded by things that gave her joy." As we worked, each of us on separate tasks but together in the same room, we chatted about dozens of things. It was a sad occasion and a working one in more ways than one, but the Shane women were together, and that part of it was good indeed.

There was a marked absence of real clues there, though. After we'd stripped the room of everything personal in it, Sara Lynn carried the last box of donations out of the room. I jumped on the opportunity and said to Lillian, "I was expecting to find something in here that might help."

"Jennifer, there may not be anything of use to us in the entire house. After all, we've already discovered something."

I nodded. "The missing scrapbooks—I know—but it's going to be hard to tell if it means something or not if we don't know why they were stolen."

"There's more to do yet," Lillian said as Sara Lynn rejoined us.

With a little more delight in her voice than I'd expected, she said, "We'll be at this half the night. Let's do the kitchen next. I'll make coffee."

"Make it strong," I said, fighting a yawn. It had been a long day, and it looked to be an even longer night.

I found something while I was working in the kitchen at the desk where Maggie did her bills. Sara Lynn was disposing of the food, keeping a few things to the side for a late-night snack while Lillian cleaned out the cabinets full of pots and pans. In a letter holder on the desk behind a few bills, I found a distinctive envelope I recognized from the shop with Jeffrey Wallace's name and address printed on the front.

"Does this look familiar?" I said as I held it up to Lillian.

"It's from one of those ghastly new papers you've been making recently," she said.

I nodded, though I didn't agree with the "ghastly" designation. "That means Maggie made this card within the last week."

Sara Lynn said, "It's got a stamp on it, so go ahead and mail it."

"But it's not sealed, is it?" I said as I started to lift the back flap. Many of my card makers enjoyed cutting out their own envelopes so they'd have matching stationery, and Maggie was no exception.

Sara Lynn snatched it out of my hand. "You can't read that. It's private."

Lillian said, "More private than what we're doing now? Let me see it."

Sara Lynn hesitated, but the tone of Lillian's voice was no doubt hard to refute. My sister handed her the card, saying, "I still think you should mail it."

"Perhaps after we've seen what it says," Lillian said. As she pulled the card from the envelope, I moved beside her so I could read it along with her. Sara Lynn kept working, her silence showing all the disapproval she needed it to express.

On the front of the card, there was an anatomically correct stamp of a heart split in two, shaded the ghastliest red hue I'd ever seen. The heart had been cut right down the middle, and as I studied the card closer, I could see that she'd glued the pieces in place. The front said, "My Heart Is Broken." I wasn't sure I had the heart to read the rest of it, but Lillian didn't hesitate. Inside, Maggie had written,

Jeffrey, we're finished. Leave me alone, I mean it. Don't take the last thing I have left between us: my memories, Maggie.

So she'd broken up with him recently, and he wasn't taking the hint, from the look of the card. Funny that Jeffrey hadn't mentioned the fact that he'd just been dumped to me when we'd talked about Maggie that afternoon. It appeared that he'd taken it pretty hard, too. I couldn't help wondering if he'd been angry enough to kill her. I took the card from Lillian and tucked it into my purse.

Sara Lynn saw what I was doing. "What on earth are you going to do with that?"

"You said I should mail it. I'm going to do one better. I'm going to hand deliver it myself."

"Is that wise?" Lillian asked.

"Probably not, but I want to see what he has to say for himself."

We were still clearing out the kitchen when the telephone rang. I reached to pick it up without thinking.

"Hello?"

In a muffled voice, I heard someone say, "Get out of there or I'll kill you all."

Chapter 14

"Excuse me," I said. "What did you say? I couldn't understand you. Your voice is too muffled." I motioned Lillian and Sara Lynn to me, holding the phone out so they could hear, too. I had no idea whether it was a man or a woman. Maybe they'd be able to tell if I got the caller to repeat the threat.

"You only get one warning. Stop this second or you're all going to die."

Lillian grabbed the telephone out of my hands before I could stop her and said, "Grow up, would you? If you've got a problem with what we're doing, the front door's open."

And then she slammed the phone down.

"Do you think that was wise?" Sara Lynn asked. "Whoever was calling was obviously deranged."

"So think of it as a random crank call," Lillian said. "Some fool with too much time on her hands, a bad case of insomnia and a twisted sense of humor."

I looked at my aunt. "I don't believe that for a second, do you?"

To my surprise and Sara Lynn's shock, Lillian said, "Actually, I'm delighted by that telephone call."

"What? Why on earth would a death threat make you happy?" Sara Lynn was watching Lillian as if she were on fire.

"It means we're on the right track looking into

Maggie's death," she said. "Why else would someone threaten to kill us?"

"And you call that progress," Sara Lynn said, shaking her head. "Do you two have a death wish?"

"No," I said. "We want to see justice for our friend, though."

"Bradford ruled it an accident," Sara Lynn protested, obviously uncomfortable with the direction our conversation had taken.

I shrugged. "Sara Lynn, nobody on earth is a bigger fan of our brother than I am, but he can't be right a hundred percent of the time."

"Then we should call him right now," Sara Lynn said, reaching for the telephone.

Lillian wasn't about to let go of it, though. "Let's think about this. If we get Bradford over here this late, he's going to make us leave, and we haven't finished the job yet, have we?"

"What about that threat?" she asked.

"Nobody's going to attack us while we're here together. It was meant to scare us off. I say we stay. Jennifer?"

I nodded my agreement. "I want to finish this tonight more than ever. If there is something here that the killer missed, what are the odds it will still be here tomorrow if we have to come back?"

Lillian nodded. "I hadn't considered that possibility." She turned to my sister and said, "Sara Lynn, we certainly won't hold it against you if you want to go home now. This isn't your fight, and there's no reason you should stay if you feel you're in danger."

"I'm not going anywhere," Sara Lynn said, the Shane stubborn streak out in full force. "I just thought it might be prudent to call Bradford, but you're probably right. So let's see what else we can uncover."

I wasn't about to comment on that declaration. If Sara Lynn wanted to join us in our search, it was her right and she'd be most welcome. I had to wonder, though, if a part of her would rather be at home instead of sorting through a dead woman's things.

We had the kitchen cleaned in record time, and after a short break for coffee and cookies, it wasn't long before we were in the living room, the last place we hadn't fully searched yet. Outside on the front porch there were three distinct piles of boxes, but if there was anything all that incriminating still inside, either we'd missed its significance or we hadn't gotten to it yet.

As we worked, Sara Lynn stood in the middle of the room, a large frown on her face. "What's wrong?" I asked her. "You look like you just ate a bad turnip."

Lillian said, "Is there such a thing as a good turnip?"

"Shh," Sara Lynn said. "Something's not right."

I stopped packing books in a box and listened intently. "I don't hear anything."

"It's not a noise, you nit. Something's missing, though."

"It's the most recent scrapbooks," Lillian said. "We've already been over that."

Sara Lynn's expression suddenly changed. "Where is all of Maggie's equipment?"

I had to hand it to my big sister. Lillian and I had been all over the house, but not once did either one of us notice that everything Maggie used to make scrapbooks and greeting cards was gone.

"How did we miss that?" I asked Lillian.

"I could claim old age, but I won't," my aunt said. "I simply overlooked it."

Sara Lynn looked pleased by the admission. "It's a lot harder to spot what isn't here than what is."

"So where did it go?" I asked. "I don't know how much equipment and supplies she bought from you, but I know I've sold her a ton of stuff myself."

Sara Lynn nodded. "Yes, Maggie always was one

to buy a better tool whenever it came along. I can't imagine anyone stealing her things, though."

A sudden chill went through me. "Unless it was another card maker," I said.

"It could have been a scrapbooker," Sara Lynn said, obviously trying to make me feel better.

I shook my head. "No, you said it yourself before. Maggie still enjoyed scrapbooking, but she'd been focusing mostly on cards for the last few years."

Lillian said, "I'm afraid you're right, Jennifer. It appears that whoever killed her was most likely a card maker as well. Why else steal the most valuable items in the apartment? Who else would even realize it? I suppose the real question is, who would be desperate enough to kill her for her tools?"

I shook my head. "You're not seeing it right. The tools were a bonus. The real reason had to be something else. Like jealousy." I was thinking of Betty or Howard, two of my favorite card makers in the world.

Lillian said, "Wait a second, maybe we're jumping to a conclusion the killer wants us to. What better way to divert suspicion than to point it in an entirely different direction? Let's say that Jeffrey Wallace killed her. Wouldn't it make sense that he'd try to point the blame toward another part of her life? There are lots of card makers we could suspect, but if we focus solely on those, we'd miss him entirely."

Sara Lynn slumped down onto the couch. "So we're back where we started from. I don't know how Bradford does this. It's impossible, isn't it?"

"No, but it's not easy," I admitted. "We do know one thing we didn't before."

Lillian said, "If you mention those missing scrapbooks again, I'll scream, I swear it."

"Besides those," I said. "Whoever killed her came to this house and tried to cover their tracks. We can't be sure which thing we discovered is significant, or even if any of them are, but we do know one thing:

Maggie was surely murdered. Why else would anyone try to cover it up?"

"So now it's time to call Bradford," Sara Lynn said after a few moments of silence between us. "He'll know what to do."

Lillian shook her head. "We don't have anything to give him that's concrete, and if anyone in the world should know what a pragmatist he is, it should be you."

"I do, believe me, I do," Sara Lynn said. "I don't know what good we accomplished here tonight, but at least Maggie's possessions have been sorted and boxed. What should we do with the few boxes of keepsakes? I don't care if anyone goes through the other boxes, but what's left is all of Maggie's memories."

"Let's bring them back inside and lock the door," I said. "Lillian, would you call the Salvation Army tomorrow and have them pick up the clothes? I'll call somebody about the trash."

She nodded. "And I'll take Maggie's personal items to Patrick tomorrow when I return the key to him. They'll be fine here in the meantime."

The three of us walked outside together into the night. Sometime while we'd been inside it had started to rain, and everything glistened from the streetlight's illumination. It was getting colder—there was no doubt about it—and soon enough the rain would turn to snow. I saw a movement down the street, and for a second I could swear I saw someone peeking out from behind the bushes. Was it my imagination? Were we were being watched, or was someone just out for a late-night stroll? I started walking in that direction when Lillian asked, "Jennifer? Where are you going?"

"I thought I saw someone," I said, but by the time I got there, either she was gone, or more likely, she'd never been there in the first place. It was amazing what my imagination could do when I was tired.

"Is anyone there?" Sara Lynn called out.

"No, I probably just imagined it." I started to look for my Gremlin when I remembered I'd ridden over with Lillian. "Would you give me a ride back to my car?"

"I can take you home, if you'd like," Sara Lynn said.

"Thanks, but then I'd be stranded in the morning."

Lillian said, "I'll take her. Thank you for your help, Sara Lynn. You were a real asset tonight."

My sister nodded. "I was glad to do it."

Then I remembered what had brought Sara Lynn to us in the first place. "Listen, all I've got is a couch, but you're welcome to it."

Lillian piped up. "I can do better than that. I've got a guest bedroom just begging to be used."

"Thank you both, but I'd better get back home," Sara Lynn said. "It appears I might need to get used to being alone."

After we saw her safely to her car, Lillian and I drove through the deserted streets of Rebel Forge toward the shop. I'd parked close to the front, something I hardly ever did when we were open for business, but for once I was glad I was under a streetlight and not tucked away in the alley behind the shop. "That was a productive evening, wasn't it?" Lillian said.

"I'm still not sure what we discovered, but we're better off than we were, so that's something."

She patted my arm as she pulled in behind my car on the deserted street. "Have faith, Jennifer. We'll get to the truth sooner or later."

"I hope you're right," I said. "Good night, Lillian, and thanks for everything."

She looked up at me through her open window. "Jennifer, I should be the one thanking you. Since you brought me into your shop, my life's been full of excitement just when I thought I was going to be consumed by boredom forever."

"That's me, never a dull moment," I said. "I'm glad you're working with me, too."

After she drove away, I could swear I felt someone's gaze on me. There was a creepy feeling on the nape of my neck, and I fumbled my car keys trying to get inside. As I raced away, the feeling left me, but I still didn't stop rushing until I was safely upstairs, locked in on one side with the world on the other.

As tired as I was, I couldn't just go to sleep. Not only was I wired from the massive amounts of coffee we'd put away, but I was truly filthy from working. A shower was in order if I was ever going to go to sleep. Unfortunately, it only woke me up more. I paced around the place, wishing I could get some sleep before another big day tomorrow. The clock read just after midnight. Maybe some chilly night air would help. I wrapped my wet hair in a towel and opened the window onto the small porch. It was too cold to go out there, but I enjoyed the sudden chill when I poked my head out through the window. I rested my forehead on the sill, and I could feel myself start to drift when Oggie jumped on my back, something he liked to do occasionally and a habit I couldn't break him of. I pulled my head back as a reflex, and less than a second later, the window crashed down, jarring the glass with the force of its impact against the jamb. It shook me; I couldn't deny it. "Did you cause that, or did you just save me?" I asked him as I stroked his fur.

He sneezed once and squirmed out of my grip, a "no comment" if ever there was one. I looked at the window again, lifted it and tried to see if it was at all loose. The odd thing was that it took both hands to lower it once it was open. So why had it fallen unbidden? Was it a warning from Frances that I was in danger, or was she trying to kill me? Either way, I wasn't happy about the message. Before I'd risk my neck out that particular window again, I was going to saw off my broom and use the shaft to hold it open.

My heart was still furiously pumping a few minutes later as I curled up on the couch. As I sat there with a single small table light illuminating the room, I thought about reading or watching television, anything to take my mind off the world and get some rest.

I was still considering the possibilities when I heard someone outside my door. Go away, I thought to myself. It could only be Jeffrey or Barrett, and I wasn't in the mood to talk to either one of them at the moment.

Then I heard a drunken voice, and I was suddenly wishing for either one of my neighbors. "Jennifer, let me in. We need to talk."

Should I answer Wayne, or pretend to be asleep?

That fiction died soon enough as he slammed the door with his fists. "Let me in, or you'll regret it. You know you want to see me. Admit it."

He hit the door again, this time hard enough to shake it on its hinges. Though Ethan had pronounced the lock solid and the door secure, I knew it could only stand so much of such a fierce assault.

I shouted, "Go away, Wayne."

"Good, you're up. Now open the door so we can have a party." He pounded on the door again, and I wondered where my nosy neighbors were now. I grabbed my baseball bat, then called Bradford at home.

"This better be good," he grumbled when he picked up.

"Wayne Davidson's trying to break into my apartment," I screamed, despite my pledge to myself to stay calm.

"Sis? Hang on, I'll be right there."

At that moment, I heard a horrid splintering sound and saw the door swing inward. I threw the phone down and grabbed the bat with both hands.

Wayne dropped an iron bar on my couch. "You're

not being very friendly," he said as he started toward me.

"Don't," I said, my fingers clenched to the grip of the bat.

"You've got to be kidding," he said. "You can't stop me."

I waited until he was within reach, then I did what Bradford had taught me as a kid playing my first game. I swung from the dirt up into him. Though I'd been aiming for his chin, it was a good thing I didn't hit him there. The force of the blow would have probably killed him. As it was, I managed to catch him squarely in the stomach, and there was a huff of alcohol-laden air as he collapsed on the floor.

Barrett was there thirty seconds later, with Jeffrey on his heels. "We came as soon as we could," Barrett said, faltering at the door when he saw Wayne's unconscious form on the floor.

"My God, did you kill him?"

"I don't think so," I said.

Jeffrey nudged Wayne's unconscious form with his toe, then bent down and checked his breathing. As he stood again, he said, "He's still alive, but when he wakes up he's going to be sore in places he didn't know he had."

"What took you two so long?" I asked. The shakes were starting to hit me hard, the way they usually did after something frightening happened to me. After the phone call at Maggie's, the falling window and now this, I was nearly out of adrenaline.

"We got here as fast as we could," Barrett said, snugging his robe tighter.

"Barrett, are you coming back to bed?" I heard a voice call out through my open door. I didn't need to see that blonde hair to know that it was Penny.

"Yes, why don't you go back downstairs," I said. "I'd hate to break up your date."

"It's not what it looks like," he said.

"Oh, did you two decide to have a slumber party and make s'mores? I didn't get my invitation, did you, Jeffrey?"

Jeffrey backed up. "Leave me out of this. If you're okay, I'm going back to bed."

"What about him?" Barrett said as he pointed toward Wayne.

Jeffrey said, "Fine. I'll stay with her until the police get here, but do you honestly think he's going to give her any more trouble tonight?"

Barrett was saved from answering by my brother's sudden appearance. His gun was drawn, and he came off that landing like he was ready to shoot somebody, and he didn't much care who.

He took one look at Wayne, then holstered his gun. "Well, I'm sorry if you had to kill him, but just because of the nightmares you're going to have because of it." Bradford had been forced to kill two different men since he'd become sheriff, and it was no secret he still was haunted by their faces from time to time.

"He's not dead," I said, and Wayne snorted once to prove it, then quickly settled back into his baseball-bat-induced coma.

"That will save me a ton of paperwork, thanks," he said, trying to diffuse the situation with a grin. Bradford turned to the two men and said, "Thanks for watching out for her."

I was about to protest that they hadn't done a thing when Barrett did it for me. "He was like that when we got here."

Jeffrey added, "I don't envy him that. May we go, Officer? There's nothing we can do here."

"Go on. I'll need your statements, but that can wait until morning."

After they were gone, Bradford leaned down and cuffed Wayne, though he was now snoring fitfully.

"Do you think that's really necessary?" I asked him.

"Don't want him waking up and catching me off

guard," Bradford said. He gently took the baseball bat from me, then wrapped his arms around me. "Are you okay, Sis?"

That's when I let it all go and started to cry.

After a while, I pulled back and wiped my cheeks. "I swear, sometimes I can be such a girl."

"That's one of the things I love most about you," my brother said. "You surprise me all the time, and I'm not that easy to shock anymore. Why don't you grab some stuff and come home with me? Bring your roommates too. Where are they, by the way?"

"If I had to bet, I'd say they were sound asleep on my pillow. Listen, I appreciate the offer, but I don't want to leave my apartment tonight."

He looked at the door, barely hanging on to its frame, then stared at me. "Jennifer, stubborn is one thing, but this just isn't happening. There's no way I'm letting you stay here until we get a steel door to replace that one."

I looked at the door and realized that he was right. "Just let me get Oggie and Nash. So what are we going to do about him?"

"Jody and Jim are both coming. They'll be here any minute, so they can take Wayne to jail and I can take you home. Let me call Cindy and tell her what's happening. She's worried sick."

As Bradford called his wife, I looked in on my roommates. I couldn't find them at first, but when I glanced over at their carriers, I saw that they'd crawled inside and were waiting patiently for me. I didn't know what was up with them, but for once I didn't care. It made my life easier, and that was what counted. I grabbed a change of clothes and a few toiletries, stuffed them into an overnight bag, and by the time I came back out, Wayne was gone.

"They got him already?" I asked.

"He wasn't any problem, and I told them if Wayne

tripped a few times, well, we can always claim it happened because he was drunk."

"They're not going to hurt him, are they?" Though I was not one of Wayne's biggest fans, I didn't want to see him beaten up. Well, not any more than I'd already pounded him, anyway.

"No, they're good men, both professional. Don't worry. He won't bother you anymore."

I smiled weakly. "Because of the law, or because of my baseball bat?"

"If I had to guess, I'd say a little bit of both. Do you have everything you need?" he asked as he gestured to the carriers and the bag slung over one shoulder.

"I'm set. If anybody wants what's left, they're welcome to it."

We drove in silence to my brother's place, and I was glad it was dark outside. I couldn't control the shakes, but I'd stood up for myself when it had counted.

Cindy was standing near the door when we got to their modest ranch, and she ran out to hug me before I could even get inside. "I just got off the phone with Lillian and Sara Lynn. They wanted to come over."

Bradford shook his head. "You told them not to, didn't you?"

"I said it was you-all's decision, but if you want to stop them, I suggest you call them right now before they can get dressed."

Bradford turned to me and made what I knew was a heavy sacrifice for him. "Do you want them here, Sis?"

I shook my head. "I just want to go to bed and forget this ever happened. Give me your phone. I'll call them."

Bradford said, "Don't worry, I can handle those two."

I waited, my hand outstretched, and he finally handed me the telephone. "I swear I don't know what I did to deserve so many stubborn women in my life."

Cindy kissed him on the cheek. "You're just a lucky man, I guess."

Bradford laughed softly. "Are the kids still asleep?"

"Are you kidding me? I don't think an explosion would wake them up right now. I just wish I could sleep like that."

I called my sister and aunt, making our conversations as brief as possible. Yes, I was fine; no, I didn't want any company; and yes, we'd talk about it the next day.

Cindy waited until I was finished, then said, "Jennifer, I'm so glad you're okay."

"Me too," I said, the fatigue suddenly overwhelming me.

Bradford said, "There's just a few questions I want to ask you, and then you can go to bed."

His wife wasn't about to stand for that. "Bradford Shane, your sister is our guest. She's obviously worn down to the bone. She'll be here in the morning, so you can ask your questions then. In the meantime, let her rest."

I thanked Cindy, promised Bradford we'd talk later, then walked downstairs to the guest room in the basement. Once I was there, I opened Oggie and Nash's carriers, but the rascals wouldn't come out. Too much excitement, I supposed as I crawled onto the bed without even taking my clothes off.

Sometime in the night they got out and joined me, and when I woke up, I felt two small sets of engines purring against my ribs.

HANDCRAFTED CARD TIP

Don't know what to say inside your carefully crafted card once you've made it? Sometimes I use lines from my favorite poems, quotations or songs, and there are other times I think simplicity works best. Over the years, I've sent cards that say "Simply Because," "You Are in My Thoughts" and "Missing You." In handcrafted-card making, it is, above all else, the thought that counts, and that you care enough to make it yourself.

Chapter 15

It always throws me off when I wake up in a strange place, not that I've made much of a habit of it over the years. Once I was oriented, I gently nudged Oggie and Nash far enough so I could get out of bed. When I glanced at the alarm clock, I saw that I'd slept in till nearly nine, a modern-day record for me. Ten minutes later I walked into the kitchen, led there by the ambrosia of fresh pancakes.

"Am I too late for breakfast?" I said, stifling a yawn.

Cindy was sitting at the kitchen table reading the newspaper, and Bradford was working at the griddle. My brother had on his police uniform with an apron over it that said KISS THE COOK.

"You're just in time. Are you ready for some flapjacks?" Bradford asked. "If you don't like those, we've got pancakes and hotcakes. It's your choice." It was an old family joke, offering me three names for the same thing.

"They smell so good, I'll have one of each." He poured three circles of batter onto the griddle. "Coming right up."

Cindy handed me a cup of coffee when I sat down. I said, "You actually let him cook?"

She smiled. "He handles the grilling outside and the pancakes in here, and that's about it. I wasn't about to say no when he offered."

I took a sip of coffee, then asked, "Where are the kids?"

"They've been out playing for an hour," Bradford said as he flipped the pancakes. "I didn't think you were going to ever get up."

Cindy swatted at him with the paper. "Now be nice. Jennifer had a late night."

"And too much excitement," I said. I started to get up when Bradford said, "Sit back down, young lady, your breakfast is almost ready."

"I've got too much to do before I open the shop," I said. "Thanks for thinking of me."

Cindy said, "Jennifer, if you think he's going to let you get out of here without breakfast, you don't know your brother very well."

Those pancakes did smell awfully good. "I suppose I've got time for one."

He slid all three off the griddle, then put them on my plate. "If you've got time for one, you've got time for three."

Then he poured more batter onto the grill.

"Three are plenty," I protested as I poured some warmed syrup on the short stack.

"These aren't for you, little piggy," Bradford said. "The cook has to eat too, you know?"

"You've already had one breakfast," Cindy protested.

"Hey, I've been slaving over a hot griddle all morning. I deserve a little extra."

She got up and moved in behind him, and I could tell Bradford was expecting a hug. Instead, his wife pinched his love handles. "I'd say you had more than a little extra, wouldn't you?"

"Just more to love, woman," he said. "Tell you what, I won't eat all four of these. I'll show remarkable restraint and just have three."

"One," she said firmly.

"Okay, but you drive a hard bargain. I'll limit myself to a measly two."

Cindy gave him a narrow glance, then said, "Just this time, and only in honor of your sister's visit."

Bradford winked at me as I ate. "You can stay as long as you want; you know that, don't you?"

"So you can keep grabbing extra portions?" I asked.

"Hey, it's a win-win situation as far as I'm concerned."

I took the last bite of pancake, finished off my coffee and stood. "As much as I'd love to hang around, I really do have to get back to my place and find someone to fix my door."

"If that's all you're worried about, Ethan's been working on it since seven. I'm willing to bet that he and his carpenter friend have that new door hung already."

"What do you have on him, anyway?" I asked.

Bradford shrugged, but Cindy said, "Stop trying to be so mysterious. They've been friends forever, though neither one of them is likely to ever admit it."

He rolled his eyes toward his wife, then said, "Either way, you're covered. Do you want these two? I hate to just throw them out."

I glanced at the two orphan pancakes and was ready to give in, despite my promise to cut back, when Cindy said, "Stop picking on your sister. Jennifer, they freeze great, and the kids eat them as after-school snacks. Have some if you'd like, but he'd never just toss them."

That helped. "I'm going to stop then, as good as they were." I stood and kissed my brother on the cheek. "Thanks."

"Wow, you're easy. I got a kiss with just three pancakes? I bet you're a popular girl at the breakfast table."

I slapped him gently on the arm. "I wasn't thanking

you for the pancakes. I just wanted you to know I appreciate everything you did last night."

He put the spatula down and said, "Jennifer, I honestly didn't do much of anything. By the time I got there, you'd handled him all by yourself."

I shook my head. "You're the one who taught me to swing like that."

"Well, I'll accept your thanks for that, then. Seriously, though, you don't have to rush off. You and your two roommates are welcome to stay as long as you want."

I looked into my brother's eyes and said, "Thanks, but if I don't go back right now, I may lose my nerve altogether."

Cindy said, "Would that be such a bad thing? How can you live there now after what happened?"

"You'd be amazed what you can deal with if you have to," I said. "I was going to ask to leave Oggie and Nash here, but since you've arranged to have my door fixed, we're going home."

Bradford started to say something, but Cindy glanced at him and he shut right up. I swear, those two had a level of nonverbal communication going on between them that never ceased to amaze me.

Bradford said, "Fine, but at least let me hang out with you a few minutes before you go." He took the apron off and threw it over the back of a chair.

"You can come back while I get the cats into their carriers," I said.

Cindy said, "You two go on. I'll finish this batter."

Bradford told his wife, "I expect fresh pancakes after Jennifer leaves. It's the least I deserve."

She laughed. "Do you really want to talk about the least you deserve with me?"

"No," he said. "You're right. Forget I said anything."

My brother followed me back to my room, and as

I suspected, Oggie and Nash were still soundly asleep. "Come on, you two, rise and shine." At least they were pretty docile just waking up, and I didn't have too hard a time getting them back into their carriers.

Bradford took one from me, then grabbed my bag, too. "Listen, I really do need to ask you a few things about last night. I'm truly sorry."

"Don't be; it's your job." I took a deep breath, then said, "I was on the couch when Wayne started pounding on my door just after midnight. He tried to get me to let him in, and when I refused, he started banging on the door. That's when I grabbed the bat and called you. What did he use, anyway?"

"He had his equalizer," Bradford said softly.

"What does that mean?"

My brother looked embarrassed, but he admitted, "Wayne used to brag about his personal protection device, a chunk of iron bar he carried around in his truck. I thought he was all bluff and steam, but I was wrong. Jennifer, I'm sorry. I never should have let it get that far."

I touched his arm. "You can't be responsible for his behavior any more than I can control these two cats. Is that all you need from me? I really am running late."

"You're free to go," he said. "I'll take you home." We walked outside and I waved good-bye to Cindy. The best decision my brother had ever made had been marrying her. I wondered if I'd ever get that lucky myself.

Outside, I stowed the cats in the back of his patrol car, then climbed in front with him.

"I'm proud of you, Jennifer," Bradford said as he drove toward my apartment. I wondered how proud of me he'd be if he knew Lillian, Sara Lynn and I were conspiring against him.

"Thanks, but I don't deserve it. I didn't have much choice. Honestly, I was scared to death."

"But you didn't freeze up," he said, "You did what you had to in order to protect yourself."

I couldn't take another ounce of his niceness, not with what I was doing. "Listen, there's something you should know."

I was ready to tell him when he said, "What, that you and Lillian are looking into Maggie Blake's death?"

"Now how on earth did you know that?"

He smiled. "I *am* the sheriff here. I knew you couldn't just leave it alone, and when Lillian asked me to come to the funeral, it didn't take much to figure out what you two were up to."

"Sara Lynn's helping too," I blurted out, and that news seemed to surprise him.

"How'd you manage to get her involved?" he asked, his gaze steady on the road ahead.

"Well, we were at Maggie's house last night and—"

"What?" he snapped. "Jennifer, you had no right. That's trespassing, and you know it. How did you get in? Did you break a window?"

So much for my brother's sympathy. I should have kept my mouth shut. "We had every right to be there," I said.

"How do you figure that?"

"Patrick Benson hired us to clean the place up and sort Maggie's things into boxes."

"Do I even want to know how you managed to get that assignment? Forget it; ignorance is truly bliss at the moment." He pulled up in front of my place and shut the engine off, though Bradford made no move to get out of the car. I normally parked in back with the rest of the tenants, but my brother had a mind of his own. "So what did you find?"

I wasn't about to give up my hard-earned information that easily. "I thought you ruled it an accident."

Bradford swiveled and stared at me. "Don't be petulant. I'm the first person in the world to admit that

I'm not perfect. Knowing the three of you, I'm sure you think you've got something."

I blurted out what we'd uncovered. "Some of Maggie's scrapbooks were gone, her tools and supplies for card making were all missing, and we found a card she'd made about breaking up with her boyfriend."

"She could have given the tools and scrapbooks away," Bradford said, "but I didn't realize she had a boyfriend. Who was the mystery man?"

"Jeffrey Wallace, the man who lives downstairs."

"Are you talking about the young guy from last night? You're kidding."

"No, I mean the other one," I said, not wanting to get sidetracked about who was appropriate dating material for a middle-aged woman and who was not.

"That still doesn't mean anything. People break up all the time. Do you have anything else a little more concrete?"

I considered telling him about Howard and Betty and my other suspicions, but I had even less solid proof about everything else. If the missing equipment and books weren't going to convince him, nothing else was either. "I'm working on it."

He shook his head. "That's the problem with this business. There are too many amateurs wanting to get involved without formal training. How in the world did you rope Sara Lynn into this? I thought she was more sensible than that."

"She's having trouble at home," I blurted out, silently asking my sister's forgiveness in my head.

"I know." Bradford nodded. "It's been brewing for a while."

"You knew about it and didn't tell me?" I asked, outraged. "I have a right to know, she's my sister, too."

"Take it easy, Jennifer; the signs have been there for quite a while. I've been wondering when it was going to blow."

"Do you think it's serious?" I asked. Sara Lynn and Bailey had been married forever. I couldn't imagine the two of them apart, no matter what the justification.

"It's always serious when it goes on too long," Bradford said. It was obvious he was uncomfortable with our discussion topic. "So do you want some help with those two felons of yours?"

"Thanks, that would be nice," I said. I was perfectly capable of handling both carriers and my bag, but if I was being honest with myself, it might help me to climb those steps with my brother beside me.

Instead of the sound of drills and saws upstairs, it was dead quiet.

"I guess Ethan couldn't make it first thing after all," I said.

"Don't bet on it," Bradford said. "Do you mind if I go up first?"

"Lead on," I said. The vision of my shattered doorframe was strong in my mind, and I wasn't at all certain I could handle seeing it again.

Ethan was sitting on the top step, spinning a set of keys around one of his fingers. "Took you long enough," he said, smiling at Bradford. "I've been waiting for hours."

"If you finished that fast, you didn't do a good enough job," Bradford said.

"Let's see you try to get through it, I dare you."

I looked and saw that the door was replaced as well as the frame. "That must have been a lot of work."

"Honestly, it's easier to replace the entire unit than repair a frame, but that's not why I did it this way. Your brother insisted on steel all the way around."

I thought about the bill and wondered if I'd have enough in my account to cover it. "Let me get my checkbook," I said.

"No need to," Ethan said.

I turned to Bradford. "You're not paying for this. I won't let you."

Ethan grinned. "He doesn't have to. I'm billing the owner of the building. After I leave you two, I'm trotting right over to Hester's to get my check."

"She's the realtor," I said. "She doesn't own the place."

Ethan raised an eyebrow. "Last I heard her name was still on the deed."

"But I thought—"

He cut me off. "Lots of folks around here think she's just scraping by, but Hester's loaded. She's worth a mint, and it's not just in property." He tossed me the keys, then said to Bradford, "See you."

"See you," Bradford said, bobbing his head for a split second in a country boy's wave.

"You never know, do you?" I said as I let the cats out of their carriers. They scudded away the second they were free, and I had a feeling they'd be ripping through the place, examining every fresh sight and smell until they were satisfied that everything was as it should be. I just wished it were that easy for me.

"You want me to hang around awhile?" Bradford asked. "I've got time."

I shoved his chest. "No, go on, I'm fine. I know you've got work to do."

"You kidding me? This town practically polices itself."

"Then you're grossly overpaid," I said, walking him through the new door.

He paused outside the threshold. "I'd trust Ethan with my life, but dead bolt this thing for a second, would you?"

I did as he requested, then heard him throw himself into the door. It didn't even quiver.

I opened it back up and Bradford was rubbing a shoulder. "It'll do," he said.

"Go on, you big goof."

Once he was gone, I dead bolted the door again after him. The place was remarkably tranquil after the events of just a few hours ago. Would I ever be comfortable there again? At that point, I just couldn't say. The clock caught my gaze, and I realized if I was going to open my shop before noon, I'd better get moving.

But I had a phone call to make first. If Gail found out what had happened last night without hearing about it from me first, she'd be crushed.

"Hey, I hope I'm not calling too early," I said when she answered on the fourth ring.

"No, I was awake," she said, but I could hear her masking a yawn.

"I'll make it quick. Do you remember me telling you about Wayne Davidson?"

"The creep that works for your brother? What about him? He didn't make another pass at you, did he?"

"It's worse than that. He tried to break in last night."

There was silence on the other end. "Gail? Are you still there?"

"Jennifer, what happened?"

"I took him out with my baseball bat," I said. "No big deal, but I wanted you to hear it from me first."

"There's no way I'm letting you get away with leaving it at that. Scoop, girl."

"I will later, I promise, but I'm running behind as it is. I just wanted you to know that I was all right."

She chuckled softly. "It sounds like you're a whole lot better than that. Call me soon. And Jennifer?"

"Yes?"

"Thanks for letting me know."

"You're welcome."

Forty minutes later I was ready to face the world again. Sometimes the only solution to a problem is a long hot shower or an equally cleansing soak in the tub. As I walked down the stairs, I saw Jeffrey's door start to open. I didn't know if he'd been waiting for the sound of my footsteps on the treads, but as far as I was concerned, his timing couldn't have been better.

"Good morning," I said. "Do you have a second?"

He nodded, and it looked as though my neighbor hadn't gotten much sleep the night before, either.

"Sorry about the noise so early this morning."

Jeffrey shook his head. "Nonsense, it's perfectly understandable. I want to apologize again for my delay in helping you last night." He cast his gaze to the floor, then said, "I thought I'd need reinforcements, and it took me forever to get Barrett to the door."

"He was busy," I said, not wanting to discuss his liaison with Penny. "I need to talk to you."

Instead of inviting me inside as I'd expected, Jeffrey stood in the opening, one hand on the door.

I looked at him and said, "Do you really want to do this out here?"

He glanced at his watch. "I really don't have time for a long discussion, Jennifer; I'm late as it is."

"Fine," I said, "we'll do it in the foyer, then. Why didn't you tell me Maggie broke up with you?"

He looked as if someone had hit him with a bat instead of Wayne. "I don't know what you're talking about," he stammered.

"Come on, Jeffrey, don't lie to me."

"I don't care enough about what you think to lie," he said. "Besides, it's none of your business."

"You're wrong there," I said. "Maggie made it my business before she died."

"What did she tell you?" he asked, suddenly very defensive. "Certainly we had our share of tiffs from time to time, but we were two adults in an adult relationship. Things were good between us."

"Then why did she make this for you?" I pulled out the card we'd found at Maggie's the night before and stuck it in his face.

He read the front, then opened it and stared at the

words she'd written inside. "How do you explain that?"

Jeffrey's face was almost white. "I don't have to, not to you or anyone else." He took a step inside and slammed his door shut. "Hey, I want that card back," I protested. It was the only real evidence I had that there had been trouble between them.

"It's mine," he said sullenly.

I knocked again, but Jeffrey ignored me. So much for his urgency to leave the building. I could spend the rest of the morning waiting him out, but I was pretty sure that card had been shredded by now. I'd really blown it, confronting him without anyone there to back me up, and worse yet, ·I'd let him take what might have been the only real evidence I had against him. If it turned out that he'd killed Maggie and I couldn't prove it because of my negligence, I'd never be able to forgive myself.

I walked out back to the Gremlin and noticed an odd car parked behind Barrett's. It was a Trans Am I'd never seen before, but as soon as I saw the license plate, I knew who it belonged to. The personalized plate said PNY URND. How clever. I wondered what Penny had done to earn it, then tried to dismiss her from my thoughts. I had other, more important things on my mind.

Lillian had opened Custom Card Creations without me, a fact I was thankful for. To my surprise, she and Sara Lynn were sharing a cup of coffee at my worktable.

"Good morning," I said as I put my purse behind the counter. "I'm glad you're both here. I only want to have to tell this once, okay?"

Sara Lynn hugged me, and Lillian moved in on the other side. "We're just glad you're okay," Sara Lynn said.

Lillian added, "I hope they fry him for this."

I enjoyed their embraces, then backed away. "I'm willing to bet he's in pretty rough shape after I hit him."

Lillian looked delighted. "Oh, I hope you broke a few of his ribs. I know how much that hurts; it can be sheer misery to breathe."

Sara Lynn asked, "When did you break a rib?"

"Skydiving," she explained. "I took a bad tumble. It was entirely my fault. But enough about me. Talk to us, Jennifer."

I related the night's events to them, trying to skim over the facts and leave the commentary out, but with those two, it was practically impossible. What should have been a five-minute story ended up taking half an hour, and by the time I'd declared the subject closed and off-limits forever, I was finished with it. If there was anything I could do about it, Wayne Davidson would never haunt my dreams again.

I looked at my sister and asked, "Don't you have a store to run?"

"My staff can take care of things while I'm gone," she said. "I've got good people working for me."

I hugged Lillian's shoulder. "I do too. Listen, I appreciate you being here, but I'd kind of like to let things get back to normal if I can, okay?"

"I understand," she said. "We'll talk later."

After Sara Lynn was gone, Lillian said, "So that's that. What do we do now?"

I told her what had happened with Jeffrey Wallace, not able to meet her gaze as I admitted how badly I'd fouled things up.

"Nonsense, all is not lost. Sara Lynn and I both saw that card, so it's not a matter of your word against his. Jeffrey's reaction is interesting, isn't it? The real question is if the man's in denial or if he truly believes what he told you."

I said, "You saw that card. Was there an inch of room to allow them to reconcile?"

Lillian thought about it a few seconds, then said, "If it had come from anyone else, I would have to agree with you, but we both know that Maggie had a flair for the dramatic."

"I know," I said. "When I tried to tell Bradford what we found, I could tell her past behavior was on his mind."

"So you shared everything with your brother?" Lillian asked. "Do I even need to ask you what he thought?"

"We don't have enough evidence," I said. "I didn't even have the heart to tell him about Howard and Betty, not without more proof than we've got."

"Jennifer, I think it's time we went back to the marker board."

I looked around the shop. "So have we completely given up on running this place as a business?"

Lillian shook her head. "If a customer comes in, we'll help them, of course, but are you going to be able to put your heart and soul into this place with Maggie's death weighing on the back of your mind?"

"Probably not," I admitted. "Let's try it again."

"Good," Lillian said, retrieving the board. "Now where were we?" She studied it a few moments, then said, "Do you know what, Jennifer? This is useless." Before I could protest, Lillian wiped the board with a paper towel.

"Hey, I wasn't done with that," I said.

"Jennifer, we know so much more now than we did. It's time for a fresh look at things."

I nodded reluctantly, since it was too late for my protests to do any good. It was time to figure out who had murdered Maggie Blake, and why.

Chapter 16

"So where do we start?" I asked Lillian as she retrieved a marker.

"There's the prime question," she said as she wrote, "Who killed Maggie and why?"

"We had that on the board before," I said.

"Patience," she said. "We're going to approach this differently."

As she wrote names down the right side of the board, Lillian said, "Okay, we've got our main suspects as Betty, Howard, and Jeffrey Wallace. Who else should we list?"

"All of the names in the club," I said, "including ours."

I'd said it as a joke, but Lillian wrote down "Hilda," "Lillian," and "Jennifer." "Who else?"

"I was kidding," I said as I got up and wiped out our names.

"What about Hilda?" Lillian asked. "Should we erase her name too?"

I thought about it a second, then said, "Let's leave her up there until we can figure out a reason to take her name off the list."

"Is that it, then?" she asked.

"I can't think of anyone else," I said. "Now what do we do?"

Across from the names, she wrote in headings that spelled "MOM." I said, "Do you honestly think her mother did it? If the poor woman's still alive, she's at least eighty."

"Jennifer, you should read more mysteries like I do." As she touched each letter, she said, "Motive, Opportunity, and Means."

"Why isn't 'Means' first? After all, they both start with *M*."

"Are you trying to be difficult, or does it just come naturally to you?"

I shrugged. "I was just curious." I looked at the board. "Let's go ahead and do Means first. We don't even know how Maggie was killed. How in the world could we know if any of them had the capability of doing it?"

"So we do that one later," Lillian said. "Let's tackle Opportunity."

I pointed to Howard's and Betty's names. "They couldn't have done it."

Lillian frowned at the board. "Why not? They admit they were the last ones to see her alive. It makes perfect sense to me. You know what kind of mind-set Betty's had lately. The two of them have been on the brink of divorce for years because of her jealousy."

"That's exactly why I think they're innocent. Can you honestly see the two of them working together to kill Maggie and make it look like an accident? I doubt they could agree to a grocery list, let alone such an elaborate cover-up."

Lillian paused, then said, "You've got a point." As she put question marks by their names, she added, "So do you think Jeffrey Wallace could have done it? There's no love like a scorned love."

I thought about my downstairs neighbor, and the different sides I'd seen in him in a short period of time. "He could have done it," I said. "But I don't know if he would."

Lillian said, "Unless we learn otherwise, we have to assume he had the means to do it, and the opportunity.

He had the motive too, if she'd just dumped him and he was beginning to realize that she was earnest about it."

"So we convict him now? Let's at least wait until we finish the board."

Lillian sighed. "What possible reason would Hilda have to murder her? They were dear friends, from what we've heard."

"They weren't best friends for all that long," I said. "Before Hilda, Maggie was best friends with Frances." I shuddered as I thought about the prospect of that window coming down on my neck. If she was a ghost inhabiting my apartment, Frances was trying to make a point, and I wanted to figure it out before she tried something even more dramatic to get my attention.

I took the marker from Lillian and wrote "Frances Coolridge" beside Maggie's name. "What if their murders are tied together somehow?"

"Jennifer, are you still on that? I can't imagine why a suicide would be a part of Maggie's murder. If Maggie had died first, I could see there might be some remorse there, but it was the other way around. Frances's death didn't have anything to do with Maggie's."

Something clicked in my head, but I couldn't say what. There was something we were missing, some connection that was slipping past. Then it hit me. "Wait a second. Frances's death did impact Maggie."

"Certainly it's difficult to lose a close friend, especially to suicide," Lillian said.

"Humor me, okay? Let's say Frances was murdered. So what happened to all her stuff?"

Lillian spoke as if she were talking to a small child. "Maggie inherited it. It's not all that odd, you know. After all, they were both widows with no children. Who else would they leave their possessions to?"

Then I remembered what had been bothering me. "What was it that Patrick said on the telephone last night?"

"Which time?" Lillian asked.

"When he told you about Frances's will, he said he did them all at the same time."

"So? What's wrong with that? He had no reason to lie to me," Lillian said. "And all the motivation in the world to be absolutely straight in his answers."

I tapped the marker on the table. "He didn't have any reason to volunteer any information either, but I think he let something slip without meaning to."

"Go on. You've certainly got my attention."

I twirled the marker in my hand a second, trying to recall Patrick's exact words. "He said he'd done all of them the same way, but shouldn't he have said 'both of them'?"

"So he chose the wrong word," Lillian said. "We do it all the time."

I wasn't buying that. "We're not sticklers for language usage like he is. I could hear it every time you talked to him. Lillian, what if there were more women involved?"

"Now you think it's murder for profit?" she asked incredulously. "You heard Patrick yourself. Frances didn't have anything all that valuable to leave Maggie, and I doubt Maggie did either for the next in line, if there is such a person. How do you explain that?"

I couldn't. "I didn't say I knew everything, but it does change the way we look at things, don't you think?"

"If we can get Patrick to admit there are other members of the Widows Club, and that's a big if."

I picked up the telephone and handed it to her. "So call him and find out."

She shunned the phone. "I think I'd better handle this in person."

"Great, let me grab my jacket," I said.

Lillian shook her head. "Jennifer, I hate to exclude you, but he's more likely to breach his professional oath with me if we're alone. I doubt he'd want a witness to it."

"I want to go," I said firmly.

"I'm sure you do, but I'd better handle this on my own. In the meantime, why don't you keep the shop open? I won't be long, I promise you that."

"How can you say that?" I asked as I walked her to the door. "He could be with a client; he could be in court; the man might not even be in his office."

Lillian smiled. "His secretary will be able to find him, believe me, and once she passes my message on, he'll see me, no matter what."

"Come straight back here," I said reluctantly as I watched her leave.

"I will," she said, and then Lillian was gone. She had a point about getting Patrick to open up to her in private, but I didn't like missing out on the conversation. There was nothing I could do about it but take her advice, but it was going to be one of the longest waits of my life.

I waited on a few customers, but even selling a nice set of alphabet stamps with a hefty price tag didn't help my general disposition. Despite Lillian's pledge, she was taking much longer than she'd promised, and I was going crazy pacing the aisles of my shop. Finally I put the BACK IN FIFTEEN sign on the door and locked it behind me. If nothing else, I needed more room to pace. My steps led me naturally to Greg's pottery shop, and I nearly went inside when I noticed that he was with a customer. I might have gone inside and waited anyway, but she was a good five years younger than I was, and, if I was being honest with myself, quite a bit prettier. It was no time to talk to Greg about our failed relationship. He nodded as he saw me through the window, but I just waved and kept walking past.

Ten seconds later he was out on the sidewalk with me. "Jennifer, are you all right? I heard what happened last night, and I couldn't believe it."

Before I could avoid it, he wrapped his arms around

me in a bear hug. I could swear I felt my spine crack under the pressure. But I'd be lying if I said I didn't enjoy it.

"I'm fine," I muttered. "If I could just breathe. You shouldn't leave your customers alone in your shop."

He released me from his embrace, but didn't step back much at all. "She'll be all right. I'm worried about you."

"Believe me, Wayne's the one feeling the pain this morning." I gestured to Greg's shop. "So you trust her that much?" I asked. "How well do you know her?"

"She's signing up for lessons, so I doubt she'd try to steal from me on her first day," he said.

"You don't give private lessons," I said.

"Yeah, well, I make exceptions sometimes."

"Still, you shouldn't just abandon her." Greg had taught me to throw pots once, and I knew it was part of his technique to reenact scenes from *Ghost* with his more attractive female customers.

"I need to talk to you," he said.

"We can do it some other time. Go on."

He nodded reluctantly, but before he went back inside, he said, "We'll finish this later, okay?"

"Okay," I agreed, willing to say just about anything to get him to go. So what did he want to talk about? I had a friend who used to say, "The horse is dead; dismount." Maybe it was time to do what Greg was obviously trying to do, to look forward and not back.

Lillian was waiting for me inside the card shop. "How'd you get past me?" I asked.

"Are you kidding me? When I saw you standing there wrapped up in Greg's arms, I doubted an elephant would have gotten your attention."

I blurted out, "He's giving private lessons. To a woman. She's young and she's pretty and from the look of her clothes, I'm guessing she's rich, too."

"Jennifer, don't read more into it than is there," she said calmly.

"I'm not, but if he can move on, so can I. So what did Patrick say? Did you even find him?"

Lillian flashed a brief smile. "Oh, I found him all right, though it was obvious he was ducking me. Jennifer, I was wrong."

"Does that mean I was right? I surely hope so. I could use an ego boost about now."

"Very well, I'll say it. You were right and I was wrong. It appears that greed might be the motive driving this after all."

"Don't leave me hanging," I said. "What did he say?"

"After no small amount of persuasion," Lillian said, "Patrick finally confessed that there were four women involved in an odd will structure."

I felt the hair on my neck stand up. "What happens? Does the last one standing get everything?"

"Actually, it's something like that," Lillian said. "There's a stipulation that each woman write down her preference of beneficiaries to be included in each will. If any of the people named are already dead, they're dropped until one woman gets everything."

"So who are these two women left?"

"That's what Patrick was so fussy about. They're both clients, and he was worried he was breaching their trust. He demanded full deniability, and I promised I wouldn't tell a soul."

"And yet you're going to tell me," I said. "Aren't you?"

"Of course I am," Lillian said. "But you have to give me your word that no one knows where we got our information, and that includes your brother and sister. You have to promise me, Jennifer, or we're going to drop this right here and now."

I hated keeping anything from Sara Lynn or Bradford, but there was no way I was going to miss out on Lillian's information.

"I promise," I said.

"That easily? You're making no demands, asking

for no stipulations or loopholes? I'm deadly serious about this."

"I know you are. So am I," I said. "They won't hear it from me. So who are they?"

"If your theory is correct, either Hilda is the murderer, or Hester Taylor."

"So let's go pressure them both," I said. I couldn't see either woman as a murderer, but it was the only thing that made sense. If one of the dead women owned something that was valuable—perhaps without her having realized it—then killing off the remaining members of the pact was the only way to have sole possession of it, whatever it was. I said, "You take Hester and I'll talk to Hilda."

Lillian said, "No, we'll question them together."

"We don't have time to do this as a team," I said. "One of their lives could be at stake right now."

"And if we split up, it could be one of us. We're doing this together, Jennifer, or I'll call your brother with some feeble excuse to lock them both up until we can figure it out, if we ever manage to."

"You're serious, aren't you?"

She nodded. "You'd better believe it. I've lost too many people I love in this world, and I'm not about to lose any more, or risk my own neck if I don't have to. Are you ready?"

"Okay, we'll do it your way. Who do we talk to first?" I asked, knowing from Lillian's tone that she wasn't about to budge. Truly, I was happy she was so resolute. With the odds right at fifty-fifty, I hadn't been thrilled about confronting a possible double murderer by myself, either.

I was still waiting for an answer when I glanced over at Lillian. She'd gone as white as I'd ever seen her, and for a second I thought she was having a heart attack.

"What is it?" I asked her as I grabbed her shoulder. "Are you all right?"

"Jennifer, I think I know who did it."

"Don't keep me in suspense," I said. "Talk to me."

"It had to be Hester. I never would have believed it."

I led Lillian to a chair. "Sit down and I'll get you some water."

"I don't need a drink," she protested, "at least not one of water."

"Sit," I commanded, and to my great surprise, she obeyed. I came back a few seconds later with a bottle of water from the refrigerator in back.

"You know I don't like it so cold," she said.

"Just drink it." I swear, sometimes dealing with her was like having a three-year-old.

She took a few sips, then sighed heavily. While she was composing herself, I said, "You know, I think you're right about Hester."

"Why do you say that?" The color was coming back to her cheeks, and I forgot about calling 911 for the moment.

"When we searched Maggie's house, I thought I saw someone in the bushes outside, remember?"

"Of course I do. I'm not senile."

That was Lillian's next stage of recovery. Snapping at me was a good sign. At least that's what I told myself.

"Well, I didn't say anything at the time because I thought I was probably imagining it, but I could have sworn I spotted Hester in the bushes watching us."

"That makes sense, if what I'm thinking is correct. We had a conversation at the funeral that I thought was a little odd, but it's making a lot more sense now under this context."

I remembered their talk, and how I'd eavesdropped. "She said before long it would just be her, and she didn't sound all that broken up about it, did she?"

"You heard that?" Lillian asked pointedly. "Jennifer, you know that listening to other people's conversations is rude."

I smiled at my aunt. "Hello Pot, my name's Kettle."

She didn't think I was all that amusing, but my aunt was a great eavesdropper from way back. If she didn't like the fact that I'd turned the tables on her, that was just too bad.

"If you're quite finished, we need to go," Lillian said.

"I'm ready if you are. Should we have Bradford meet us there?"

Lillian scowled. "On what pretext? Let's hold off for now. After all, she can't suspect we know what she's been doing."

I flipped the sign to CLOSED and we headed for Lillian's Mustang. When she started driving away from town and Hester's shop, I asked, "Where are you going?"

"Before we talk to Hester, we have to warn Hilda. If there's one person on earth Hilda trusts, it's her, and I won't have it on my conscience if anything happens to her."

"Okay, I'll buy that," I said. "Hey, how do you know where Hilda lives? I've known her longer than you have, and I don't have a clue."

"She invited me over for coffee the other day," Lillian admitted. "She even drew me a map. Since we had Maggie's memorial, that woman's been doing her utmost to be my new best friend. You didn't have anything to do with that, did you?"

When I didn't answer right away, she pushed. "Jennifer, what did you say?"

"Your name came up in conversation," I admitted. "She asked, so I told her a little about Uncle Roger. That's it, I swear."

"Yes, I got the feeling she was going to invite me into their Widows Club. Good thing I didn't get to know her sooner, or my name might have been on that list as well."

I touched her shoulder lightly as she drove. "You didn't qualify," I said.

"I most certainly am a widow, even if I did have a husband or two after Roger."

"I'm not disputing that," I said, "but none of the other women had any family they're close to. That was kind of the whole point."

Lillian shared a warm smile, lacking any hint of the acidity she could usually muster at will. "We are an odd group ourselves, aren't we? But it's nice belonging to someone."

"I agree," I said as we pulled up to a modest house on the outskirts of town. The lawn was well kept, and the bungalow had been freshly painted a charming shade of pale blue, with royal blue shutters and a white front door. It looked perfect for one person.

"How are we going to break the news to her?" I asked.

"The same way we do everything else," Lillian replied. "Direct and without doubt."

I touched Lillian's arm before we got out. "What if we're wrong?"

"Jennifer, warning her doesn't hurt anything but our pride if we're off base, but on the positive side, we may just save her life. Isn't that worth the risk?"

"It is," I said.

We walked to the door, but our repeated summons went unanswered. "Either she's not home or she's ducking us," I said.

"Let me leave her a note, and we'll find Hester. I just hope we're not too late."

Chapter 17

"Are you sure we shouldn't call Bradford first?" I asked Lillian as we pulled up in front of Hester's shop. It had started to rain, coming down in sheets, and the darkness of the day matched my view of the world. "We can make it a casual request."

"Call him if you'd like," Lillian said, "but I can tell you what he's going to say."

"You're right," I agreed as I got out of the Mustang. "I'm just not sure what we're going to say to Hester."

"Let me do the talking," she said. "I've known her forever, and if someone's going to accuse her of murder, it should be me."

We dodged as much of the rain as we could and walked into the combination copy store/apartment rental agency/ice cream shop. Hester was alone behind the counter, no doubt because of the onslaught of rain. Part of the place had seats and tables near the freezers, while the other half was devoted to copiers and printers and one lone computer. I didn't know where she handled the real estate end of her business: out of the back room no doubt.

"Ladies," she said softly, not meeting our glances. Behind her, she'd mounted a bulletin board for notes, announcements and general information, which covered a lot, given the scope of her business. "I'm sorry, but a lease is a lease. I can't let you break it and move out."

"We're not here about that," Lillian said, and Hester looked relieved. "We're here about your little Widows Club. That's what you meant at the memorial, isn't it?"

Hester looked shocked. "How did you know about that? It was supposed to be a secret."

I took a deep breath, then said, "How long did you think you'd be able to get away with killing them for their money?"

"What? Have you lost your mind?"

Lillian was looking at me with the exact same expression, but I decided to bull on through. "Don't try to deny it. I saw you stalking us outside Maggie's house last night."

"I can explain," Hester said, nearly hyperventilating. "I wanted to come in—I swear it—but you know how nervous I get around people."

I said, "So you're denying you had anything to do with the murders?"

Hester screeched, "Murders! Why do you keep saying that? Maggie's death was an accident, and Frances killed herself. Everybody knows that."

Lillian said, "Hester, you can stop lying. We know the truth."

"You don't know anything," she screamed. I'd never heard her speak above a whisper before, but she was certainly coming out of her shell. It was amazing what a little accusation of double homicide could do.

Lillian was still talking to her when my gaze drifted back to the board behind the counter. Something had caught my eye earlier, but I hadn't been able to isolate it from the clutter. I walked back to get a better look, then felt my heart chill as I pulled a handmade card from the collage of facts and information announcing that someone was moving.

"Where did you get this?" I asked as I studied the distinct edging that had been Maggie's latest personal pattern. "Did she send you a card, too?"

"Of course she did. It just came in the mail today, but what has that got to do with anything?"

"You know exactly what I'm talking about," I said as I opened the card. Instead of finding Maggie's handwriting, though, I saw that someone else had made the card using those specialty scissors. Inside was an announcement that someone I knew was leaving town, and they hadn't uttered the slightest word to me about it.

I grabbed my aunt's arm. "Lillian, we've made a mistake."

"What? That's impossible. The facts are all there."

I showed her the card without saying a word and waited while she read the inside. "And we just tried to warn her," she said.

Lillian turned to Hester and said, "I'm so sorry, but you're going to have lock up your shop and leave."

"Lillian, I swear I think you've lost your mind. First you accuse me of killing my friends, and now you're telling me to close my business. What's gotten into you?"

"There's no time right now; I'll explain it to you later. Listen to me carefully. No matter what you do, don't answer the door, even if it's someone you think of as a friend." She took Hester's hands in her own and said, "Now this part is extremely important. There's one person you must not let inside, even if she acts like she's dying. Do as I say, or Hilda will kill you, just as surely as she killed Frances and Maggie."

It took some convincing, but after a few more minutes, Hester agreed and dead bolted the place up as soon as we left. I'd tried to get her to come with us, but she wouldn't hear of it. It appeared that she wanted to believe Lillian, but I had the feeling she was locking us out as well as anyone else who might want to hurt her. I wasn't sure why Hilda was moving—running was more like it—but I knew if we didn't get to her in time, there might be another "accident" so she could have it all before she vanished.

"Call him now," Lillian said as she handed me her cell phone. I dialed Bradford's number, and got through to him immediately. "Bradford, we need your help."

There was a ton of interference on the phone, and the rain was pounding down on the roof of the ragtop so hard I could barely hear my own voice.

"Jen, is that you? I can't hear you, you're breaking up." There was a pause; then we were disconnected.

"You didn't tell him what we were doing," Lillian said.

"He couldn't hear me," I said. "This rain is miserable. I'll call him again when we get there."

We were on the outskirts of town when Lillian's eyes lit up as she said, "Look behind us."

Coming out of the rain and the gloom, I could see Hilda speeding toward us in her white truck. As she hit our back bumper, I felt the Mustang start to skid off the road. She was trying to kill us!

"Hang on," Lillian shouted as she fought the wheel. We were near a hillside with a pretty steep drop-off, and I doubted we'd survive the fall if Hilda managed to force us off the road.

"What are we going to do?" I asked, trying not to scream as I looked back at Hilda's furious expression.

"We're going to survive," Lillian said curtly. "Now stop yapping and let me focus."

Lillian took another hit, this one spinning us sideways, jamming us for one moment against a telephone pole and caving in part of the side before she managed to regain control.

"She's not going to stop until we're dead," I said loudly.

"Quiet," Lillian snapped.

She needed to concentrate on her driving, but time seemed to come to a standstill as I saw Hilda prepare to ram us again. I could barely recognize her. Her face was twisted into a mask of fury, and it looked like the only thing she wanted in the world was to see us die.

Hilda slammed into us again, and after a harsh jolt that slammed my head forward, I could feel the back of the car start to skid toward the trees. I didn't know how Lillian managed it, but she corrected at the last second and somehow straightened us out of the fishtail.

Hilda was growing more furious by the second, and I could see her face redden as she shouted at us. No doubt she was frustrated that we refused to die.

She was nearly to us again and I braced myself for what might be the final impact when Lillian did something with the gas, the brake and the steering wheel all at the same time. The Mustang responded to her touch and we were suddenly turned facing the other direction and out of danger, at least for a moment or two. Hilda's reaction time wasn't nearly what Lillian's was, and her vehicle kept going straight, though the road curved abruptly. The truck hit a tree, started to tip, then was upright again as another massive trunk caved in the passenger side entirely. I hoped and prayed that Hilda was still alive, but not out of any humanitarian spirit. If she died, the secret of why she'd behaved as she had might die with her, and I didn't think I could stand not knowing for the rest of my life.

Lillian looked at me and asked, "Are you all right?"

"I'm a little shaky, but I'm alive, thanks to you. Where did you learn to drive like that?"

Lillian offered a partial shrug as she unfastened her seat belt. "Did you forget that my husband Hank raced stock cars when he was younger? He made sure I knew every trick he did before he'd let me out on the road. I'll have to thank him for that. Maybe I'll send him a card."

"Was Hank your third husband or your fourth?" I asked as I got out of my side.

"He was my second husband, and you know it."

I was about to say something smart when I saw the side and the back of Lillian's car. "Oh no. It's pretty bad, isn't it?"

Lillian shrugged. "Jennifer, it's only a car. I was getting tired of it anyway. Call your brother again, and then we'll go check on Hilda."

There hadn't been any movement from the truck, but I still kept a wary eye on it as I hit the redial number on the cell phone.

Bradford answered. "Jen, did you just hang up on me? This weather's driving me nuts."

"There's been an accident. We're on route twenty-seven, just out of town. Call an ambulance."

I could hear my brother's breath explode. "Jennifer, are you all right?"

"I'm fine. Just hurry," I said.

"I'll be right there."

After we hung up, I saw Lillian walking toward the truck. I called out to her, "Wait a second; Bradford's going to be right here."

"Jennifer, she might need our help."

"She tried to kill us," I said, shouting through the pouring rain.

"That doesn't matter right now," Lillian said, and I followed her to the truck. I was braced for another attack, but when I got to the vehicle, I could see that I needn't have worried. Hilda was pinned neatly against the steering wheel, and there was a steady pulse of blood coming from her forehead. I knew head wounds could be bloody, and Hilda's was shaping up to be a real beauty.

I leaned forward, still staying out of her reach. "Hilda, are you all right?"

She seemed to come out of it. "Jennifer? Is that you? What happened?"

Lillian stood beside me. "You tried to kill us," she said flatly.

"I know that," Hilda snapped. "How did I miss?"

"You can curse my second husband," Lillian said. "He taught me evasive driving."

"Wish he'd have taught me," Hilda said. "You two would be out of my hair now."

I took a deep breath, then said, "You don't have any remorse for trying to kill us and succeeding with Maggie and Frances?"

Hilda said, "I'm sorry I didn't get away with it, but that's not what you want to hear, is it? So you figured Frances out, too. I was afraid the two of you were too clever for me. Can you get me out of here? My chest is killing me."

"The paramedics will be right here," I said, not wanting to help free such a dangerous woman, despite the current evidence to the contrary. "So why did you kill them?"

"Why do you think? It was all about the money. Frances was part of a rich family, and I wanted my share of it. I've been sick of living on a widow's pension. She'd told us all that she might as well have been orphaned, but I didn't believe her. I thought for sure I'd be her first choice, but then she named Maggie instead of me in her will. I couldn't believe it! After Frances was taken care of, I cemented my friendship with Maggie. I waited until she had time to change her will to reflect our new relationship; then I decided I had to take care of her. That part of it worked, anyway. The daft woman even sent me a card from beyond the grave like she did the rest of you. I knew I had to kill her. It was the only way I was going to get my hands on Frances's money."

"Maggie didn't get any money from her estate," Lillian said simply.

"That's what she tried to tell me when I confronted her. She was lying, though, and I knew it."

"So you decided to kill her too," I said as the rain

finally started to ease up. I couldn't hear the sirens yet, but I knew I didn't have much time if I was going to get the truth out of her face-to-face, and suddenly it was very important that I did.

"I couldn't trust her, so she had to go next," Hilda said calmly. The steady cadence of her voice sent chills through me that had nothing to do with the icy rain. "I waited in the back of her van, and I was ready to deal with her when I noticed she was driving to Howard and Betty's house. If news of our arrangement got out, I knew I'd be a prime suspect, so why not muddy things up a bit? They must have had some row inside, because Maggie was shaking when she got back to the van. She drove about a mile up the road, then pulled over so she could calm down. It was easy taking care of her; she wasn't expecting me."

I wanted to throw up, but the sirens were coming in the background, and I knew we didn't have much time. "So you made it look like an accident."

"I thought I did a pretty good job too," she said. "How did I slip up?"

"My brother told me he found Maggie with her seat belt unbuckled, and a friend of hers told us that she was an overly cautious driver, so I knew there was no way it was an accident like you'd staged it."

"But what led you to me?"

"A greeting card," I said as the first ambulance pulled up. "You used Maggie's scissors to cut the edges of the card you just sent to Hester."

"They were rightfully mine," she said, showing emotion for the first time since we'd been talking. "She left them to me."

As the EMTs worked on getting her out of the truck, Lillian and I walked back to the road and waited for Bradford.

After what seemed like forever, I was finally back in my apartment. I could have gone out and faced the world if I had to, but for the moment, I just wanted to lock the door and keep everyone and everything out on the other side. I called Gail and brought her up-to-date, then turned down her offer to get together. I knew we'd talk about it later—we discussed everything happening in our lives—but for the moment, I just needed to be alone. The peanut butter sandwich I ate as the cats dined on their own victuals was finer than any other meal, since I didn't have to leave to get it. By the next morning, I was feeling somewhat human again, ready to see what the day held.

I'd taken my shower, had gotten dressed, and was drying my hair when there was a knock at my door. I could think of a dozen different people who could be on my doorstep, and I didn't want to talk to a single one of them. I glanced through the peephole and saw Barrett standing out there with a dozen roses in his hands.

"Go away," I said through the door.

"Jennifer, I want to talk to you."

"Well, I don't want to talk to you," I said.

"Penny and I are finished. Can we start over?"

This guy was out of his mind. I threw the door open after I grabbed my baseball bat. "Would you like a little of what Wayne got last night, or are you going to leave me alone?" I asked.

"These are for you," he said, holding the roses out like they were some kind of shield.

"I don't want them. Barrett, if you'd turned Penny away the other night, things might be different between us now, but you made your choice."

"It was the wrong choice," he said. "Can't I have a second chance?"

"Sorry, I'm fresh out," I said. Maybe I was a little hard on him, but I wanted to be sure there was no doubt in his mind where we stood.

"At least accept these as an apology."

He dropped them at my feet, then started down the

steps. I picked them up and threw them at him before
he could get to the bottom. "Thanks, but no thanks."

As he dodged the cascading flowers, I saw that I
had another visitor just coming in. Greg had a bouquet
of Shasta daisies with him, but when he saw the roses
careening down the stairs, he started to back up.

"If this is a bad time, I can come back later," he
said.

Barrett looked at him like he wanted to kill him.
"That would be great. We're not finished here."

Before Greg could leave, I said, "You're wrong
there. We never even started. Come on up, Greg."

He stepped over the roses and walked up the steps.
In a lowered voice, he said, "Seriously, if this is a bad
time, I can always come back later."

"I think your timing is perfect," I said as I led him
inside, bolting the door behind him.

Greg started toward me, and I backed off a few
steps. I asked him, "What do you think you're doing?"

He looked confused by the question. "I thought we
were making up. I was wrong. It's not over between
us."

"You bring me flowers once and think that makes
everything all right? Have you lost your mind?"

"But they're daisies," he said, obviously grasping
for something, anything, to make things right.
"They're your favorite."

"I don't care if they're solid gold. You know what?
Maybe you should just go."

He didn't budge. "Listen, I don't know what I
walked in on, and I'm not sure I want to know, but
whatever issues you have with that guy don't involve
me. I'm one of the good guys, remember?"

"It's hard to tell you-all apart without a program
sometimes."

He looked so pitiful I couldn't leave it at that. Trying to soften my voice, I said, "Listen, Greg, I really

do appreciate you coming by, and the flowers are beautiful, but what's happened in the past between us can't be fixed by a dozen bouquets."

I unbolted the door and held it open for him. "Thanks for stopping by, though."

He shook his head as he walked out. "You're welcome, I guess. See you later."

"Sure," I said as I closed the door behind him. As I put the daisies in water, I wondered what I was going to do about Greg. When he'd been in my life, I'd enjoyed great swooping highs, but I'd also seen more than my share of despair. Did I really want to go through all that again? The history between us was so strong that he was a comfortable choice, despite the way I felt when I was with him. But was I going to let myself be satisfied with comfortable anymore?

I still wasn't sure what I was going to do when I left my apartment and headed for the card shop. Thankfully neither of my neighbors were in the foyer, so I could make a graceful departure without any more confrontations. Penny's car was gone from our little parking lot, but after seeing Barrett's track record with her, I didn't doubt she'd be back in his life again soon, at least for a little while.

Lillian was already at the shop when I got there, a strange and nearly unique occurrence.

"I didn't think you'd be coming in today," she said.

"Why not? We're open, aren't we?"

She shrugged. "It's just that after what happened yesterday, I thought you might want some time to deal with it."

I hung my coat up. "You're here, aren't you? Why does everybody think I'm such a delicate flower?"

"I've accused you of many things, Jennifer, but that's not even on the list."

I wanted to scowl, but Lillian's good humor infected my sour mood. "Can you believe what happened yesterday?"

"I can't quite grasp what's been happening for months all around us. We had a murderer in our card club and neither one of us picked up on it."

I straightened a stack of cards that didn't need it. "I don't think a trained psychologist would have spotted anything. Hilda must have had a lot of practice fooling the world."

"I suppose this means we'll have to disband the club," Lillian said.

"Not on your life. In fact, I'm going to start trolling for new members. Do you remember Daniel, the stay-at-home dad who's been in here a couple of times? I'm going to ask him to join us."

Lillian frowned. "Honestly, Jennifer, do you think it will ever be the same?"

"Is that such a bad thing if it's different?" I asked. "I'm getting tired of the same old same old. I think it's high time we shake things up a little."

I was ready to teach some lessons, wait on customers and make some new cards. It was my life, and I wanted to get back to it. So I was excited when the front door chimed, but a little disappointed when I saw it was just my brother.

"I've had warmer greetings from prisoners in my jail," Bradford said as he joined us.

"Sorry," I said. "What brings you here? Have you finally decided to let me teach you how to make cards? Come on, it will be fun."

"Yeah, I'll put that on my list. I just wanted to stop by and let you in on something."

I saw Lillian perk up. She loved getting the inside scoop. "Go on, we're listening."

Bradford ignored her as he told me, "I was talking to Patrick Benson this morning." He waited a beat for one of us to say something, but I wasn't about to rat him out, and I knew Lillian wouldn't either. Though our reasons were different, neither one of us wanted him exposed for sharing privileged information with us. After all, he'd saved Hester's life; there was no doubt in my mind about that.

When Bradford saw we weren't going to comment, he continued. "There's something interesting about Hilda's claims. It turns out she was right, at least about one thing."

"I can't imagine what that might be," I said, remembering the look on her face as she'd tried to kill us the day before.

"Frances inherited some property when she died, and I'm sure her family thought it was worthless, because Frances never put any store in it. When she died, it passed on to Maggie, but she didn't know any better either and left the deed with Patrick, along with some other official documents. Anyway, Patrick ran across it again last night while he was doing an inventory and he found it. He called around first thing this morning and pretty soon he discovered that it's smack in the middle of a chunk of land that Undrian Manufacturing wants to build their new plant on. It's worth half a million, at least."

I couldn't believe it. "Hilda won't see a dime of it, will she?"

Bradford stroked his nose, something I recognized from our childhood when he was perplexed about something. "No, you can't profit from murder, and that's a fact. The odd thing is, though, she could have kept it tied up in court for years and Undrian would have had to pick somewhere else to build their place, but she signed a quitclaim on it the second Patrick approached her."

"She wasn't angry she'd been so close to that much money?" I asked.

"You'd think so, wouldn't you? As a matter of fact, she was crowing about it as she signed the document. All she kept saying as she did it was, 'I told you-all I was right, and nobody believed me. I was right.' It was kind of creepy how she focused solely on that, and not on all the lives she'd destroyed." He paused a few moments, then said, "Anyway, I just wanted to let you-all know before it got out to the world. It was the least I could do after getting it so wrong with Frances and Maggie."

I touched his shoulder lightly. "You're human, Bradford. Anyone can make a mistake."

He pulled away. "Yeah, but most mistakes don't kill people. If I'd seen through Frances's murder, Maggie might still be alive."

I started to say something when Lillian spoke up. "Bradford, you are one of the finest men I've ever had the privilege to know, and the best sheriff this county could hope for."

Coming from my aunt, it was the strongest declaration of support Bradford could receive. He reddened slightly, obviously uncomfortable with the unexpected praise. "Thanks. Well, I'd better get going. See you two later."

Before he could get out the door, I called out to him. "Bradford, I've got one more question for you."

When he turned to look at me, I could see the dread in his face of what I might ask.

"Go ahead," he said solemnly.

"Do you know of any places I might move into? After what happened the other night, I don't think I can stay where I am much longer."

"I'll keep an eye out for something," he said, then quickly left us.

After he was gone, I asked Lillian, "Do you think Hester will mind if we break our lease?"

"Jennifer, we could paint her red and she wouldn't care today. Don't worry, dear. I'll take care of everything." She paused, then added, "You know, you could always stay with me. I've got plenty of room at my place, and your roommates would be welcome, too. I'm certain we can all find a way to coexist."

I hugged my aunt quickly, then said, "Lillian, as

much as I love being around you, I think our time at the shop is enough every day, don't you?"

She shrugged. "I suppose. So where do you think you might live?"

"I don't know," I said, laughing. "And that's the real beauty of it, isn't it?"

I was ready to start living my own life, one day at a time, looking forward and not back. And if I sold a card or two along the way, so much the better.

HANDCRAFTED CARD TIP

Embossing can be a fun way to add fancy, decorative touches to your cards without a great deal of skill or effort. With the right kit, you can edge, add ornate flourishes or even embed complete designs within your cards.

Embossing is normally achieved by using two identical templates, with the paper sandwiched between them. A bone or embossing tool is then used to trace around the edges. The tool resembles a pen with small balls attached to either end. Don't worry if the results you see as you work don't look absolutely perfect. In fact, from the side of the card that faces you, there's not much to see at all. But when the card is flipped over, it's amazing how beautiful the subtle additions of raised images make your finished card. A dry brush with the slightest hint of paint can then highlight your patterns in complementary colors, making the designs jump off the page!

Read on for an excerpt from the next
Card-Making Mystery

Murder and
Salutations

By Elizabeth Bright

Available from Signet in December 2006.

For Eliza Glade's entire life, she somehow always managed to steal the spotlight from my sister and me, and wouldn't you know it, she kept her record perfect, even in death.

"You look absolutely radiant," I told my aunt Lillian, who was elegantly dressed in a formal evening gown. She's more than my aunt, though—Lillian is also my only employee at Custom Card Creations. My name's Jennifer Shane, and I own the shop of my dreams, a little handcrafted-card store tucked away on one end of Oakmont Avenue in the heart of Rebel Forge, Virginia. It's a place where customers can select one of our own handmade cards, or buy the materials to make one themselves.

After Lillian and I had worked at the store all day, we'd changed into more formal attire, and now we were ready to attend the Chamber of Commerce's annual awards banquet. The organization had held the ritual religiously for the past sixty-seven years, but it was the first time I'd been eligible to attend. The dinner was slated for Hurley's Pub, an easy walk from the store and a place I'd been many times.

Lillian was wearing an evening gown made of a pastel material that was so sheer, it was nearly translucent. The emerald green tint of the dress complemented her richly dyed henna hair, and I'd never felt so dowdy in my thirty-something years of life. While my aunt was petite and graceful, I tended to feel big-boned and gawky, and it was never so obvious than when we were both dressed up.

"You look lovely as well," Lillian said. After casting a critical glance at my simple gray dress, she added, "Though I do wish you'd let me treat you to a new outfit sometime." Lillian paused, then added enthusiastically, "I've got a wonderful idea, Jennifer. Why don't we go to Richmond in the morning, shop all day, and then eat somewhere delightful tomorrow night? I know the most charming place we could stay, and we'd be back in time for lunch the next day. What do you say? I'd be delighted to treat." With several ex-husbands and a shrewd mind for investing, Lillian could easily afford the gracious gesture. She worked at my shop for materials and instruction in lieu of a salary, and to my delight, my aunt had grown to love making cards nearly as much as I did.

"I'm tempted to take you up on it sometime, but you know I can't afford to close the card shop that long."

She waved a hand in the air, dismissing my protest. "Yes, I know how thoroughly wed you are to your business. Speaking of marriage, I'm still not certain you should have invited me to this banquet as your guest. Surely you could have found a suitable young man to escort you."

I wasn't about to have that conversation with her again. I hugged my aunt and said, "We both know that I probably wouldn't still be in business without your help. There's no way I could have asked anyone else tonight."

She raised an eyebrow in consternation. My aunt had perfected the look from a great deal of practice over the years. "At least promise me you'll find some time to chat with the eligible young men there. Will Greg be attending?"

Greg Langston was my two-time former fiancé, but never my husband. He ran a pottery shop a few doors down from Custom Card Creations, and we were just starting to manage the awkwardness inherent in our proximity. Lillian had a dream that we'd make the third time a charm someday, and I was getting tired of trying to rid her of her delusions. "I suspect so, but I really don't know. We quit coordinating our social calendars a long time ago."

There must have been something in my voice that told her I was through talking about it. "Shall we go then?"

"Just let me lock up and I'll be ready."

As I secured the last dead bolt on the shop's front door, I heard my sister's voice calling me from up the street. "Jennifer, wait for me."

Sara Lynn had been cut from the same cloth as my aunt; they were the only two petite people in our family. She ran Forever Memories, a scrapbooking shop that had inadvertently led me to custom card-making. I'd been her employee there not so long ago, and when Sara Lynn had rejected my idea of a card-making corner, I'd gone out on my own to prove there was a market for handcrafted cards in our resort community. Our brother, Bradford, was the sheriff for Rebel Forge, though at times it seemed his main duty was keeping our family together.

"You look award-winning," I said, appreciating the effort my sister had gone to. Sara Lynn normally eschewed makeup and fancy formal wear, but she was now skillfully enhanced, from her brand-new hairdo all the way down to her expensive pumps.

"It's nonsense, and we all know it," Sara Lynn said. It was rumored around town that Sara Lynn was slated to receive the Rebel Forge Businessperson of the Year award, something that she'd yet to receive in all her years as a small businesswoman. The reason for the slight was obvious: there was bad blood between my sister and Eliza Glade, the woman who ran the chamber—along with her businesses—with a velvet fist. However, it appeared that it was finally going to be Sara Lynn's turn, and she was long past due, in my opinion.

I looked behind her and asked, "Hey, where's Bailey?" Sara Lynn and her husband had been having marital troubles for months, but I had expected him at least to show up for his wife's crowning triumph. The Bippy—as we affectionately called the award—was the Oscar, the Emmy, and the Obie combined for the folks who ran businesses in Rebel Forge, and I knew that, despite her protests to the contrary, Sara Lynn had a place ready in the display behind her checkout counter for the small golden anvil award.

"He's not coming," Sara Lynn snapped. From the tone of her voice, it was pretty obvious she was finished with that particular conversation.

Not that Lillian was going to accept the dismissal. "When are you going to kick him to the curb like he deserves?"

I was shocked by the harshness of my aunt's comment. "Lillian, that's out of line, even for you."

Our aunt was prepared to protest, when Sara Lynn put a hand on my arm. "She's right, Jennifer." She took a deep breath, let it out slowly, then said, "You'll hear about this sooner or later, so it might as well be from me. Bailey and I have decided to split up."

I couldn't believe it. They'd been married forever, and while I knew they'd had their share of problems, I never imagined it would come to this. "Sara Lynn, it will all work out. I just know you two are meant to be together."

She touched my shoulder lightly. "Thank you, Jennifer, but I don't think so."

Lillian nodded her obvious approval. "You had every right to toss him out after what he did."

"What happened?" I asked. "Is there something I don't know about?"

Sara Lynn frowned. "If you haven't heard the rumors yet, you will tonight. Bailey and I are completely and utterly finished. I could have probably forgiven him having an affair—I know he's just human—but I will never be able to get the image out of my mind of him in Eliza Glade's embrace."

I was shocked by the admission, but Lillian just nodded and said, "We're both here for you. You know that, don't you?"

I finally managed to find my voice. "Are you positive you want to go to the banquet tonight? Eliza's going to be making the presentation." I couldn't imagine my sister onstage with her worst enemy in the world. I turned to our aunt and asked, "Lillian, does your offer of a shopping trip to Richmond still stand? Let's go right now. What do you say, Sara Lynn? We'll have a blast."

"That's an excellent idea," Lillian said. "The three Shane women loose in the capital city. Let's do it."

Sara Lynn stood her ground, though. "I won't let that woman deprive me of this evening. I did nothing wrong, and I won't scuttle away to a corner and hide. Now, are you two coming or not? There's a banquet I'm determined to attend."

Behind her back, Lillian looked questioningly at me, and I nodded to signal my acceptance. If Sara Lynn still wanted to go, then I would be right there beside her.

"Let's go," I said with as much enthusiasm as I could muster.

As we walked to Hurley's Pub, the three of us chatted about the weather, the mutual states of our businesses, and just about everything but Sara Lynn's husband and his new paramour. I thought of myself as a strong woman, but I couldn't touch my sister's grit and determination. She was right, of course. The best way to handle the gossip and the scandal in our small town was to face it head-on. That had always been her approach to life, and I'd constantly done my best to emulate her behavior, with varying degrees of success over the years.

Hurley's was closed to the public for the night, and the second we walked in, I could see why. Jack Hurley had opened up the dividers between the dining areas, making his restaurant one big open space. There was a temporary stage set up in front, with a pair of tables split by a podium. Several people were mingling around the room, sharing drinks and quips. Was it my imagination, or was there a momentary hush when everyone realized that Sara Lynn was there? I looked over at my sister, her head held proud and her gaze unflinching, and I couldn't remember ever being prouder of her than I was at that moment. In less than a second, the crowd went back to their drinks and previous conversations, and I squeezed Sara Lynn's hand. "You are probably the bravest woman I know."

She shook her head briefly, and I could see that she was trying her best not to show any emotion at all. "Nonsense. I have every right to be here." As she spoke, I saw someone approaching us out of the corner of my eye. The relief I'd felt in seeing someone join us dissipated in an instant when I realized who it was.

Eliza Glade was heading our way, and it wasn't my imagination this time. The room was as quiet as a soft kiss; everyone was holding their breath. Eliza wore a red dress that showed just a little bit too much of her voluptuous figure for a Chamber of Commerce dinner. Her blond hair had been teased and sprayed, and her makeup was more than just a smidge overdone. Truthfully, she looked as though she would have been more at home in a Las Vegas lounge than in Rebel Forge. Before Eliza could reach my sister, Lillian disengaged from us and headed straight for the woman, effectively cutting her off from us. They shared a few whispered comments, then Lillian said something that rocked Eliza in her tracks. Her face reddened as if she'd been slapped, and I saw her back quickly away.

When Lillian rejoined us, there was a look of smug satisfaction on her face.

Sara Lynn said, "I don't need you to fight my battles for me. I'm perfectly capable of handling that woman myself."

Lillian just laughed. "What, and let you have all the fun? That's hardly fair."

"What did you say to her?" I asked. "You must have really spanked her hard."

"Me?" Lillian asked, her tone as innocent as she could summon. "I don't know what you're talking about."

About the Author

Elizabeth Bright is the pseudonym for a nationally best-selling mystery author. Though never credited with solving a murder in real life, Elizabeth's alter ego has created scores of handcrafted greeting cards over the years.

Invitation to Murder

A Card-Making Mystery

by Elizabeth Bright

Jennifer Shane's brainchild of a shop, Custom Card Creations, hasn't been all glitter and tinsel. Customers are scarce and—after finally landing a client—Jennifer hears a murder over the phone. And when she receives a threatening note, it's clear someone has designs on her life, too. Now, between holding cardmaking lessons, trying to scissor her ex-fiancé out of her life, and piecing together a murder, Jennifer has really got her work cut out for her.

"Elizabeth Bright shines in this crafty new series."
—Nancy Martin, author of the
***Blackbird Sisters* mysteries**

0-451-21634-2

Available wherever books are sold or at
penguin.com

Nancy Martin

The Blackbird Sisters Mystery Series

Cross Your Heart
and Hope to Die

At the unveiling of the most miraculous bra
in fashion history, Nora's boss is found
trussed up in pantyhose and shot execution
style. To find the killer, Nora must
shadow the most glamorous suspects in
Philadelphia—including a bad-boy designer
and a pair of luscious twin models. Though
they're used to "murder with style"
(Pittsburgh Magazine), cross your fingers
for the Blackbird sisters, because this time,
high society has never stooped so low.

0-451-21532-X

"A LAUGH-OUT-LOUD COMIC MYSTERY
AS OUTRAGEOUS AS A PINK
CHINCHILLA COAT."
BOOKLIST

Available wherever books are sold or at
penguin.com

Cynthia Riggs

The Martha's Vineyard Mystery Series

At 92 years of age, Martha's Vineyard native Victoria Trumbull is about to take on a new vocation—solving murders.

Deadly Nightshade
0-451-20816-1

The Cranefly Orchid Murders
0-451-20961-3

"Poet-detective Victoria Trumbull [is] an unforgettable character."
—Sena Jeter Naslund

"A welcome debut...Everyone should have such a terrific grandmother."
—*Publishers Weekly*

Available wherever books are sold or at penguin.com